JACK'S HEIR

JACK'S HEIR

Michael Litchfield

ROBERT HALE · LONDON

© Michael Litchfield 2013
First published in Great Britain 2013

ISBN 978-0-7198-1155-5

Robert Hale Limited
Clerkenwell House
Clerkenwell Green
London EC1R 0HT

www.halebooks.com

2 4 6 8 10 9 7 5 3 1

Typeset in 11/14.5pt Palatino
Printed in the UK by the Berforts Group

Acknowledgements

A special thank you to the brilliant newspaper and magazine columnist Faith Eckersall for the seedling idea, albeit unwittingly.

1

Friday, August 31:

Death was on the prowl; a sly, anonymous demon of the night, swathed in the menacing cloak of hooded darkness. Unsuspecting innocence went about its abandoned business of partying, unaware of the sneaky predator whose satanic mission had been honed by the grim harvester of sinless souls.

There is no such phenomenon as an act of random, psychopathic madness. Every psychopath is consumed by his compelling logic and is driven by his sense of righteous purpose. He crusades on behalf of virtue. His self-sacrifice is solely for the benefit of humanity. He is the addled egg that somehow defied nature and got born; both scrambled and hard-boiled. The yolk of the Devil.

The moon had a night off and the town was dimmed by a grey blanket of rainless cloud. The day had been hot and jungle-steamy. The air was no fresher now that twilight had been smothered by airless darkness, which had descended like a suffocating pillow over the face of this sprawling urban conurbation.

Mary Walker, just one week from her 21st birthday, hurried with friend Sally Wingate along the amber-lit streets of Bournemouth, with the heaving town centre, and the less lively seafront, disappearing behind them. They had been to a cinema to see the movie, *Yesterday Is Always Too Late*, which had finished at 11.30 p.m. Before heading home, they picked up burgers and fries from an all-night takeaway, eating as they climbed Bath

Hill, away from the twinkling pier, illuminated promenade, and decorative street lights.

Even away from the heartbeat of clubland, the periphery rocked to the frenetic beat of Friday night fever. Hundreds of young women, in short skirts and high heels, flocked like migrating birds in one direction, the trade winds of the night-economy under their fledgling wings. Pub-drinkers spilled out into this seemingly endless high-tide of human flesh. Playful screams from the sea told of carefree youthful gambolling.

Although Mary and Sally could have caught a bus, they enjoyed walking, especially at night in summer; when the scent of jasmine and the salty smell of the sea hung heavily in the air, mixed with the mouth-watering aromas from beach-barbecues, and the heat of the day was no longer a burning issue.

From the top of steep Bath Hill, they forged onwards against the incoming swell of revellers making for funland. At the junction with Derby Road, Mary pointed towards the Lillie Langtry Manor Hotel, where her partner, Jamie Roper, was going to treat her to a birthday celebration dinner in a week's time.

'Lucky you!' Sally cooed, suitably impressed. 'That's what I call *really* living it up. I wish I could find a man who'd take me to places like that. Will you be sleeping there, rounding off your big night with sex in a royal four-poster?'

Mary giggled. 'I don't think our budget will stretch that far, but what a wicked idea.'

Lillie Langtry had been one of the infamous mistresses of Edward, Prince of Wales, before he was crowned King. What was now a restaurant and hotel, had been built in the late 1870s as a dirty weekend retreat from London for actress Lillie and 'pork chop' Edward.

From the intersection with Derby Road, the young women found themselves tottering downhill towards Boscombe Gardens, which threaded through a shallow gorge to the sea. And it was here that they separated, with Sally crossing the road at the traffic-lights to head for her bedsit a couple of blocks away, while Mary continued, uphill now, towards the tacky suburb of Boscombe.

In Edwardian times, Boscombe had been something of a fashionable quarter, gentrified and genteel. More recently, however, it had gone the way of so many neighbourhoods with largish, multi-occupied old houses on the outer limbs of large towns and cities. There were brothels, drug-dealers and street-corner prostitutes and their pimps, mixed with the good and devout in a cosmopolitan mishmash. However, for couples like Mary and Jamie, the cost of rented accommodation reflected the reputation of the area. Hence they were able to afford a ground-floor flat that would have been way beyond their means in the more salubrious districts.

There were still plenty of people milling around in Boscombe High Street, which had been constructed on level ground. Being propositioned while walking home after dark had become something of a running-the-gauntlet ritual for Mary and this night was no exception.

'Looking for business?'

'Looking for a trip?'

'Looking for some ecstasy in your life?'

As always, she kept walking; erect, head held high, chin up, avoiding eye-contact.

Some men were more persistent than others. None ever fazed her.

The precinct of shops was well-lit; clubbers queued in a well-behaved, orderly line outside a popular rave joint. Bouncers, built like bulwarks, guarded black reinforced doors leading to venues of ear-blitzing entertainment.

Mary pressed on relentlessly, soon peeling off to the right and into a much quieter and darker scene. More residential; few people about now. Plenty of cars, but none on the move. In just a few strides, she had abandoned the night-players. Now she was among the sleepers. Already she could see the iron-gate that led to the front door of the house where she lived. No more than a hundred yards away on the opposite side of the street.

She stopped and looked both ways before crossing the road. Not another pedestrian in sight. The click-clack of her heels striking concrete was the only sound.

Fifty yards to go now.

Instinctively, she opened her handbag for the door-key, without missing a stride. Although she looked forward to the day she and Jamie could afford to own their own home, she was comfortable and happy in their rented flat. It was her sanctuary, where she felt safe.

'Home!' she sighed, contentedly.

Three nights a week, Jamie Roper worked as a barman from 8 p.m. until 4 a.m. at the Rambo nightclub in the town centre. Friday was one of those nights, and always the busiest.

By day, he was a student at the local university, two years into a media degree course. He was hoping for a career in radio or TV, starting locally.

Mary, a lover of animals, had a full-time job as a receptionist and assistant at a veterinary surgery. On Friday nights, because she didn't work weekends, she often stayed up late, waiting for Jamie to return, which usually was around 4.30 a.m. Jamie wasn't allowed to drink at work, so he had no qualms about driving to and from the club in their two-door, MG sports car that they'd snapped up second-hand (fifth-hand to be pedantic) for £480.

When Jamie arrived home that Saturday, September 1st morning, he was surprised to find the flat in complete darkness. Even when Mary was too tired to wait up for him, she always left on the hall-light. *Perhaps the bulb has blown,* he thought, stumbling over the doormat and cursing mildly to himself.

Assuming that Mary must be asleep in bed, he tiptoed into the lounge, situated on the right-hand side of the truncated entrance-hall, and switched on the light. He was quickly struck by the unoccupied quietness of the flat. There was an overpowering and overwhelming emptiness.

With a sense of urgency and inexplicable foreboding, Jamie hastily headed for the next door on the right and into the main bedroom, where the couple slept, hoping to discover Mary asleep.

The bedroom was in darkness, but the bed was empty; no contours and undulations of a human body beneath the sheet. Now clammy with anxiety, he flicked the switch to fill the room with yellow, artificial light and almost scampered to the other side of the bed, fearing that Mary might have fainted, hitting her head on something hard when falling and ending up unconscious on the carpet. Still there was no sign of her.

Panicky and sweating profusely, he hurried to the spare bedroom which had been converted into his little study, equipped with desk, computer, printer, filing-cabinet, bookshelves, and a couple of plain, upright chairs. No Mary. Neither was she in the kitchen at the end of the corridor or in the bathroom that was next to Jamie's den.

Mary wasn't at home.

Next, Jamie searched all over for a note. Nothing.

He listened to the answer-machine in the lounge. Just two messages:

One: '*Hello Mary darling, this is Mum. Dad's none too well – one of those awful summer viruses; worse than winter 'flu, they are – so I doubt that we'll be able to get down this Sunday. Hope to make it the following weekend. Give me a call when you have a moment. Love you. Remember me to Jamie.*'

Two: '*Hi Jamie, it's Dave. Just calling to see if you're going to the gym tomorrow. If you are, give me a bell and I'll meet you there. Perhaps watch some footie in the afternoon, if you're not being dragged around the shops.*'

Both incoming calls had been made early evening. If Mary had been back since finishing work at 8.00pm after evening surgery at the vet's, she would have played those messages and the tape would have been wiped, he reasoned.

'My mobile!' he exclaimed aloud. While on duty at the nightclub, he always had his mobile phone on silent. Usually, he returned it to 'normal' mode on leaving the Rambo, but tonight he'd forgotten.

Taking the phone from the breast-pocket of his black, silk, short-sleeved work-shirt, he saw immediately that he had missed a text.

Darling, going 2 flicks with Sal. Be home long before u. x x x

Now Dave was no longer worried: he was frantic.

She must have had an accident or been taken ill, he told himself, simultaneously thumbing through the telephone directory for the numbers of the two local general hospitals – Poole and the Royal Bournemouth – that had A&E departments.

Stupid! He berated himself. *Why don't you just call her mobile? I'm not thinking straight. Get a grip!*

Using the landline phone, he punched the numbers of Mary's handset. As soon as he heard the ringing tone, he thought, *Good, it's switched on.* After six rings, he pleaded vocally, 'Come on, Mary, answer for Christ sake!' Another two burrs and Voicemail kicked in. 'Mary, where are you? Are you OK? I'm worried sick. As soon as you've played this message, please call me to put my mind at rest.' As an afterthought, he added, 'I love you.'

Maybe she's gone with Sally to her place. But she wouldn't have done that without letting me know. And if she'd stayed this long, she'd have asked me to collect her on my way home from work.

He'd dropped the telephone directory on the floor. Now he resumed flicking through the pages frantically. It made sense, he decided, to call the Royal Bournemouth Hospital first.

'No,' he was assured, 'the name Mary Walker doesn't appear on the list of patients treated here or admitted tonight. Of course, she could still be in A&E waiting to be seen, but if she'd been involved in a serious incident, the police would have made contact with you. I assume she is in possession of some form of identification?'

'I'm sure she is,' Jamie said weakly.

The response from Poole Hospital was similar.

Before contacting the police, he decided to walk the route that Mary almost certainly would have taken from the town centre. *Maybe she passed out and passers-by have mistaken her for a drunk or junkie. Thank God it's not a freezing winter's night!*

Before setting out, he scribbled a note, which he deposited on a bedside-table, on which Mary always kept the latest book she was reading. *Darling, gone looking for you. Call me to let me know you're home if you beat me back. Me x x x*

He deliberately left on the lights in all rooms as a sort of warm, welcome home gesture, in the genre of a yellow ribbon.

For the next two hours, he padded the streets of Bournemouth as dawn's pale yolk fractured the black night-shell. He made a point of detouring to explore Boscombe Gardens, where the sentinel pines hid many a sin between sundown and sunrise. He inspected every inch of the rippling stream that coiled through the Gardens towards the sea.

He didn't believe for one moment that Mary would have ventured into the St Paul's underpass, a notorious muggers' lair. Nevertheless, he checked it out, dismissive of any potential threat to himself. Several derelicts, men and women, were slumped against graffiti-defaced walls, snuggled up to empty bottles, their drunken snores echoing along the draughty tunnel; the whiff of urine in the dank air. No Mary, of course.

If only I knew where Sally Wingate lived. I don't even have a phone number for her, damn it!

The cinemas were in darkness, of course; locked and bolted hours earlier. Even the roulette-wheels of the numerous casinos had stopped spinning.

One more possibility: the Lower Gardens, a green oasis threading through the town's midriff to the pier and seafront, and the epicentre of numerous sexual assaults on women.

Nothing.

On reaching the deserted promenade, he again tried to reach Mary on her mobile, only despairingly to find himself diverted directly to Voicemail. He dictated yet another panicky message. He contemplated ringing Mary's mother, who lived miles away in the East Midlands, to see if she had heard from her daughter, but he didn't want to alarm her, especially at this early hour and while her husband was unwell.

Overcome by a compulsion to be at home, at the root of their relationship, he sprinted all the way back to Boscombe, passing early-risers who were already on their way to work. The lights of the flat were still blazing. Nothing had changed since Jamie had embarked on his fruitless mission. Every room remained a vacuum, a hollow reminder of the essential missing ingredient that made this a home rather than a mere building.

After ensuring that there had been no new messages left on the answer-machine, he knew that he could no longer delay calling the police.

'I'm desperate. My partner has vanished … into the night … into thin air….'

The veteran who took down details from Jamie over the phone sounded as if he'd left his brain in bed.

'I'm sure there's a simple explanation; nearly always is,' he said, trying to assuage, but fanning the flames of anxiety, rather than dousing them.

'Something's very wrong, take my word for it,' Jamie countered, everything about him tremulous.

'Have you a valid reason for assuming that, sir?'

'She's disappeared! What more valid reason could there possibly be?' Jamie was almost screaming into the mouthpiece. 'She went to a cinema with a girlfriend hours ago and now she's missing.'

'Is your partner in possession of a mobile phone?'

'Yes, but she's not answering. I've left two messages.' His patience was running on empty.

The desk-bound uniformed plodder wearily asked for the number of Mary's mobile phone and the name of the service-provider. 'I'll pass on this information and someone will be in touch, *eventually*,' he said.

'How soon?' Jamie pressed.

'Impossible to say. These things have to run their routine course.'

Jamie feared that the report would be filed and forgotten.

'One last thing,' said the officer. 'If your partner should turn up, please inform us without delay.'

Jamie had heard enough.

*

But he was wrong about the report being assigned to the archives. Within an hour, two cops were on his doorstep. Detective Chief Inspector Mike Lorenzo had a thumb stuck on the front door bell-button. Detective Constable Matt Valentine tapped his feet restively.

Jamie, by now resembling a cross between a cadaver and a scarecrow, was instantly impressed by the prompt action of the police. However, his first reaction was quickly overtaken by one of foreboding. Such speed could mean only that they were there as harbingers of bleak news, he cautioned himself.

After the usual doorstep-formalities, the detectives invited themselves indoors and as soon as they were camped in the lounge, Lorenzo said, 'It's my understanding you phoned your partner twice during the night?'

'That's right,' Jamie confirmed. 'But neither call was answered, something I keep repeating.'

Lorenzo squeezed the bridge of his nose and then, with two fingers, massaged his forehead, just above his coal-black, seemingly soulless eyes. 'And you were here when you made the first of those calls?'

'Yes, I was,' Jamie said, his eyes darting to and fro between Lorenzo and the detective constable.

'And your partner, Mary Walker, hadn't returned from going to a cinema with a friend?'

Jamie was beginning to become frustrated again by what he perceived as plod, plod repetition. 'I went over and over, again and again, about all this stuff on the phone with one of your officers.'

Lorenzo raised a halting hand. 'Bear with me just a few moments longer, please, Mr Roper. This is all very important, as will become apparent. We've already been in contact with the service-provider of your partner's mobile.'

Now Jamie Roper's antenna was primed.

'They were able to tell us quite a lot very quickly, backing up what you've said about the two calls you made, one from the landline and the other from your mobile. They also verified a text from your partner to your handset earlier, when, presumably, she was on the way to town and a cinema.'

'Where is this leading, Inspector?' said Jamie restlessly.

'Not very far,' Lorenzo replied cryptically, the double entendre lost on Jamie. 'You see, the service-provider was able to pinpoint amazingly accurately the location of your partner's mobile, and presumably her, when she received both those two calls from you.'

Now Jamie Roper came alive. 'Where was she?' he demanded, almost hysterically.

The theatrical pause that followed was fully justified.

'Here, Mr Roper. On these premises. Right here, with you! How about that for a turn up?'

2

'This is crazy!' fumed Jamie Roper, slapping his thighs, before running his shaky fingers through short, dark, spiky hair. He began ambulating nervously. 'There must be a mistake. She's not here. Look for yourselves. If my partner *was* here and I'd harmed her, would I be sending for you guys, bringing you to the scene of the crime? Use your loaf!'

'Why don't you sit down, Mr Roper, and take the weight off your feet,' Lorenzo said, conciliatory, stroking the black jungle-undergrowth on his chin. He hadn't shaved that morning, but even if he had his face wouldn't have looked much cleaner. Within half an hour of shaving he would be in need of more pruning; it was a daily losing battle against the growth of facial weed.

Roper flopped into an armchair opposite the two detectives, head buried in his hands now. Lorenzo was eager to empathize.

'We have some sorting to do.' His eyes never roamed from Roper, not even for a split-second. 'We're all on the same side.' This wasn't necessarily true, of course, but Lorenzo was playing the bonding game. 'You're desperate to be reunited with your partner. We also want to find her.' He smiled. 'We like happy endings.' More than anyone, Lorenzo recognized how glib he must have sounded.

'But....' Roper gathered himself, preparing to make some sort of protest, but nothing materialized.

'Is that Mary?' Lorenzo asked, nodding towards a framed portrait photograph on the mantelpiece, next to a carriage-clock and under a delicate Monet print.

'Yes, that's *my* Mary,' said Roper, his eyes misty.

Lorenzo mentally noted the blonde hair, blue eyes, ruddy, healthy complexion, cheeky mouth and moderate use of makeup.

'We might have to borrow that photo if she doesn't show up soon.'

'Anything,' Roper muttered, like a lost soul.

Lorenzo casually extracted a flick-over notebook from the jacket-pocket of his blue suit that resembled an unmade bed. He patted his jacket, looking for a pen, a habit that always made Valentine smile. Historically, Lorenzo never remembered to pocket a pen before leaving his desk. Valentine was so used to this ritual that he was already proffering a ballpoint.

'The service-provider isn't wrong, so get that out of your head,' Lorenzo said peremptorily. 'How many flats are there in this property?'

Roper steeled himself for the inevitable catechism. 'Just two. Ours and the one upstairs.'

'Are the flats self-contained?'

'Yes. Our entrance is via the front-door, the way you came in. The door to the upstairs flat is at the side.'

'And who lives upstairs?'

'Dave.'

'Dave who?'

'Timms.'

'Is he the house-owner?'

'No. He rents, just like us.'

'Do you have access to each other's flat?'

Roper reacted startled. 'Grief, I hope not! We don't have a key to Dave's pad. In fact, I've never been inside his place.'

'Has he been in here?'

'Not while I've been home,' Roper said emphatically, a reply that prompted Valentine to scribble a note.

'Who *does* own the house?'

'It's managed by a letting agency, Drone and Markham. The actual owner, a Mr Marsh, lives in London, apparently.' He shook his head and threw his arms despairingly into the air. 'Why these questions? You're just wasting valuable time.'

'Ticking boxes can be frustrating, I accept, but tried and tested procedures work, believe me,' Lorenzo said equably. 'Now, does the letting agency keep a duplicate key?'

'Of course.'

'How do you get on with the upstairs occupant?'

'I don't.'

Lorenzo gave him a searching look. 'Why's that?'

'It's no big deal. Mary and I are both out all day in the week. I work a number of nights. I don't even know what Dave does for a living, if anything. I can't have seen him more than a dozen times since we've been here. And then it's only just been in passing.'

'Was he already in occupation when you moved in?'

'Yes, he was.'

'And he lives alone?'

'As far as I know. I've never seen anyone else going in or coming out.'

'What kind of age is this Mr Timms?'

'Around fifty. Now, please, can you do something to find Mary?'

'OK,' said Lorenzo, slapping his knees, 'now give us the grand tour.'

'What's the point?' Roper balked. 'I've already been through every room myself. Don't you believe me?'

'I have to see for myself,' Lorenzo explained, patiently but firmly. 'If I didn't, I'd be guilty of negligence. So let's go.'

Within five minutes, the detectives had satisfied themselves that Mary Walker wasn't in the flat.

'OK, now we'll knock-up Mr Timms,' Lorenzo announced. 'You stay put, Mr Roper.'

Loose wire hung from the upstairs flat's doorbell, so Lorenzo resorted to fist on wood.

A gruff, irked man's voice wafted down the stairs. 'Coming, coming, keep your hair on!'

The detectives heard weighty, descending footsteps, followed by, 'Who is it? What do you want? I don't open the door to no cold-callers.'

'Police,' said Lorenzo, his tone mimicking art. He, like everyone else, had seen too many cop movies and TV detective series. Fiction set not only the fashion but also the agenda.

A security-chain rattled, a bolt was wrenched sideways, and a deadlock turned.

Dave Timms sported an untidy, budding beard and an untrimmed, ragged moustache. His dark eyebrows resembled a couple of prickly bushes, while his hair was an unkempt shrubbery. Sleepwalker-eyes were having difficulty focusing. Squinting, he said, 'Are you local?'

'Very,' said Lorenzo, quickly moving on. 'We want to ask you a few questions about your neighbour, Mary Walker.'

Timms, who wore a food-stained black jumper, with sleeves rolled up to the elbows, peered over Lorenzo's shoulder to Valentine.

'Never heard of 'er.' His voice was unattractive, though there was no obvious regional dialect that Lorenzo could detect.

'She occupies the downstairs flat with her boyfriend,' said Valentine, deciding he deserved to be more than Lorenzo's silent shadow.

'Oh, 'er,' Timms said disparagingly, sniffing. 'What's she been up to? Doing naughty favours for makeup-money?'

Taking an instant dislike to Timms, Lorenzo said challengingly, 'Nothing like that, unless you have evidence to the contrary.'

'Well, I don't have much to do with anyone around 'ere,' Timms explained himself uncomfortably. 'I don't reckon I've said more than a dozen words to them two downstairs since they moved in.'

'When did you last see Ms Walker?'

Timms angled his head skywards as he calculated, a scabrous finger pressed to his fleshy mouth.

'To be honest, it must've been several days.'

'Not last night? Not this morning?'

Timms was shaking his head before Lorenzo had even reached his second question.

'Where were you last night?'

Now Timms eyed the detectives cannily. 'I think I'm entitled to know what this is all about, seeing as you're getting all personal and nosy.'

'Mary Walker has been reported missing,' Lorenzo elaborated.

'You mean she's pissed off and left 'er fella with an aching dick and he's making a song and dance of it? Well, last evening I went for a few jars in Boscombe.'

'Where *exactly* in Boscombe?'

'The Blue Bottle pub. I'm what you might call one of their regulars, especially on a Friday night, when it rocks.'

'*Rocks?*'

'Yeah, there's "live" entertainment and the whole place swings.'

'Were you alone there?'

'Hardly! It was wall-to-wall carpeting with sweaty flesh, most of it well-oiled by kick-out time.'

'You included?'

'I can hold my liquor. I'm no southern wimp.'

'What time did you leave?'

'I'm no clock-watcher either, when it comes to giving me liver a good belting. But I guess it must have been elevenish. Not late. An early night for me, especially for a Friday.'

'Then where did you go?'

'Home sweet home.'

'Did you happen to see Ms Walker on your way back?'

'You trying to trick me, or are you just dim? I've already told you I haven't seen 'er for several days.'

'So you did,' Lorenzo said sardonically. 'Did you notice if there were lights on downstairs?'

'I didn't take much interest in anything. I'd had a skinful, something else I've already told you.'

'You were drunk?'

'Isn't that what I just said?'

'OK, but do you think you'd have noticed if there had been lights on downstairs?' said Lorenzo, trying to avoid confrontation.

'Not if the curtains were drawn.'

'Had you company?'

'That's my business, no one else's.'

'Did you go straight to bed?'

'I made coffee; watched a movie.'

'What movie?'

'Some late-night crap. No idea what it was called. It was already halfway through when I switched on.'

'Did you hear any noises from downstairs?'

'Nope. Rarely do. They must have a bed with well-oiled springs.' He guffawed at his own coarse humour. 'Different from my old bouncy banger. When I'm having fun the whole neighbourhood shakes.'

'Mr Roper tells us he works late several nights a week.'

'Is that so?'

'But you didn't hear him return?'

'I 'eard nothing. How many times do I 'ave to tell you things? When I went to bed, I bombed out. Dead to the world until about 'alf an hour ago, when I was rudely disturbed.'

'OK, Mr Timms, we're going to have to take a look around your flat,' Lorenzo announced assertively. 'It'll take only a few minutes.'

Timms stiffened, his body-language telegraphing hostility and resistance.

'What for? You won't find nothing illegal in 'ere.'

'You're not suspected of any wrong-doing, Mr Timms,' Lorenzo said patiently. 'We're not searching for drugs. This isn't a raid. We're simply going through the motions in respect of Mary Walkers' reported disappearance.'

Timms mimicked a mocking laugh. 'And you reckon I might 'ave kidnapped 'er? 'Ave 'er stashed away in the attic?'

'We have a procedure to follow, Mr Timms; a process of elimination, that's all. Nothing for you to worry about.'

Timms snorted contemptuously. 'I'm not worried about nothing, but you're not stepping over this threshold into my castle without a search-warrant. I know me rights.'

Both detectives threw daggers with their eyes.

'Looks like we have a barrack-room lawyer here,' Lorenzo said to his partner, smirking, before addressing Timms provocatively, 'What have you to hide that you don't want our seeing?'

'That shit is falling on deaf ears,' Timms sneered. 'But for your information, I'll tell you exactly what I 'ave to hide: privacy. *My* rightful, legal privacy. Something you're not going to invade. You say you're looking for the tart from downstairs. Well, as I said before, most likely she's buggered off with some bloke or is stoned under the pier. Instead of pestering me on a precious Saturday morning, you'd be better off 'aving your dogs sniff her scent to whoever's bed she's shacked-up in.'

'Tell you what I'm going to do, Mr Timms,' Lorenzo said menacingly. 'I'm going to arrest you for obstructing our investigation. I'll have my colleague here handcuff you and we'll bang you up in a cell while we obtain a search-warrant from a magistrate. I trust you haven't anything planned for the weekend.'

'Bastards!'

'That's an irrelevant issue,' Lorenzo retorted passively. Then to Valentine, 'Cuff him!'

Without warning, Timms aimed a kick at Valentine's genitals.

Valentine was off-balance and unprepared, but not Lorenzo, who reacted with the speed and dexterity of an expert in martial arts, intercepting the kick and propelling Timms onto his face on the concrete path.

'Now we really do have something to charge you with and detain you for,' Lorenzo puffed gleefully, pinning Timms to the floor, while Valentine snapped on the handcuffs.

As the detectives frog-marched Timms to their car, he continued his futile struggle. His last act before being locked in the rear of the car, was to spit at Lorenzo, who sidestepped the airborne spittle.

'Send for back-up,' Lorenzo instructed Valentine. 'Let someone else have the pleasure of tossing this dross in the slammer. We've important work to do here.'

Roper had heard the commotion and emerged quizzically from his front-door.

'Just a little spat with your neighbour,' said Lorenzo, dusting himself down.

Roper looked beyond the detectives to the police car. 'Is that Mr Timms you've got in there?' Before Lorenzo could reply, Roper continued, 'Does he know something about Mary's whereabouts?'

'So far it's just a matter of his being out of order,' Lorenzo said low-key. 'We'll sort it.' Then, 'Is there a garden to this property, Mr Roper?'

'Yes, only a small one, mind you; out back.'

'Do you share it with Mr Timms?'

'No, it comes with our flat. We have exclusive use of it. There's not much to it; just a patch of grass and a tool-shed.'

'Let's take a look.'

The wooden gate to the garden was just a few yards beyond Timms' front-door.

'Do you keep the gate locked?' Lorenzo enquired casually, as Roper led the way.

'No, it's just on a latch,' said Roper, clicking open the entrance to the modest back yard. 'Nothing much to see really,' he added apologetically, stepping aside.

The diminutive lawn was fenced-off on three sides from neighbours' properties. The timber shed was on the right-hand side at the bottom, some twenty yards from the house. The shed had one window, covered in dust, and an ill-fitting door that faced the house.

'What's kept in there?' said Lorenzo, as they ambled over grass that was in need of a trim.

'Mostly rubbish that's been discarded from our flat, plus a lawnmower, spade and clippers.'

There was resistance to the door opening.

'That's funny,' said Roper, pushing hard. 'Something must have fallen down, getting in the way. It's usually harder to keep shut than to open.'

'Let me help,' said Lorenzo, putting his shoulder against the shed-door.

The combined beef of the two men gradually inched open the door, a weighty obstacle on the floor being forced backwards.

The only illumination inside the shed was borrowed from the sun. A single sliver of gold cut through the dusty gloom, throwing hazy light on the mystery that had brought detectives Lorenzo and Valentine to this unremarkable property in an unpretentious part of town.

Mary Walker was no longer a missing person.

3

There was little mystery surrounding the cause of death. The gaping wound in Mary Walker's neck, ear to ear, had been evident to Lorenzo the moment he stepped inside the garden-shed. The pool of blood around Mary's head, soaking her upper clothing, was consistent with an artery severed by a knife.

'Not a frenzied assault,' said Dr Savannah Moran, the pathologist, her manner as clinical as her job. 'One cut. Deep. In a nutshell, she bled to death.'

'No evidence of a fight for life,' Lorenzo commented, making a statement rather than asking a question, his fingers steepled to his chin. He was standing in Dr Moran's compact office in the local general hospital, while Dr Moran leaned over her metallic desk, leafing through the post mortem report.

'The lack of resistance is easily explained,' she said dismissively. 'There's a fracture to the base of her skull, the result of a blow to the head with a round, blunt implement.'

'Such as a hammer?'

'Very likely a hammer,' agreed Moran, who was suddenly looking wan and weary, having carved and sliced through Saturday night; a glorified butcher in all but name. With her adrenaline receding in an ebb tide, fatigue was kicking in fast.

'But the blow to the head didn't kill her?' Lorenzo said pedantically, pressing the point for clarification. He hated grey areas. As quickly as possible, he wanted the sequence of events in black and white, sharp definition.

'No, it was the slit-throat that prompted a massive and fatal haemorrhage.'

'So the killer came upon her from behind, catching her unawares, knocking her unconscious with a single strike,' he said thoughtfully. 'Did that hit cause much loss of blood?'

'No, hardly any; just enough to matt her hair slightly.'

'I'm finessing with these questions because there was no blood-trail leading to the shed,' Lorenzo explained. 'I'm trying to get my head around the last few seconds in this young woman's life.'

'There wouldn't be a trail if her throat wasn't cut until she was inside the shed,' Moran pointed out.

'This is the scenario I'm picturing, Doctor: the victim is almost home when she's bludgeoned unconscious. She's then dragged, like a lamb to the slaughter, through the garden-gate to the shed, where she's executed.'

'*Executed!*' exclaimed Moran, fluttering her eyelashes. 'Strong word.'

'Well, what would you call it?'

'It's not my business to be emotive, Inspector – not when I'm at work, anyhow. *All* hearts are cold in morgues. So anything other than cold facts would also be out of place. But as for your speculation, it sounds about right to me.' Her unusually lifeless, sapphire eyes longed to be shut at home on one of her silk pillows.

'Was she sexually assaulted?' Lorenzo pressed on.

'No signs of it; no semen on the swabs we took; no bruising or tearing in the vaginal cavity; no mutilation.'

'I'm not surprised.' The strain of a night without sleep was showing on Lorenzo's gaunt face; a good match, in that respect, with Moran's features.

The pathologist looked up sharply, some brightness refreshing her face, as if a light had been switched on in a dark room. 'What makes you say that?'

'No great Sherlock Holmes intuition. It's just that none of her clothes appeared to have been interfered with. The attack lacked frenzy, the reason I used the word *executed*. Everything about it cold-blooded. Elementary, dear Moran!'

Dr Moran smiled politely. 'I tend to agree,' she said reflectively. 'In crimes motivated by sex, revenge, hatred or jealousy, I'd expect to see evidence of hacking; a plethora of stab wounds and slashes; a desire to desecrate. A demolition job. The destruction of something once regarded as sacred. Citadel-smashing.'

'So what kind of weapon should we be looking for?'

Moran again referred to her notes. 'The blade had a pointed tip and was straight-edged; no serration, no unusual features.'

'Such as a dagger?'

'Or hunting knife; even some kind of kitchen-tool. Can't even guess at the length because the wound was relatively shallow, a curved cut and not a plunging stab. But the width of the blade was about an inch at its widest.'

'How about a fix on the time of death?'

Moran flicked through more pages of the file.

'She had a takeaway meal between 11.30p.m. and midnight, right?'

'That's what the girlfriend told us.'

'Confirmed by my autopsy. Digestion had only just begun, so she died shortly after eating. Assuming the timescale info you've been given is accurate, she was dead by 1.00am'

Eliminating the boyfriend, Jamie Roper, Lorenzo told himself. *Just as long as his alibi stacks up.* Lorenzo wouldn't have a chance to talk with the manager of the Rambo club until that evening, after the night-owls had flown their nests.

'I understand you already have a suspect in custody,' Dr Moran said idly.

'The tenant of the upstairs flat.'

'Think he's your man?'

'I hope he is. Oh, how I hope!'

Dr Moran shot Lorenzo a curious, quizzical look.

'He's an uncivilized animal,' said Lorenzo, answering the unasked question. 'Being caged is where he belongs. Could the killer have avoided being heavily bloodstained?'

28

'Not a chance. A fountain of blood would have surged upwards and outwards, like water from a fire-fighter's hose, the moment the artery was severed. Is that a problem for you?'

'It is in making a case against Dave Timms, the piece of excrement we're holding. No body-fluid on any of his clothes, including footwear. Of course it's possible for bloodstains to be invisible to the naked eye.'

'But not when the amount is so copious,' said Moran, following Lorenzo's reasoning.

'Exactly.'

'And there were no bloody footprints leading away from the premises?'

'Nothing obvious. Forensics are still working it, of course. But I'm not holding out much hope.'

'He must have been very careful, very DNA aware,' observed the attractive pathologist. 'Especially as it was night-time. Would there have been much lighting?'

'The street was reasonably lit. Amber lights, all operational. But the electric-light in the shed hadn't worked for months, apparently. And as for the back-garden, well, that would have been as black as a rabbit-warren.'

'Unless he had a torch,' said Moran. 'Which might suggest he was prepared and the crime was premeditated.'

'We didn't think there'd be any need to look beyond Timms when we discovered a woman's body in his flat,' said Lorenzo, tantalizingly deadpan.

'You mean there's a second victim?' gasped Moran, astonished.

'No, this female body was a live one, a fact that took a while to establish, however.'

Dr Moran pinched her slender waist with both hands and cocked her head spaniel-fashion, preparing for a punchline that she knew Lorenzo must be preparing to deliver.

'Why do I have that feeling of being a catch on the end of a fishing-line that you're playing with, before reeling in?'

'Because you're naturally suspicious,' said Lorenzo, reaching out to her with a smile of camaraderie. There was a genuine, cosy rapport between them. Although they had never socialized, Lorenzo had recognized from their first professional encounter a couple of years ago that their chemistry meant they gelled. However, although they were undoubtedly kindred spirits, Lorenzo had interpreted her knuckle-duster wedding-ring as a 'Beware of the bull' warning. Recently, he'd lost his appetite for locking horns with cuckolds, though his personal life remained no less complicated. 'The woman in Timms' flat, Sonia Martin, has history: a part-time, petty whore.'

'Whoring is a lifestyle choice and state of mind,' stated Moran, sermonizing, which wasn't her usual style. 'I don't see how it can ever be *petty* or indeed *part-time.* Irregular and spasmodic, maybe. But once embarked upon, you're a prostitute for life, even if you become sexually abstinent. Same way a reformed alcoholic is always just one drink away from alcoholism.'

'So a retired whore is just one paid-fuck away from being back in business,' Lorenzo finished the homily for Moran.

'I couldn't have put it more succinctly myself.'

'Sonia Martin has a habit that has to be fed,' Lorenzo continued. 'Whenever she's desperate for a fix, she turns a trick – or two. She was out cold in Timms' bed. Naked and white as a peeled banana.'

'The reason why you thought you had a second cadaver?'

'It was also the reason why Timms made such a fuss about our wanting to look around his dump. He banged on about his rights, demanding we have a search-warrant before putting a foot on his grubby territory. Of course, as soon as we found Mary Walker, the entire property became a crime-scene and we were able to bust in with impunity.'

'And that's when you came across the other woman?'

'Yep, the living corpse! We weren't able to talk to her until yesterday evening. We had her brought here, but she discharged herself around ten last night. Her story tallied with Timms' account: he picked her up in the pub and they took drink back to his place. She'd already done a couple of tricks and had bought cocaine on the street, then snorted the stuff in Timms' flat, while boozing.'

'Is Timms a dealer?'

'We've no record of that. Basically, he's just a bum. A small-time fence, handling anything nicked. He's a parasite without the balls or skill to do the burgling himself. Martin insists she bought the cocaine before going to the pub.'

Moran ignored the character-assassination. 'Were they indoors before Mary Walker was murdered?'

'Probably. No way of being absolutely certain, but it'll be hard to make a case against him, unless Martin was already out cold, in the upstairs flat, when Mary Walker arrived at the front-door downstairs and Timms saw her from one of his windows. But what would he have done with his bloodstained clothes?' This question was as much for himself as the pathologist.

'Burned them. Buried them.'

'Right now there's a scene-of-crime team digging up the garden. If anything's been buried there, they'll unearth it. Anything burned, they'll find the ashes.'

'Don't forget that bleach destroys DNA evidence,' Moran reminded Lorenzo.

'Timms isn't that smart. But neither is he dumb enough to shit on his own doorstep and that's what killing Mary Walker would amount to.'

'Unless he's a sicko and couldn't control himself.'

'He's a sicko, all right,' said Lorenzo, scowling.

Moran waited for more, but Lorenzo held back. There were two elements to the investigation that presented conflicting perspectives and, on the need-to-know principle, there was no reason for Lorenzo to share this information with Moran.

Timms was on the national Sex Offenders' Register, something Lorenzo had known about within an hour of the body being found. Five years previously, Timms had been convicted of sexually assaulting a 16-year-old girl and her mother, who was a prostitute. He'd been sentenced to five years in prison, but had earned full remission, being released after serving barely half the tariff imposed by the rather lenient trial judge.

No point looking any further was the mood among most of the detectives assigned to this investigation, but Lorenzo had no such confidence. More than most, he knew only too well the danger of allowing desire to override logic.

Only a small inner circle within Lorenzo's team knew of the note that had been stuffed between Mary's bra and breasts:

Sorry about the date: blame circumstances beyond my control. How smart are you? We'll soon find out. This is your challenge of a lifetime. Think big. Think about dear John. Bye for now – until the next time!

4

Next morning, at ten o'clock, a press conference was convened in the main briefing-room at the Central police station where Timms was detained. Lorenzo, with Valentine sitting beside him, fielded all questions from the dozen or so reporters, a few of them from regional TV and radio stations, but mostly print journalists, representing local and national newspapers.

Q. Is it correct that you've made an arrest and have a suspect in custody already?

A. We have someone helping us with our inquiries.

The journalists snickered in unison. 'Helping with inquiries' was universally accepted as cop code for a 'hot suspect in the can'.

Q. Can you confirm that the man you're holding is Dave Timms, a neighbour of the victim?

A. No, I cannot confirm that.

From this point the questions were fired with machine-gun rapidity, in the manner of an ambush.

Q. Are you expecting to charge him today?

A. Not with murder.

Q. You mean it'll be a holding-charge, until you've harvested more evidence against him?

A . No comment.

Q. Was the victim raped?

A. It would appear not.

Q. Sexually assaulted in any way?

A. We are not currently treating this as a sex-motivated crime. Please note currently.

Q. Is her lover implicated?

A. He is not the man we have in custody.

Q. Does that mean Jamie Roper is in the clear?

A. These are early days, as you'll appreciate. Far too early to rule people in or out.

Q. Who found the body?

A. I did.

Q. So she'd been reported missing?

A. Correct.

Q. Yet she was discovered in the grounds of her own home?

A. That's right.

Q. So she wasn't missing, after all? What are we missing here?

A. In the fullness of time, it will become clear, for me too, hopefully.

Collective sniggers.

Q. Had she at any time run off?

A. Nothing like that.

Q. Who reported her missing, though, apparently, she wasn't?

A. Her partner.

Q. So he's key to everything?

A. Please be more explicit.

Q. They were living together, right, as a couple?

A. Right.

Q. How long had she been missing, according to the boyfriend?

A. Only a few hours.

Q. Yet, in truth, she was at home all the time?

A. It's not as simplistic as that. Things will become more transparent when I'm at liberty to unlock further information for you.

Q. Had she been abducted, then returned dead?

A. I cannot answer that.

Q. Why are you withholding so much?

A. I'm not withholding: truth is, there's still so much we have to bottom-out. I've no intention of speculating – that's your trade.

A ripple of light laughter helped to dilute the discord. These press conferences were always a combative stand-off; tantamount to a frenzied attempt to milk a reluctant cow that would dry-up if squeezed too hard.

Q. Is it true that she was stabbed to death?

A. No. Her throat was slashed, severing an artery and she bled to death, very quickly.

Q. So she *was* stabbed?

A. No (wearily), she was cut; big difference. Look in the dictionary.

Q. What kind of knife was used?

A. That's where you can all help. We're looking for a knife with a sharp-tipped point. A blade without a serrated edge and about an inch wide.

Q. A dagger?

A. Quite possibly. Also could be a common kitchen-utensil.

Q. How long?

A. Not known.

Q. Do you reckon it was discarded near the crime scene?

A. Might have been. Nearby drains, rivers, streams, woodland and wasteland are being searched. We desperately need public co-operation. People should check their dustbins and gardens. If they come across a knife, which may be heavily bloodstained, it's essential it shouldn't be touched, unless gloves are being worn. Fingerprints could be crucial and evidence mustn't be contaminated. We're also interested in a blunt instrument, such as a hammer. We believe that Ms Walker was knocked unconscious before suffering the fatal wound.

Q. Was she definitely murdered where found?

A. That's the opinion of our medical expert.

Q. Was she being stalked?

A. That's another loose-end that has to be tied.

Q. Had she been threatened, then?

A. Not to my knowledge.

Q. She hadn't made a complaint to the police?

A. About what, exactly?

Q. You know, about being harassed, by a pest, something like that?

A. I've no information of that, but all records will be checked, of course.

Q. Where do her parents live?

A. It would be inappropriate for me to disclose those personal details. They obviously wish to be left alone to grieve privately in peace, for as long as possible.

Q. (From the mouth of a representative of a red-top) The victim's flat is near a red-light district. Is there any connection? I mean, was she moonlighting as a hooker while lover-boy was slaving in the sweat-shop, otherwise known as the Rambo?

A. (Frowning grimly) From all accounts, Mary Walker was a very respectable young woman, without a blemish on her character. She worked at a veterinary practice, she loved animals and people, was caring and compassionate, and any attempt to tarnish her name and reputation will be repudiated vigorously. Further, you should be ashamed for floating such a scurrilous proposition without any grounds for its veracity.

Q. Are you working on the theory that she knew her killer?

A. It's far too soon for theories.

Q. Are there witnesses?

A. Maybe – and that's how the media can assist further. We'd like to hear from anyone who might have seen Mary Walker between 11.00pm on Friday and 1.00am Saturday. We know roughly the route she took home from town, where she'd been to the cinema, and she may have been trailed. We'll be releasing a photograph of her to newspapers and TV companies. Posters will be displayed throughout the conurbation and there's the possibility of a reward being offered for information that leads to the conviction of her killer.

Q. Where *is* Mr Roper now?

A. Staying with family.

Q. Where?

A. A place where he hopes press bloodhounds won't sniff him out. OK, time for just one more question.

Q. Isn't it a fact that most murder victims know their killer?

A. Yes.

Q. Have you any reason to suppose that this crime should be one of the exceptions?

A. I stipulated just one more question and that's a second. Sorry, time's up, ladies and gentlemen. Our press office will keep you updated, within reason and subject to my approval.

Lorenzo turned on his heels and marched from the room, with Detective Constable Matt Valentine shadowing him closely, leaving a uniformed sergeant and a constable to shepherd out the restless and truculent media mob.

As Lorenzo and Valentine settled opposite one another with coffees at a corner-table in the police station's canteen, they made a striking contrast. Although suited, Lorenzo appeared unkempt and dissipated, but there was an innate shrewdness about him, a hidden depth, like Loch Ness, where legend had it that a monster patrolled the murky waters. Many a woman had been tempted to hunt the demons lurking in the labyrinthine network of Lorenzo's complicated psyche, hoping to unlock the mysteries of his dark and brooding make-up. They'd all failed, of course, many of them ending up emotionally damaged. His marriage had gone beyond the rocks; now a shipwreck on the sea-bed. Not only was he divorced from Pat, but also his two teenage children; all kinds of emotive flotsam were washed up from matrimonial disasters.

A two-year on-off-on-off affair with a detective sergeant, Sarah Cable, who had also been his work-partner at Scotland Yard, had petered out acrimoniously, in keeping with the conclusion of so many of the different chapters in Lorenzo's rollercoaster life. He was bad at relationships, something he was honest about, always warning women not to get too close to him emotionally because it would be something they'd both regret. But they never believed him; he was an irresistible challenge to them and each one was convinced that she would be the exception; that she would nail and slay the monsters in his Loch Ness head, discovering only too late that the demons were invincible. He could be loved, but not lived with. He wasn't an animal that could ever be content in captivity. He had to remain wild, free to roam, to explore as a free agent. The F-word – freedom – was his indestructible mantra. His roguish, raffish lifestyle bizarrely was a magnet, especially to women from middle-class, mundane backgrounds, for whom he represented a dangerous joy-ride, the chance for an outré expedition into a culture that had always been off-limits to them.

Lorenzo had made promise upon promise to reform and, to be fair, he'd made a genuine effort to tame himself. He no longer gambled, except occasionally in his job; risk-taking had the thrill-potency of the turn of a card, the spin of a wheel or the rattle of dice. Long ago, psychologists had identified casino-gambling as a sex-substitute for some people, especially masochists, who derived more pleasure from losing than winning, ejaculating at the tables as their chips were scooped away by the dealer's stick. The joy came from the concept of being beaten by a leggy and busty croupier.

Lorenzo was no masochist and for him there was certainly no adequate substitute for sex; faking it was fraud; a hanging offence in his book. There had been nothing sexy about blowing his salary on a succession of slow racehorses and dice that refused to dance to his tune. He had curtailed his drinking and even given up smoking, but those habits were mere accessories; they weren't the man. But women would always be his Achilles' heel.

Lorenzo had requested a transfer from Scotland Yard to the provinces to make a fresh start after the messy breakdown of his marriage and the turbulent affair with Sarah Cable. Already new temptations were nibbling at his weak spot and his resistance was wearing thin. He was finding that being good was bad for his self-esteem; perverse maybe, but perfectly understandable to those who knew a thing or two about Jack the Lads. Notoriety did something for certain men's egos, endowing them with a swagger, if only spiritual, their swashbuckling confidence a beacon for large swathes of the opposite sex. But no woman wanted to live with such a man, so the stratagem was to catch and change. Then, if a woman succeeded in changing her catch, the original attraction dimmed, because she'd killed the allure: Catch-22 of the mating game.

As for Valentine, he was much more one-dimensional and looked like a clone of the FBI; tall and athletic, with light-brown hair cropped short, fair complexion and soulless, steely eyes. He was always nattily dressed in a sharp-cut suit, freshly-laundered white shirt, sober tie, and highly-polished black shoes. He'd never been seen on duty unshaven and he kept a battery-operated shaver in his desk to deal with that crepuscular-grey that crept across his boyish face every day around sunset. He was one of the new-breed of ex-university cops, who no doubt would be fast-tracked to a rank that Lorenzo hadn't a hope in hell of attaining. Valentine's redolence – not just his aftershave – was right for the times: he had a young family, his wife was a teacher, he'd never smoked, he'd never been inside a betting-shop or casino, and when he did occasionally drink, it was wine and not beer. Most importantly, he was a one-woman man, loyal to the core, having married the sweetheart of his youth, the daughter of a chief constable; a fact that provided him with bullet-proof protection in his career, much to Lorenzo's chagrin.

Although Valentine boasted academic qualifications, he would never be as astute or intrinsically cunning as Lorenzo; only one of them would ever be a *real* cop – and it certainly wasn't the one who *looked* like a smart detective. Appearances so often were the mother of mistakes.

Despite the chasm of their differences, Lorenzo and Valentine rubbed along without too much friction, each of them reasonably tolerant of what they saw as foibles in the other.

'Time for a quick appraisal,' said Lorenzo, his manner brisk and all business. 'What's the latest from Forensics?'

'Nothing to excite.'

'What did you make of Sally Wingate?'

'Reliable.'

Valentine had interviewed Sally on the Saturday afternoon.

'She's mortified, of course,' Valentine added.

Mortified! Lorenzo winced mentally. *A woman's word! Why can't he simply say she's in shock? I'm 'mortified' by what comes out of universities and gets into police uniform!*

'And her story fits the overall narrative?' said Lorenzo, without rancour.

'A perfect fit, I'd say. They met after work and went together to the Odeon cinema in town. It was something they did often on Fridays.'

This set Lorenzo thinking. 'So it was a regular thing?'

'I know what you're getting at, Mike. You're wondering if it was such a ritual that someone else might have cottoned on to it and perhaps followed them or waylaid Mary later.'

Clever bugger! 'Something like that,' said Lorenzo, still relaxed.

'It wasn't a routine set in stone. Some weeks, they'd give it a miss completely or go on a different evening. When Sally had a boyfriend, they went months without meeting, except perhaps for a drink at lunchtime. Another factor was the irregular hours Mary worked, but she was normally needed for evening surgery; that's why they went to the late-night show.'

'Anything noteworthy happen while they were in the cinema? Anyone make a pass at them or try to chat them up afterwards?'

'No, nothing.'

'And they walked together from town until Mary was almost home?'

'As far as Boscombe Gardens.'

'Which meant Mary had about a quarter of a mile left to hoof it on her own,' said Lorenzo, evaluating. 'The crucial segment. The last lap. Did Sally see Mary after they'd parted?'

Valentine was puzzled by this question and it showed on his face.

'Did she look back over her shoulder to wave, something like that?' Lorenzo clarified his query. 'I'm just wondering if she noticed anything remotely suspicious, like someone behind Mary who she recognized from the cinema-queue or just a face in the crowd in town?'

'Sally didn't mention anything and I'm sure she would have if something had bothered her.'

They both paused to drink more coffee before Valentine said, 'No holes in Mr Roper's alibi?'

Lorenzo had spent a couple of hours talking to people at the Rambo club between nine and eleven the previous night.

'Tight as a miser. Bar staff were swept off their feet all night. Roper didn't even take his legal break. The bar staff there are a close-knit team. They even notice every time one of them slopes off for a leak. And on Friday night none of them had time even for a pee. From the time the doors opened until they closed, it was a marathon-sprint for the workers. No, Roper's clean and in the clear, unless there was a conspiracy and unless someone did the business for him.'

'What possible reason could there be for him to want Mary dead, the woman he lived with, loved, and was going to marry?'

'Absolutely none that I can think of,' Lorenzo agreed sullenly. 'We have to look elsewhere, I'm afraid. Start being creative. '

'Something did strike me as a little odd, though, when we were interviewing Roper before Mary's body had been found,' said Valentine, in partial reverie.

'Let's hear it,' Lorenzo prompted.

'When you asked him if Timms had ever been in their flat, he replied, "Not while I've been at home". It seemed to me that he might have been harbouring a suspicion that Mary was up to something while he was out of the way.'

Lorenzo stroked his prickly chin thoughtfully.

'Probably nothing in it,' Valentine continued awkwardly, as if ashamed of speaking ill of the dead.

'No matter, very observant of you,' Lorenzo grudgingly congratulated the young detective, though genuinely impressed. 'However, I don't think we can read anything mean-ingful into it. I should imagine it was just a technically accurate answer from a man too stressed to concern himself with avoiding clumsy sentences with innuendo.'

'I suppose,' said Valentine. 'Especially after talking with Sally Wingate who was adamant they were a devoted couple who lived for one another.'

She shall not grow old to wither under the strain of divorce, Lorenzo thought cynically, before saying aloud encouragingly, 'You're right to concentrate on the way people speak. For example, when Timms asked if we were "local", I knew he was on some force's radar for something nasty. But the most disturbing feature of all for me about this case is the note.'

'Don't you think it shows that this is a game for the killer?' said Valentine.

'Undoubtedly. It also strongly points to Mary Walker having been pre-selected for some specific reason. Nothing random about it at all.'

'But what does he mean by: *Sorry about the date: blame circumstances beyond my control?*'

'Dunno. That's the riddle we have to decipher. He's throwing down the gauntlet to us when he writes: *How smart are you? We'll soon find out.*'

'Making it personal, a contest, duel even?'

'Reads like that to me,' said Lorenzo.

'But he couldn't have known who'd be the lead detective. He wouldn't have been aware you'd pick up the tab.'

'You're right, it can't possibly be *that* personal,' Lorenzo concurred, still affably. 'It's more generic – him against the police per se, against the law and authority in general. He's out to prove he's smart and we're stupid. On that score, I guess he has a head start!'

Valentine didn't do humour, so Lorenzo's little self-deprecating dig sailed over Valentine's head.

'There could be a clue in this,' Valentine reasoned. '*He* could have done time and perhaps was wrongly convicted and this is his warped way of getting revenge.'

'If a grievance was the motive, the grudge would be specifically against the victim,' said Lorenzo. 'So we start with Mary: why *her*? His challenge to us is supplementary; kind of icing on the cake or cherry on a cocktail-stick. He tells us to *think big*. To think about *dear John*. What does that suggest to you?'

'A *Dear John* letter is one of goodbye; the ending of a romantic relationship,' said Valentine. 'The ditching of a lover. Maybe we should be taking a close look at Mary Walker's old flames.'

'That's my interpretation, too – except for one fact.'

Valentine waited expectantly for Lorenzo to finish.

'The last seven words of the note: *Bye for now – until the next time!* Don't you see, Matt, this is only the beginning. When he tells us to *think big*, he really means that *he's* thinking big – as in serial numbers. And every serial killer starts with his tally at just one.'

'You really believe....' Valentine's voice trailed away before he could finish articulating his fear.

'Oh, yes, Matt: this fella means business. He's proved what he can do. He's set the template and he's forewarned us about his machinations.'

'But forewarned is to be forearmed,' Valentine said glibly.

'Except that he has an insuperable advantage over us: he knows exactly what's going on in his addled head and we haven't a clue; despite the note, the autopsy report and the distinctive MO: not a clue.'

5

Since migrating from London, Lorenzo's rented home had been a converted barn in the grounds of a farmhouse, about six miles out of Bournemouth, under the flight-path of the regional airport. The owners, Luke and Tricia Lockwood, weren't farmers. The land that went with the old, grey-stone property was sold years ago to developers and the crops grown thereafter were houses and shops. The Lockwoods, like most of their neighbours, weren't rural folk by birth or temperament. They'd bought into the country culture as an investment and perceived prestige, but they'd always be townies at heart, just like Lorenzo.

Luke worked from home as a financial adviser. His office was downstairs at the rear, the lattice-windows overlooking a small courtyard and stables. Tricia kept half a dozen horses and ran a small riding-school with Kylie Roche, the 19-year-old daughter of a local vicar. The converted, two-tier barn was at the side of the farmhouse, within the courtyard complex.

Tricia, a handsome 40-year-old, had been born in Virginia and for ten years worked for the FBI as a language profiler within the agency's Behavioural Science Unit. She'd met Luke when he was in Washington on business from the UK while employed by one of the world's largest financial institutions. Their first encounter had been during the 'happy hour' in the hotel where Luke was staying and Tricia was attending a weekend seminar on stalkers and their trademarks. The 'happy hour' had expanded into a happy, six-week whirlwind romance, culminating with Tricia abandoning the

FBI for Luke and London, where they married a week later. Within an hour of returning from honeymoon in Italy, Luke logged into his computer to begin opening the fifty or so emails that had accumulated while he was away – one of them curtly and cruelly informing him that he was fired, a casualty of the recession. With bonuses, he'd been raking in something in the region of half a million pounds a year, so retrenchment was suddenly a priority, something to which neither of them was accustomed. Proceeds from the hasty sale of their Mayfair apartment had comfortably covered the purchase of the Dorset farmhouse, horses, and all necessary tack, leaving a handy surplus.

Lorenzo wasn't privy to Tricia's FBI background until at least a month after moving into his rented accommodation, appropriately named 'The Barn'. Since then, he'd exploited Tricia's expertise on several occasions, but no time had ever been as compelling as the present.

'Saw you on TV,' she said, casually, her American accent undiminished.

They were in the low-beamed but modernized farmhouse-kitchen, Lorenzo slouched in a chair at the stolid, oak-varnished table, under harsh spotlights embedded in the undulating ceiling. Tricia postured by the hob, hands on jaunty hips, waiting for the coffee-percolator to start rattling.

'I have an aversion to press conferences,' Lorenzo said miserably.

'I thought you handled it rather well; got across what you wanted to, conceded nothing, kept the rabid bloodhounds in check, and didn't allow them up your nose; not noticeably, anyhow. The plug for public co-operation always goes down well, but I suspect you were holding back on something or things. And if you weren't, then you're in trouble.'

'Very astute.'

The coffee came to the boil. It wasn't until Tricia had delivered two stout and cheerful mugs to the table that the conversation was resumed.

'When I see you like this, in the sticks, just having mucked-out in the yard, it's easy to forget that you were at the forefront of helping to crack some of the toughest serial killer cases in history,' said Lorenzo, his awe sincere.

'That's something of an exaggeration,' she said, blushing a little from the compliment, bringing a pink glow to her otherwise pale cheeks. 'I was very much a backroom girl; recruited from academia, not dealing in exact science like the DNA profilers. A language profiler, as I'm sure you know, is an interpreter of sorts. Defence counsel will always try to rubbish our input as nothing better than crystal-ball gazing.'

'Defence counsels would shamelessly rubbish the testimony of the Disciples.'

'Except that of Judas,' said Tricia, with irony. 'Mind you, everyone loves a Judas these days; a whistle-blower or spy who's been turned.'

'Where's Luke?'

'At the pub – where else?' Her face hardened and resentment burned in her flinty, perceptive eyes. She was a natural blonde and the outdoor life had even further lightened the parts of her hair most exposed to sunshine. Her features were small, but her lips were full, and clever use of pink lipstick enhanced and enlarged the definition of her mouth. Because her hair was styled to frame her face, its angular outline was obscured. In floppy jumper, jodhpurs and riding-boots, she looked as if she must have been born and reared in a stable.

Obviously Luke wasn't the special of the day on Tricia's menu, so Lorenzo moved on quickly.

'I want to pick your brains.'

'Don't be apologetic about it, Mike. I'd rather have my brain picked by you than have Luke picking a fight when *eventually* he staggers in.'

Lorenzo deliberately missed his cue. Instead, he said, 'You were right to suspect I was holding back on something at the press conference. Take a look at this; it's a photocopy, so it doesn't matter how much you finger it. All I ask is that you don't mention it to anyone, even Luke.'

'*Especially* Luke, you should have said. He keeps secrets like bottomless buckets hold water.' There was no humour in her voice or eyes. 'Where was this found?' she asked gravely, while reading.

'On the body.'

'A gambler, for sure.'

'What makes you say that?'

'It's been a long time since I last saw a handwritten calling-card of this nature. He's either a reckless thrill-seeker or very dim; could be both, of course. On the other hand, he may have a reason to feel secure; can't see that, though. Handwriting's as good as a latent fingerprint; not that I need to tell you that. Let's give him credit, where it's probably not due, and assume he's of at least average intelligence. If that's the case, he must be reasonably confident that you won't ID him via his handwriting.'

'But what can you tell me about him, apart from being a chancer?'

She sighed resignedly. 'I can't help you at all about his character from the physical style of his writing, Mike; you'll need a graphologist for that. Language profilers draw conclusions from content, nothing else. My comment about his being a gambler was only an aside really; my surprise at his daring to use a pen rather than a computer-printer or a compilation of letters cut from newspapers.'

Lorenzo nodded, sipped his coffee, reclined and listened. Tricia was as absorbed and intense as a soothsayer in a trance, suddenly totally one-dimensional.

'He really rates himself. When he writes "How smart are you?" he's really bragging that he's a lot smarter than you. He desperately wants recognition, to be noticed.'

'He wants to be identified and caught?'

'No, that's not what I mean. He probably leads a mundane life, perhaps trapped in a boring job and considers himself under-appreciated. Perhaps he's been passed over for promotion a number of times or maybe he's unemployed and keeps getting rejected for jobs.'

47

'Married?'

'There's insufficient here to make a call on that, but I'd guess not. The *Dear John* reference suggests he might have been jettisoned by the love of his life.'

'That figures,' Lorenzo murmured thoughtfully.

'"Sorry about the date" – he might have planned to kill on the anniversary of the break-up, but something prevented that, hence "circumstances beyond my control".'

'So his ex-lover must have been the victim?'

'Except he makes it plain that he intends to kill again. It could be, of course, that his failure in love could have deranged him, resulting in a pathological hatred of all women.'

'Turned into a psychopath, but not psychotic?' said Lorenzo.

'Well, in lay parlance he must be mad, but he won't be an axe-swinging madman running amok. On the contrary, he's more likely to be very quiet and withdrawn, blending unnoticed into the wallpaper of society. He could be married, with a family, but I'd rule out that; it doesn't fit with his malevolence towards Mary Walker, a twenty-year-old – not if he's found happiness since the break-up with her.'

'What's the age-range?'

'Over 25, under 50. Sorry, there's too little to go on to narrow it down further.'

'Gut instinct tells me we're dealing with a stalker, Tricia, but those closest to Mary Walker are adamant that she wasn't living in fear and had never talked about a feeling of ever having been followed.'

'In these kinds of killings Mike, there's nearly always a traceable connection between the perp and the victim, however tenuous. They may have met only once, but for one of them that moment was earth-moving, while the victim would not have even remembered the encounter. A major problem is that stalking isn't always visible. In other words, the target is unaware that she's a quarry and, metaphorically, is in sharp focus in someone's telescopic sights. The public generally think of stalking as the nightmare only of celebrities, but, in reality, celebs are just the tip of the iceberg. For example, studies show that a fifth of all GPs will be stalked during their career. The statistics in the UK mirror very closely those in the US: eight per cent of all women and two per cent of the male population will be stalked at least once.'

By now, Tricia had Lorenzo hooked. He was strapped to a learning-curve.

'When I was with the FBI, I learned that 40 per cent of all stalkers had had a sexual or substantial emotional entanglement with the object of their obsession.'

'*Object!* Is that how they think of the person of their dreams – an *object?*'

'Very much so; something – not somebody – to be turned into a possession. Now to another statistic: 27 per cent of all stalked women were the victims of total strangers. Do you know, it's common for stalkers to hire private detectives to shadow intended victims in order to learn everything possible about their routines, habits, likes, dislikes, friends, favourite pubs and restaurants? Phones are bugged, dustbins rifled. Homes are broken into and bugs planted in bedrooms, as near to the pillows as possible. If used condoms are garnered from the dustbin of the target, this is likely to knock the stalker badly off kilter.'

'Is there a common denominator that defines all stalkers?'

'Yes, they're all control-freaks, like my Luke.' She mimicked a laugh, but it wasn't convincing. 'They revel in the power they believe they're wielding. Often they're exacting revenge for some perceived rejection, although frequently it's imagined and never actually occurred. I've some old documents upstairs that I'd like to refer to; they might be useful to you. Help yourself to more coffee; I'll only be a few minutes.'

Lorenzo did as was invited. Tricia was away no longer than five minutes, returning with a bundle of sepia-fringed papers.

'I kept most of the research material I was privy to because I thought one day I might write a book, chronicling my experiences,' she said, slightly short of breath, having run up and down stairs. 'Here we are, this is what I was looking for.' She brushed away dust with a hand from the document she'd plucked from the pile. 'Yes ... a team of research psychologists in the US divided stalkers into five groups. The idea was to produce a model or template in chart-form that would enable the police to identify potentially dangerous serial stalkers before they escalated into killers.'

'Tricia, surely it's not suggested that all stalkers become murderers?'

'No, of course not, but research has clearly shown that *most* entrenched stalkers are capable of killing if further spurned or thwarted. They are dangerous, Mike, make no mistake about that. You underestimate their threat at your peril, believe me.'

'OK, Tricia, enlighten me about the five groups.'

Tricia read from the appropriate page of the document in her hand. 'Intimacy Seekers, Rejects, Incompetent Suitors, the Resentful, and the Predatory.'

'Now take me through them as succinctly as possible, please.'

'No problem. I'll keep to the same order. "Intimacy Seekers" fall in love with their targets, rather than hating them. I'll give you an example: a female author may autograph her book, "with love" for one of her male readers at a signing session. He takes the inscription literally, interpreting it as an invitation to intimacy. The self-brainwashing is accumulative and inexorably progressive. As the reader works through the book, he imagines that the author is reaching out to him personally, that there are coded messages and a desire for a secret rendezvous. Bedroom scenes are read as sexual foreplay between the two of them. The stalking begins very quickly. The target is idolized. No word of criticism will be tolerated against the icon. This is a classic, one-sided, unrequited love affair, but the *lover* is inflamed with unbridled passion.'

'Of which the victim is totally ignorant?'

'Naturally. The man is unknown to her. The entire fabricated nonsense exists only in the deranged male head. Most stalkers of celebrities fall into the Intimacy Seeker category, but so too those who are obsessed with say, a doctor or nurse. A certain smile or a word of kindness may be misunderstood and lead to years of harassment and misery. These stalkers are extremely persistent and usually suffer from major mental disorders.'

'I can't see *our* man belonging to that group, can you?'

'No, I can't.'

'So what's next?'

'The Rejects.'

'Sounds more promising,' commented Lorenzo, sniffing.

'Well, they're nearly always former lovers, partners or spouses, who refuse to accept the breakdown of the relationship. They won't take no for an answer and will go to any lengths to achieve their goal, which is winning back their lost love. The longer they're impeded, the more they seek revenge, just as fiercely as attempting to rekindle the flame of affection, and it's at this spiteful point that they become a danger; a volcano ready to erupt.'

'That could be a neat fit for *our* man.'

Tricia ruminated awhile. 'I agree it's possible....'

'But you're wavering, you have doubts?'

'The problem for me is that he wouldn't be invisible. He'd have been out in the open, making a nuisance of himself for months. He wouldn't have stopped at pestering Mary Walker, he'd have been a pain in the bum for the boyfriend; what's his name?'

'Jamie Roper.'

'Yes, there'd have been clashes. He'd have taunted him with explicit details of Mary's sexual track-record, true or invented. Can you remember the famous case in the late 1990s, when a guy became Britain's first convicted email stalker?'

'I've vague recollections,' said Lorenzo, scratching his chin, eyes aimed towards the ceiling, his memory hazy on this one.

'Well, he bombarded his former lover with as many as eight erotic emails an hour on her home PC, as well as sticking "Wanted" posters all over her car. You see, "Rejects" don't go from rejection to attack in one impulsive leap. They always begin with hard-sell persuasion and immature pleading; bleating, in fact. The route to revengeful aggression is usually a long, circuitous and painful one.'

'Certainly not a Cinderella-slipper fit in the Mary Walker case,' Lorenzo lamented.

'So we come to "Incompetent Suitors", who are exactly what the tag implies,' said Tricia. 'They're attracted to someone, but lack the social skills and chat-up technique to have any chance of making a successful connection. Because of their inadequacies, they're often as bad at stalking as connecting with someone. They tend to derive little or no satisfaction from harassment. A common trait is that they give up easily, only immediately falling for another *love of their life*, usually someone they've never exchanged more than a few words with or perhaps haven't even met; just someone they see every day on a bus or train. Although commonly of low intellect, they may have a high opinion of themselves, sometimes believing they're irresistible, and become disgruntled and resentful when not worshipped by the opposite sex.'

'But do they kill?'

'Can do, but clumsily and not as frequently as those from other groups. Essentially, they're big-time losers.'

'What's the fourth group?'

'"Resentful Stalkers." They feel sorry for themselves, firm in the belief they've been sinned against. They're always the innocent party in any conflict and then become hell-bent on retribution. Their victim could be someone they despise, but not always; he or she might merely be symbolic of a social class, trade, profession or political party, hated by the stalker. They're renowned for being workplace stalkers. The majority have self-righteous personalities, although some suffer from paranoia, such as schizophrenia. In their opinion, they have God and virtue on their side and are morally superior to others. One veteran of the Falklands War typified this particular species, becoming the first person in the UK to be gaoled for causing psychological grievous bodily harm to a woman he'd stalked for six years. After his release from prison, he resumed his reign of terror and even changed his name to that of the woman's last boyfriend. This was the landmark case that paved the way for anti-stalking laws.'

'Nice people you've studied!'

'The worst are still to come – the "Predators," a truly heartless, malevolent breed who really mean business, the equivalent of Great White sharks of the sea, unerringly homing-in on their prey until ready to strike. Their stalking is a pernicious prelude to a lethal attack. They're not seeking a relationship, simply violence. To these passionless hunters, it's warfare from the start, building day by day, hour by hour, towards an unprovoked and unanticipated ambush.'

'That's *our* man, I'd wager.'

'You told me you'd given up gambling,' Tricia remarked, teasingly.

They exchanged spontaneous smiles, all part of the comfortable interaction.

'You got me there!' admitted Lorenzo, wagging a finger, chalking up an imaginary point against his self.

'With these highly-motivated predators, stalking's structured along military lines, where information-gathering is an integral ingredient of the preparation. The initial groundwork comprises reconnoitring: collating as much data as possible about the target's lifestyle and habits. The evening ritual is pivotal: does she date, party, and dine out? If so, where and with whom? Finally, what time to bed? How many people live in the same house? How many silhouettes in the bedroom? In other words, is the target sleeping alone? Everything is memorized or even written daily in a special log-book. And here's the fundamental difference from the other categories: jealousy and the impulse for possession are excluded from the predator's psyche. There's no emotional traction whatsoever. For the Predator, stalking is a blood sport. He's turned on by the thrill of the chase – and most of all, by the kill.'

'You're chilling my blood,' said Lorenzo, shuddering to underscore his point.

'So I should. The Predator relishes dress rehearsals for the "big event". The anticipation makes him salivate and he's sexually aroused, even reaching a climax, merely at the prospect of what the future promises. In fact, the fantasizing over what lies ahead is almost more rewarding to these stalkers than the actual final enactment. The physical assault, which is almost always sexual in nature, can be something of an anti-climax, tantamount to bringing down the curtain for the last time on a long-running show.'

'But Mary Walker wasn't raped,' Lorenzo jumped in, seizing on the apparent faulty gene in Tricia's exposition. 'The pathologist was adamant that there was no evidence of sexual assault.'

'I know, I read all that in my daily newspaper,' Tricia said levelly.

'So doesn't that torpedo the theory that our man could be a Predatory Stalker?'

'Not at all. Sexual fulfilment can be achieved without it being shared or forced upon the unwilling victim.'

'Putting it crudely,' said Lorenzo, 'he could have *come* in his pants?'

No blush now from Tricia. This was clinical theorising, not dirty talk.

'Quite possibly. There is lust for power and control over the other person, with the woman seen as a vulnerable, helpless damsel in distress. Something else for you: are you *au fait* with erotomania?'

'Sounds like more medic mumbo-jumbo to me,' Lorenzo commented scornfully.

Tricia's laboured smile was almost patronizing, though not intended. 'Don't be put off by the pretentious lingo; it merely identifies people – women, as well as men – who get-off by hounding someone. Many people, even in law enforcement, scoff at criminal profiling, but it's been going on – and accepted – since the Jack the Ripper murders.'

'But I'm not one of the sceptics,' said Lorenzo. 'I know all about Dr Thomas Bond, a police surgeon who performed the autopsy on Mary Kelly, Jack's last victim. Bond documented the Ripper as daring, physically strong, mentally unstable and a quiet, unimposing loner. His medical peers and the cop establishment of the day were suitably impressed, apparently.'

'Indeed, and offender-profiling was born, Mike; it's not new or trendy. There's a sub-division of erotomania, known as Clérambault's Syndrome, in which sufferers have a profound narcissistic tendency. The condition is usually underpinned by schizophrenia and is hard to control; these people are very erratic, like an unstable landmine that can explode the moment it's disturbed only slightly.'

'Mind if I borrow those FBI research papers of yours for a few days?'

'Be my guest,' said Tricia, flicking them across the table, as if dealing from a blackjack shoe. 'More coffee?'

Lorenzo held up a halting hand. 'No, thanks. I've got enough on my mind to keep me awake all night without over-taxing my bladder.'

There was genuine warmth in Tricia's engaging smile.

'You've been very helpful and I'm appreciative yet, in reality, I'm still stuck in the starting-blocks,' said Lorenzo, frustration the architect of his gloomy expression.

'Because you don't yet know if stalking was involved?'

'Precisely. She could just as easily have stumbled upon her killer; a chance clash just as she was almost home. In the wrong place at the wrong time.'

'A mugging that went wrong, possibly?'

'No, nothing was stolen; contents of her handbag, including credit cards and mobile-phone, untouched.'

'And the note, of course, which I keep forgetting,' said Tricia. 'Muggers don't write and leave goading, cocky missives. So she had to be the chosen one. If not stalked, most certainly selected. Pre-selected.'

'Yet it would seem that the note was scribbled in a hurry, probably at the scene,' said Lorenzo, intrigued by his own recapitulation. 'If it was all pre-planned, why hadn't he penned the note in advance, at leisure, allowing him to scarper quicker from the crime?'

'Only one person can give you that answer with certainty and apparently, he's not the one you have in the cells,' said Tricia, reminding Lorenzo of something he'd rather be able to ignore. 'You have your work cut out.'

'Thanks!'

At that moment, the front door creaked open and banged closed.

'Luke,' whispered Tricia, a depression settling over her.

'Bloody carpet!' Luke cursed as he tripped in the hallway.

'I'd better go,' said Lorenzo.

'You don't have to,' Tricia said, rather weakly.

'It's better that I do. I'll slip out the back-door.'

Lorenzo stepped into the darkness only a few heartbeats before Luke plodded unsteadily into the kitchen.

The first thing Luke noticed was not his wife, but the two used mugs on the table.

6

Graphologist Penelope Lowen worked mainly for banks and other large commercial institutions. She vetted letters of application for jobs. The companies to which she was contracted all demanded that aspiring employees should make their initial approach by handwritten letter. They pinned unshakable faith in a graphologist of Lowen's reputation being able to identify personality flaws in applicants from their handwriting, thus avoiding mistakes in hiring. Although contracted to several international corporations, Lowen was, in essence, a freelance, so the police were able to make use of her expertise on an *ad hoc* basis, whenever she was available.

Lorenzo called her at 8.00am the day after his discussion with Tricia Lockwood. Lowen was based in the port city of Southampton, a half-hour power-drive from Bournemouth.

'Good morning, Penny,' Lorenzo began breezily. They knew one another well enough from previous assignments to be on first name terms, without the familiarity appearing contrived. Without preamble, he continued briskly, 'I'm touting for a wee favour.'

'Just how *wee*? Don't forget, I know your old blarney of old.'

'A few lines of handwriting to look at. A brief note, but very important to me. A death-note.'

'It'll be at least a couple of days before I can get to Bournemouth.'

'I'll come to you.'

'I'm flying to Scotland this afternoon to give a lecture.'

'I'll be with you in half an hour.'

'And half an hour is all the time I can spare.'

'Which is all the time I need.'

'You'd better hit the road, then.'

'Already putting on my bicycle-clips!'

Lowen was packing her overnight bag when Lorenzo arrived on the doorstep of her suburban, mock-Tudor house; a Mercedes convertible parked on the U-shaped, gravel drive.

The graphologist was dressed in a dark, business trouser-suit, her brunette hair cut boyishly short. A thick trench on a finger of her left hand was a tombstone to a dead marriage, a scar not only from a tight wedding-ring but perhaps also of the conflict that had led to its removal. She escorted Lorenzo to her rather masculine study and, as soon as they were seated, wasted no time getting down to business.

'OK, Mike, let's have it.'

Taking the tempo from Lowen, Lorenzo extracted the photo-copy of the note from his briefcase and handed it to her. Lowen swung away from the detective in her swivel-chair to switch on a desk-spotlight. From a top drawer of her antiquated, pseudo-Dickensian desk, she produced a large magnifying glass, a replica of the sort favoured by Sherlock Holmes and philatelists.

'Not much to go on,' she murmured, after a couple of minutes. 'I assume this is connected to the murder in Boscombe?'

Lorenzo simply nodded affirmation.

'I read about it yesterday. Nasty. No mention of *this*, though.'

'My ace in the hole, hopefully,' said Lorenzo.

'More like a deuce. However, OK, here we go: although I promised you half an hour, this will take five minutes, max. The author is left-handed, no doubt about that. Before I continue, there's something I must ask *you*, Mike: are you assuming this note was written in a hurry and on an uneven surface?'

'Most likely. Probably in the dark, too. Certainly he wasn't at a desk or table, if my theory has any credibility.'

'That's helpful. You see, there's a shakiness about the writing in parts, suggesting diffidence, and a scatty, spineless personality, but that would be at odds with the majority of indicators.'

'Are you saying that you don't believe this person to be mentally unstable?'

'No, I'm not saying that at all; obviously such a conclusion would be madness on my part! Now … there are long, bold strokes here. The slant to the left indicates an outgoing, well-balanced personality. However, the slant is hugely exaggerated.'

'Meaning?'

'He's flamboyant, an extrovert, a very confident showman.'

'Over-confident?'

'Oh, yes. Opinionated, too. Self-righteous. Intolerant. God's gift to mankind. Sees himself as representing the centre of gravity; life and soul of any party. Is never wrong in his eyes. A sense of humour, but only at the expense of others; can't take a joke against himself. The sort who would be an obsessive letter-writer to newspapers; that might be a line worth following up. Intolerable to live with, unless always allowed his own way.'

'Any indication of his age?'

'That's not a discipline of graphology, but I could hazard an educated guess.'

'Let's hear it, Penny.'

She pondered theatrically, making a bit of a meal of it. 'You're not looking for an elderly man, nor a particularly young one. He's out of his twenties, but not into his fifties. That's my take on it, anyhow, for what it's worth – and, to be honest, it's worth no more than your own conjecture.'

'Married? A father?'

'Again, not within my scope, but I'd speculate that's he's more likely to be divorced, because of my comment about his being impossible to live with. He's almost certainly a charmer; a smooth bastard, expecting knickers to be dropped at the flick of his fingers. Little depth to him. Fickle, but expects – indeed demands – eternal loyalty from others. A dissembler.'

'You're working well from so little,' said Lorenzo.

'Down to squeezing blood from a stone now, though. What I

can add is that he's not likely to be in a humdrum job. Artistic, I reckon. Quite possibly self-employed. But now I really am pushing the limits. At school, he'd have been a playground-bully; leader of a gang. A definite sense of drama about this note. Bear in mind local theatrical groups and writing circles. The handwriting is rather distinctive. It should be recognizable to someone. Have you considered releasing it to the media?'

'Thought about it, yes.'

'But decided against it?'

'So far, yes; mainly because of the last sentence.'

'Ah, yes; I see what you mean: "Bye for now – until the next time!" – I can see the problem: public panic at the prospect of a budding serial killer at large in their midst. Press and politicians on your back: *What are you doing? Why haven't you done this and that?* Armchair detectives pissing you off, trashing your efforts.'

'My biggest worry about going public with the note, is that it might act as an incentive to the killer, giving him a taste for what he might be encouraged to promote as his trademark.'

'If he intends to kill again, he'll kill. In that context, any note he may leave – or may not – is going to be rather irrelevant, don't you think? It's just decoration. The candy on the corpse.'

Lorenzo acknowledged that she was right. The realization that there would inevitably be another similar murder, unless the killer was arrested quickly, chilled Lorenzo to the bone. The sheer helplessness of his dilemma was the most debilitating feature of his plight; a feeling that he could do little but sit and wait, as if he was hunter converted into the hunted, just marking time, treading water. Profilers and graphologists were of zero value to him until he had credible suspects. In real terms, Lowen had narrowed the number of potential suspects to around ten million.

Lowen now read Lorenzo's thoughts. 'What's the score with the fella you've got in custody? Is he a goer?'

'Nah! He's up before the beaks this morning. He'll be remanded in custody for social and psychiatric reports. No need for me to be there. Charges don't relate to the murder.'

'Have you copies of his handwriting?'

'Only of his signature on official documents, such as his driving-licence and passport. He's an obstinate bugger, refusing to co-operate, but there's absolutely no resemblance between his right-handed writing and that of the note; even a layman like me can determine that at a cursory glance. As far as I'm concerned, he was eliminated after the first day. He simply doesn't fit, despite his history, which technically ought to make him a prime suspect.'

The damning evidence of many sleepless nights had been cleverly masked by Lowen. Cosmetic camouflage had even brought a healthy tint to the plump cheeks of her oval face. Only her liquid eyes told the truth, although the raccoon-circles had been almost entirely powdered away.

'I've time to offer you a drink now,' said Lowen, with a yawn.

'Thanks, but no thanks,' Lorenzo declined emphatically. 'I'll head straight back; might just catch the tail-end of the court hearing.'

As Lorenzo slammed the door of his car, his mobile phone started giving his hip a massage. He saw from the screen that it was Valentine calling.

'OK to talk?' Valentine queried.

'Go ahead.'

'The headmistress wants to see you.'

Headmistress stood for their martinet Chief Constable, Helen Kingdom.

'When?'

'Now.'

'Didn't you tell her where I was?'

'Of course, but you know her, she doesn't listen, except to herself.'

'She'll just have to fucking wait.'

'Shall I tell her that?' Valentine asked mischievously.

'Yes, but omit the expletive. Tell her that as soon as I have a spare moment, I'll drop by.'

'Will do; she'll love that. Do you want your P45 posted to you or will you collect it on the way out?'

Lorenzo was heartened. Perhaps Valentine had a sense of humour, after all.

'Don't worry, I'm ring-fenced. No dominatrix will ever get rid of her favourite whipping-boy.'

'If you say so, Guv. I wouldn't know about that kind of stuff.'

Lorenzo had little difficulty believing him.

'Where are you?'

'Outside court. Timms is due up in about ten minutes. I'll be on hand just in case the beaks seek any clarification.'

'There shouldn't be a problem. Diamond's been fully briefed.'

Sally Diamond was a prosecution lawyer; a rising star and destined to become the cynosure of any court.

'See you, then.'

Lorenzo decided to circumnavigate Bournemouth and head directly for Winfrith, a desolate backwater of Dorset, where the county's police headquarters and Miss Whiplash were situated, in the haunting shadow of an inoperative nuclear power station.

Helen Kingdom had bird of prey features, including an aquiline beak and hawkish eyes, while her speech and manner were as pecky as a parrot, though her build resembled more a stick insect than a feathered predator. She made a habit of never interviewing a subordinate without her trusted brown-tongue lackey beside her, taking notes or slyly operating a concealed tape-recorder. She was drinking tea from one of her Royal Crown Derby bone china cups. Lorenzo wasn't invited to join her.

'Took your time!' said Kingdom, her choleric opening salvo as Lorenzo plonked himself in the chair to which he'd been designated.

'I was in Southampton,' Lorenzo replied, unfazed. 'I think Detective Valentine apprised you of my whereabouts.'

'Made an arrest there, did you?' There was a mocking edge to her rasping voice now, Lorenzo's pay-off for his truculence.

'No, just counselling expert opinion on handwriting.'

'That brings me nicely to the reason for summoning you here this morning, Lorenzo,' said Kingdom, her claw-like hands dancing on the rim of her desk. 'You haven't gone public with the note left on the body. Why not?'

Lorenzo succinctly repeated his spiel on that issue.

'Bad call,' Kingdom decreed peremptorily.

'I beg to disagree,' said Lorenzo, holding his ground.

'Beg all you like, but you'll do as I say or I'll assign the case to someone else.'

'You're the boss.'

'And don't you ever forget it, Inspector.'

There was no mileage in biting back, so Lorenzo bit the bullet instead.

'I'll have the press office bureaucrats release to the media copies of the note, if that's your wish,' he said.

'No, it's not my *wish*, it's my *command*.'

'Very well.' He smiled to demonstrate that she wasn't getting under his skin, hoping to bug her. 'Of course, you realize we'll be inundated with half the world reckoning they recognize the handwriting?'

'Isn't that the whole point of the exercise, Lorenzo, eliciting public participation? I'd rather we were flooded with potential leads than languishing in a drought, as now.'

'All the nuts in the country – and beyond – will be flushed out of the woodwork,' Lorenzo sourly laboured his point.

'Are you including the *nuts* working for me?' Her penetrating eyes laser-beamed through Lorenzo's skull. Still he didn't react.

'I'll have the last seven words blacked out,' he said, equably, ignoring the rhetorical question.

'Remind me.'

'Bye for now – until next time!'

'Yes, I agree with you. No need to send the entire country's female population into shutdown. Not yet. In fact, it's probably best that my admin staff here liaise with the press bureau on this delicate matter, so you can focus on the sharp-end of things. Leave it with me.'

'Fine, well, if there's nothing else…' said Lorenzo, meaning: *let me out of here!*

'Keep me posted,' said Kingdom. 'And that's an order. Let's get a result – quickly. That, too, is an order.'

The harsh floodlights of the stable-block were on when Lorenzo parked in the carport beside his barn-home at just after ten that evening. Tricia was dragging a sack of feed to an outhouse. Lorenzo waited in the yard for her to return, having already noted that Luke's car was missing. At a distance of at least twenty yards, he could see that she was smiling.

'Just saying goodnight to my babies,' she said, alluding to the horses.

As she drew closer, he noticed the bruise beneath her left eye.

Tricia tracked the trajectory of his stare and tried tilting her head to an angle that put the dark swelling out of Lorenzo's line of vision, but to no avail.

'How did that happen?' he said, gently placing a finger on her face, just beneath the tender spot.

'Isn't this the moment when I should say I bumped into a door or one of the horses kicked me?' she said evasively.

'But that would be a lie, wouldn't it?'

'Leave it, Mike.' She tossed back her head irritably and brushed away his hand.

'When did *he* do it?' Lorenzo pressed.

'It was *nothing*, Mike. Let me finish my chores out here before Luke gets home. He'll want feeding. You men are more demanding than my nags.'

Lorenzo refused to be deflected. 'Did it happen last night? After I left? Was it because we'd been together talking?'

Tricia peered abstractly at a point between her feet. 'Luke gets very jealous when he's been drinking and his imagination runs riot. We had a stupid quarrel. He over-reacted. This morning, when he'd sobered up, he was contrite.'

'You mustn't put up with it, Tricia.'

Now she eyeballed him aggressively. 'This is my business, not yours, Mike. Keep out of it. You'll only make matters worse.'

Lorenzo was undeterred. 'If you don't put a stop to it now,

it'll escalate. It always does. Domestic violence is toxic. The only antidote is outside intervention or the poison spreads fast and inexorably.'

'This wasn't domestic *violence,* Mike; it was a domestic *scrap.* What are you suggesting: I should have you arrest him? Now *that* would really be toxic!'

'You should talk to professionals. You most certainly shouldn't take any more of it. And if it happened again and you came to me, yes, I'd deal with it. I'd deal with him.'

She took his hand. 'I know you mean well and I appreciate that; I really do. But a sledgehammer to crack a nut isn't the way forward; not for me, anyhow. It would only smash everything beyond repair. You must allow me to sort this my way.'

Reluctantly, Lorenzo relented, saying, 'OK, but if….'

'Shush! Don't say another word.' She planted a finger over his mouth, then stood on tiptoe to kiss his forehead. 'Goodnight, my would-be bodyguard.'

Lorenzo had just reached his living-room and was playing messages on his answer-machine, when his mobile pulled him away.

'Yes.'

'It's Dr Moran.'

'Hi, Savannah. What's up?'

'Sorry to call you so late.'

'*Late!* Some days I'm only just getting around to breakfast at midnight.'

No reciprocation of mirth the other end. 'Something I thought you ought to know ASAP.'

'Go on,' said Lorenzo, intrigued.

'I got pictures of the blood-spatter and pattern of blood-pools only a few hours ago and I've been studying them carefully all evening.'

'And?'

'It's obvious to me now that she was cut and killed while flat on her back.'

'OK, that doesn't surprise me,' said Lorenzo. 'More or less the way I had it figured.'

'I've examined the fatal wound again and I've now come to the conclusion that the killer is right-handed. This is consistent with the blow to the rear of her skull being inflicted right of centre and the starting-point of the cut and the direction in which the knife travelled. Follow?'

Lorenzo was mentally back in Southampton, hearing graphologist Penelope Lowen telling him emphatically about the note on the body, 'the author is left-handed, no doubt about that'.

7

Lorenzo was right. The circulation to the media of the killer's note triggered a tidal wave of tip-offs, most of them anonymous. Reports were made to the police from people as far away as the US, Australia, Japan, Hong Kong and Singapore. Statements were taken from those informants who had identified themselves, and then emailed to the HQ of Dorset Police. All this was in addition to the hundreds of calls to police the length and breadth of the UK.

Kingdom was delighted. 'One of these will give us the crucial breakthrough we need,' she prophesied, bloated with confidence and self-approval. Lorenzo wasn't so optimistic.

'It'll take us years to sift through this lot,' he groaned to Valentine. 'The killer will already be in his own grave by the time we get to him via this route.'

A hundred extra uniformed officers were drafted in from other police forces. Lorenzo delegated Valentine to preside over the operation of following up all *alleged* identifications of the handwriting. The media, as Lorenzo feared, went OTT, even though the all-important final sentence, foretelling of more corpses to come, had been deleted.

Lorenzo concentrated on amateur theatrical groups and writing circles in Dorset and neighbouring counties, a recommendation of his ex-FBI landlady, Tricia Lockwood. The secretaries were obliging and pledged to provide examples of handwriting from their members, where possible. He also began trawling through the letters pages of the local newspapers, looking for regular contributors and in particular, anyone who was clearly an obsessive, especially on the subject of gender issues and how women, in the writers' deranged eyes, were taking over the world. Thousands of examples of convicted criminals' handwriting were stored on a national forensic database and comparisons would be made in the hope of finding a match, a similar process to marrying two sets of fingerprints.

'Trouble is, all this publicity will have the killer salivating,' Tricia predicted. 'Suddenly he's internationally famous, with Hollywood status, albeit it for the gore genre. Ever since a boy, he's probably dreamed of being recognized as some kind of star; in the spotlight, commanding attention, having people world-wide gossiping about the murderous Mr X, building him into some kind of fearsome legend.'

Lorenzo and Tricia were chatting again in her kitchen at a few minutes before midnight and her husband had been out since before seven, announcing he was 'off to the pub for a darts match'. The bruise on Tricia's face was now well hidden behind a wall of creams and powder.

'Perhaps I should go,' Lorenzo suggested tentatively. 'If Luke returns while I'm here, he may be provoked again.'

'No, stay,' Tricia implored. 'I've resolved not to be intimi-dated any longer. No more compromising. No more making excuses for him.'

'Good girl! But don't take any chances. If he's been boozing since seven, he's unlikely to be rational, let alone coherent. He's off his rocker to have taken the car.'

'Try telling him that! On second thoughts, don't! You'll only end up in a brawl. Do me a favour, Mike. Don't tip-off your traffic division. Don't have him stopped; that really would turn him against you and, by association, me.'

'Why *you*, Tricia?'

'Because I negotiated with you the rental agreement of 'The Barn'. Because we're friends, with so much in common, and you have little to do with him.'

'Only because I hardly ever see him sober and never get the opportunity for a sensible conversation.'

'But he doesn't rationalize it that way. He sees you as *my* friend, not *his*.'

'He could kill himself. He could kill others. Turning a blind eye isn't a friendly thing for me to do – and you know that, too.'

'I just don't want him getting the wrong idea about us.'

'Would it be the *wrong* idea?' said Lorenzo.

She looked him in the eye. 'I think I should pretend I didn't hear that.'

Lorenzo blinked first, breaking eye-contact. 'I have to make another early start in the morning, so I'm going to turn in. Sorry to have embarrassed you.'

'No, no, Mike; you haven't embarrassed me at all. I'm just confused.'

'Goodnight, then,' he said softly, leaning forward to kiss her tenderly on the forehead.

She closed her eyes and when she opened them, he'd gone.

Two days later:

The crematorium in Kettering, Northamptonshire was built on a breezy hill on the western outskirts of the town and was the centrepiece of an expansive remembrance garden; always peaceful, yet also always bleak, even in a mid-summer heat-wave, when the dazzling sun and fresh, vivid flowers on lovingly-manicured graves clashed so starkly with the funereal-black of mourners and broad-shouldered pallbearers.

The first service of the day was scheduled for nine-thirty. Elspeth Hammond's last journey began ten minutes earlier from a 1930s terraced-house in the centre of town, next to a derelict factory that hadn't provided an income for anyone for almost thirty years. Perhaps the disused factory, as lifeless as Elspeth, had been spared the bulldozer to stand as an ugly monument to the town's industrial past, once the epicentre of boot and shoe manufacturing, until the Italians flooded the UK market with synthetic leather and blitzed into bankruptcy 90 per cent of the outdated industry in this southern pocket of the unspectacular East Midlands.

Elspeth's husband, John, worked in the neighbouring factory from the age of fifteen, until the overpowering fumes and smell of the corrosive dye and the dust from the leather had decimated his lungs. He'd made this same pine-box journey – the only time he'd ever been chauffeur-driven – several years before he'd been due to retire. Elspeth had lived on alone, while her son and daughter abandoned this unattractive backwater of dubious civilization for Australia and the US respectively, where their lives were so alien to that of their shackled parents they might as well have emigrated to another planet.

This short ride in a sumptuously-upholstered, crafted box and a freshly-polished, shiny black hearse was also Elspeth's first taste of luxury, something she'd waited 93 years for. Even then it hadn't come within her lifespan, of course; the irony of which wasn't something being mused over by the four occupants of the lone limousine behind the hearse.

There were two chapels within the crematoria complex, where services were held for those being cremated or buried. All denominations were catered for, from high church Anglicans to orthodox atheists.

The Rev. Theobald Lucas was posturing at the entrance to Chapel Number One, ready to receive the coffin and the pathetically meagre band of mourners: Elspeth's son and daughter – both in late middle-age – and their respective spouses. Stroking his ragged beard, he smiled benignly the way the clergy are prone to do, somewhat sanctimoniously.

The service was short; a couple of prayers, Elspeth's two favourite hymns, a reading from the Bible, and a five-minute eulogy that was cliché from start to finish. *This isn't an occasion for tears and sadness, but for uplifting joy, celebrating a long and full life.* He skipped over the poverty and hardship and how she and her husband had been pitilessly exploited by factory-barons. Even all his mannerisms and body-language were hollow clichés. That over, they migrated from the chapel by a side door, operated by remote-control, just as another hearse drew up outside the entrance. The crematorium was the one factory in town cushioned from recessions.

After a few murmured platitudes about the two wreaths that had been removed from the lid of the coffin, the Rev. Lucas led the tiny procession along the network of paths through the sweet-scented remembrance garden towards the six-foot hole that had been dug the previous day for Elspeth's final resting place. From hovel to hole. Going down in the world had been the natural pull of gravity from womb to tomb for Elspeth. At least her ending had the merit of continuity and consistency.

The birds sang. The morning-dew dampened footwear and squelched beneath feet. The sun respectfully wore a grey veil. The air had more the impact of a cold shower than a hot bath.

The minister was first to reach the grave, the pallbearers from the funeral directors closely on his shoddy heels, huffing and puffing, looking forward to releasing the load from their broad, but hunched shoulders. Lucas teetered on the edge, but didn't look into the abyss. Despite having officiated at burials hundreds of times, he always kept his eyes averted from the grim reminder of his own destiny. Holes in the road had the same effect on him; he sailed around them stealthily with the elated feeling of someone having avoided a deadly trap set specifically for him by a malevolent spirit.

It was the reaction of the head pallbearer that alerted the Rev. Lucas to the fact that all was not as it should have been. His face had turned the colour of the cadaver. And the complexion-change percolated along the line like a contagion, quickly followed by stunned paralysis.

Only then did Lucas see the cause of the stupefaction. The grave was already occupied; by a woman without the comfort of a coffin; a much younger woman than Elspeth. Even from a vertical distance of six feet, there was no mistaking the gash around her neck. Dead-eyes stared up at the living corpses gathered above.

'Oh, my God!' exclaimed Lucas, no blasphemy and fully justified.

That's when the two women mourners fainted.

Early that same afternoon, Lorenzo took a call in his office from
Detective Inspector Charlie Mountford, of the Northamptonshire
Police, based in Kettering.

'I'm lead detective on a murder that might interest you,' he
began perfunctorily. 'The victim's female. Head cracked with a
blunt instrument. Throat slashed ear-to-ear; her body dumped
in a cemetery-grave that had been dug for someone else's
funeral this morning. But the thing that induced me most of all
to make this call to you was the note left on the body, stuffed
down the bra.'

Lorenzo's heart was suddenly racing to the frenetic rhythm of
a pneumatic drill.

'What did the note say?' he said, almost gagging on the
upsurge of adrenaline into his throat.

*'Got the date right this time. Dates can be so important, can't they?
Hopefully, there'll be no more errors. Until the next time, then.* And it
was signed, *Dear John.'*

8

One thing in particular from the new note resonated with Lorenzo: *Got the date right this time.*

His eyes switched to the upright, flick-over calendar on his desk: September 9th. What the hell's the relevance of that? Something only understood by the deranged perpetrator. How do you tunnel into the muddled, labyrinthine morass of a madman's head without being moonstruck yourself? If it takes a thief to catch one....

His head was brainstorming. September 9th – 9/11; any possible association there? The Americans put the month before the day, so 9/11 represents the 11th of September, not the 9th. Maybe he's unaware of that. No, not realistic. In any case, how would that tie-in with the date of Mary Walker's murder? No, these crimes have nothing to do with terrorism, not even symbolically; it's more complicated, more convoluted, than that.

'Mind if I join you?' said Lorenzo, like seeking admission to an exclusive club.

'Welcome aboard,' said Mountford. 'Pooling resources, evidence and theories can only be beneficial for us both.'

'Where will I find you?'

'Still at the crematorium. If you approach the town from Northampton, you'll pick up signs very early.'

'I'm on my way.'

Lorenzo covered the 150 miles northwards, across country, in approximately three hours.

Two uniformed officers had been posted outside the tall, black wrought-iron gates at the entrance to the remembrance garden. Just inside the gates was a brick warden's lodge. Cremations continued as normal, but all burials had been suspended. Lorenzo was expected and one of the constables used his two-way radio to inform Mountford of his arrival.

'He's on his way,' the constable told Lorenzo, which translated into: *Stay where you are until the guv'nor escorts you in.*

Mountford was in his mid-thirties, lithe and sinewy, with short-cropped, brown hair and shrewd, grey eyes that were as restless as those of a Secret Service agent protecting the US President. In addition to being tall and pale, there was an aura of purity about him that advertised clean living. In short, he wasn't the type to have a natural affinity with an instinctive louche like Lorenzo, whose immediate impression of Mountford was that he was made more for the pulpit than the police.

Activity was the same as at any crime scene, and yellow tape made most of the garden of remembrance out of bounds to the public. People arriving with flowers for graves of their departed loved ones were turned away at the gates. Heated words were exchanged. No longer was this the most serene and peaceful location in town; the dead knew how to behave, but not their relatives.

'I'll take you to the grave,' said Mountford. 'I'll fill in the details, as much as possible, on the way. It's a fair old hike; about a quarter of a mile. Big place. Business has boomed ever since it was opened, unlike in other commercial parts of the town.'

'Is the body still here?'

'No, it was removed just a few minutes ago. A PM is scheduled for this evening. The general hospital is only a few hundred yards down the hill towards the town centre.'

'Was the note handwritten?'

'Yes, that's the point; it seems to match the handwriting of your guy. It's too soon to be absolutely scientifically certain, of course. The forensic investigation is only just kicking in here. But the entire MO is so similar to your case.'

'So what's the narrative?'

'Anne Chapman. Housewife. Thirty-six years old. Mother of two, aged eight and five; girl and boy. Qualified nurse. Worked as a matron at a nursing home. Not far from here, in fact. Home for the elderly. Clocked off yesterday evening at just after nine. When she wasn't home by midnight, Gary Chapman, her husband, sent her a text.'

'Saying?'

'Basically, "Where the blazes are you?" He got no reply, so he phoned her mobile. It rang but wasn't answered and went to voicemail. He dictated a panicky message for her to call him.'

'Didn't he contact the nursing home?'

'That came next because he reckoned there must have been an emergency just before the end of his wife's shift. But the duty manageress said that his wife had gone long ago, not much after 9 pm. I'm sure you can guess the next sequence in the process.'

'He did the rounds of the hospitals by phone?'

'Well, yes, but there's only one with an A&E department. No luck there, so he woke his wife's parents, who live in Corby, seven miles away. He wondered whether one of them wasn't well and Anne, as a nurse, had detoured there. If she had though, he couldn't understand why she hadn't told him first, unless the situation was dire. Anne's mother answered. Neither she nor her husband had heard from their daughter that day, so now they were anxious, too. The three of them debated what to do and it was agreed that Gary should call the police.'

'What response did he get?'

'He was asked for the make and registration number of her car: a red Kia. He was reassured that there'd been no report of an accident that evening involving a Kia. He was also asked for the route she would be expected to take home and also whether she suffered from a medical condition that might have struck suddenly and impaired her driving, such as epilepsy, classic migraine or a heart-defect. But Mr Chapman was adamant that his wife was in perfect health.'

'Were you on duty?'

'No, his call was handled by the night-duty sergeant, who promised Mr Chapman that a squad car would be despatched to the nursing home and the officers would then drive along the route to the Chapmans' home, which is on a modern housing estate on the opposite side of town.'

'Did they do all that?'

'Everything.'

'All negative results, I assume?'

'*Negative* for Mr Chapman, not for us.'

They broke stride as a funeral cortege crept past them towards the crematorium.

'The two officers immediately spotted Mrs Chapman's Kia on arrival at the nursing home. It was still in a parking area reserved for staff.'

'So she hadn't driven from the nursing home?'

'That had to be the conclusion. The officers questioned the night nurse. Only one member of medical staff was on duty from 9 pm. She had gone to the matron's office at 8.45pm. This was an evening ritual; sort of handing over the reins. Mrs Chapman briefly discussed individual needs of residents and updated the nurse on medication issues. Mrs Chapman finished her paper-work and said goodnight. The night nurse actually saw Mrs Chapman leave the building. At this point in the story, the officers began to suspect that their inquiries were less routine than they'd bargained for.'

'Had Mrs Chapman said anything about meeting anyone?'

'The officers pursued that line, but the answer was a definite no. Mrs Chapman had commented that it had been a "pig of a day" and she couldn't wait to get home to put up her feet.'

'Did they ask the night nurse to identify the car?'

'Yes, they did. It would appear they were very thorough. They already had the reg. number, of course, but still they requested that the nurse, a Shirley Morrisey, go with them outside. She was amazed to see Mrs Chapman's Kia still in the grounds. "I don't get it," she said. "Maybe it wouldn't start." '

'A plausible possibility,' Lorenzo observed.

'Except that *isn't* what happened,' said Mountford. 'We *know* there was no breakdown or a call for a taxi.'

Lorenzo looked blank, taking time to compute Mountford's last statement.

'Let me continue in sequence and it'll all fall into place,' Mountford continued. 'The officers initiated a search and didn't have to look far for the first big clue. They quickly came across a woman's shoe on the grass at the edge of the staff carpark, about a yard on to the lawn. There's an extensive landscaped garden there with trees, bushes, hedges and flower-beds, but there'd been no attempt to conceal the shoe. Nurse Morrisey ID'd the footwear as belonging to Mrs Chapman. The officers radioed back to base. Two traffic division squad cars were diverted there. A wider search of the grounds was instigated. Searchlights in the carpark were movement-activated and the officers noticed what appeared to be a drag-trail from the Kia towards tyre-marks about ten yards away, near the lawn. They then combed through the remainder of the grounds. No more clothing was found. And, of course, no body.'

'So she was attacked just after leaving the building and probably as she reached her car?'

'Not *probably* – definitely.'

Lorenzo treated Mountford to curious examination. 'Why is it I have a feeling you're toying with me?'

'Because I *am*, but we're getting *there* chronologically.'

Bemused now, Lorenzo said, 'OK, I'll play along. But Mrs Chapman wasn't killed in the carpark because there'd have been pools of blood and you haven't mentioned that.'

'You're right. One of the two scene-of-crime teams located the spot mid-morning where the execution took place.' Mountford stopped and pointed towards a platoon of tall, erect pines. 'Behind those trees, just inside the ranch-fencing on the western perimeter. The main gates are always locked from dusk to dawn. The killer couldn't have got in through the main entrance. Blood-splatter leads from the fencing to the grave where she was deposited, some two hundred yards.'

'Have you an approximate time of death?'

'Between 9 p.m. and 1 a.m.'

'Any of her possessions missing?'

'Not a thing, apparently. Handbag, containing cash, credit cards and mobile, tossed on top of the body.'

'Raped?'

'We won't know for sure until after the PM, but our doctor doesn't believe so. Underwear was intact. No external bruising or abrasions around her thighs and genital orifice.'

'Too much to hope that the killer discarded his weapon nearby?'

'Absolutely. Both weapons still to be located but, without wanting to sound cocky, I think we have more to go on than you do your end.'

'That wouldn't take much doing,' Lorenzo said self-deprecatingly. 'One piece of hard evidence would put you way ahead of us.'

Mountford smiled as if Lorenzo had just made his day. 'The nursing home is equipped with CCTV.'

'With cameras covering the carpark area?'

'*All* the grounds. After dark, there's an electronic tripwire that triggers the cameras as soon as there's movement. Dogs, cats and foxes even bring on the lights and start the cameras recording.'

'So the killer's been caught on camera?' said Lorenzo, astonished. 'So that's the heirloom in your attic that you've been smugly hiding from me?'

'You got it!' Mountford chuckled convivially. 'Of course, it's not cut-and-dried.'

'Rarely is,' Lorenzo empathized, but still upbeat.

'He was hooded and wore a scarf over his face, from just beneath his eyes. He was also wearing gloves. But we're able to estimate his height and build. Crucially, we know the make of the car he was driving.'

Now it was Lorenzo's turn to stop in his tracks. 'You mean you've got the whole abduction and hammer attack on film?'

'From beginning to end.'

'In colour?'

'No, black and white; a bit grainy, but fair quality. Good enough. As you know, state-of-the-art digital colour CCTV is very expensive and beyond the means of a private nursing home, especially in this moderate-income area.'

'But you must have the car's reg. number: case closed!'

'Unfortunately, not. The number plates had been covered.'

Lorenzo scowled. 'What car was it?'

'A four-wheel-drive Land Rover. Probably black from the dark images. The killer's a big guy; over six feet tall and probably weighing something between twelve and fourteen stone.'

'Wait a minute,' said Lorenzo, playing mental catch-up. 'All CCTV recordings are time-sensitive, right?'

'Right.'

'So you have not only the assault but also the *exact* time that it occurred?'

'Correct. Nine-eleven. But that doesn't establish time of death, of course. The hammer-blow didn't kill her or she wouldn't have bled here, when, presumably, her throat was cut.'

'Was she struck from behind in the carpark at the nursing home?'

'Base of the skull.'

'Which side?'

'Slightly to the right of centre. She was stooping to open the driver's door when he came upon her, appearing from behind a tree, hammer in his right hand.'

They were at the graveside now. Forensic detectives were making moulds of footprints where grass around the open grave had been flattened. Other scene-of-crime specialists were on hands and knees, combing nearby graves and paths for clues.

Lorenzo began ruminating again about the note. If Mrs Chapman was abducted just after 9.00 pm the previous evening, it was unlikely that the perpetrator waited three hours before ending her life. This was important because the killer had boasted of getting the date right on this occasion. Lorenzo had been working on the assumption that the murder had taken place this day, the 9th. However, it now seemed much more likely that Mrs Chapman died before midnight on the 8th, certainly eliminating any association with 9/11.

'Any CCTV here?' said Lorenzo, looking around him.

'Only outside the crematorium itself; none in the remembrance garden. Wouldn't be right to spy on graveside-weeping.'

'That's a main arterial road outside, isn't it?'

'Very much so.'

'A busy one?'

'In the daytime, yes. Pretty quiet though, at midnight and in the early hours.'

'Even so, the killer was taking a gamble, if he was parked on the grass-verge and dragged Mrs Chapman unconscious from his Land Rover,' said Lorenzo. 'Presumably he heaved her over the fence, before scaling it himself. A passing motorist or lorry driver might have seen something.'

'We're working on it. Top of the agenda, as far as I'm concerned, is that you'll be able to conclusively confirm that the handwriting on the note is a match with the one you have in Bournemouth. I'm sure you can see why?'

'Indeed,' said Lorenzo. 'We both have to be satisfied that you're not dealing with a copycat killer; that there's just one perpetrator and not two on the loose.'

Mountford nodded.

Copycat killings were a danger Lorenzo had foreseen when his Chief Constable had insisted on going public with the note so soon.

'Where is the note?'

'Gone to Forensics, but I have photocopies at the station.'

'Well, I'll be able to give you my opinion, but that's all it will be.'

'If you follow me to the station you can run your eye over a copy.'

'And the CCTV footage?'

'Of course.'

'Where's Mr Chapman now?'

'Barricaded in his home, comforting the kids and cushioned by family and community officers. We have a blue-ring around the house, keeping reporters and photographers at bay.'

'I'd like to speak with him.'

'I'll arrange it.'

'Let's for a moment assume there is only one killer: it's vital for me to know if the Chapmans have any association with Bournemouth, with anyone living there.'

'And if September 8th or 9th have any significance to them,' said Mountford.

They were on the same wavelength, if not in tune in other respects.

'I'll lead the way,' said Mountford, somewhat ponderously.

Not for long, you won't! Lorenzo was thinking.

9

One glance at the note was enough to convince Lorenzo that it had been written by the same hand that had penned the diabolical epitaph, thrust between the lifeless breasts of Mary Walker. Nevertheless, he would have to await official verification before strong conjecture could be confirmed as hard fact.

As for the CCTV footage, there was something distinctly voyeuristic and spooky about watching a real life, graphic assault that was a prelude to a grisly, ritualistic execution of an innocent human being. The odious drama played devilish tricks on the mind. When the hooded man sneaked stealthily and ghost-like from behind a tree, as Mrs Chapman stooped unwarily beside her car, Lorenzo experienced an urge to press the 'stop' button, illogically hoping that by freezing the frame, the *real* action could be suspended, the clock turned back, and Mrs Chapman saved. His instincts could be equated to the warning shouts of 'behind you!' by young children at pantomimes, when the villain crept up on the unsuspecting hero.

If only there had been a guardian angel, rather than a mere electronic eye, to shout 'behind you!' to Mrs Chapman in the nursing home carpark. But the world of crime was a graveyard of 'what ifs' and 'if onlys'.

'Are you a car buff?' Lorenzo enquired pensively.

'Not really,' Mountford replied curiously. 'Why?'

'The Land Rover manufacturers should be able to tell us something about this particular model. Although the reg. numbers are covered, there may be something distinctive that tells us the year of make. Then we can find out how many were sold, particularly in the Bournemouth area. Could be that it's a limited edition, for example.'

'A limited edition of just one would be very handy for us!' said Mountford. 'Good thinking, anyhow. However, I think we should be cautious about assuming the perp is based in your region.'

Cops, like so many other animal species, were protectively territorial. Mountford would fight as fiercely as Lorenzo for control; to be the main man. Both would believe that their manor was the centre of gravity in this investigation.

'It began in Bournemouth, for Christ sake!' Lorenzo seethed, reddening. 'That's fact. Bournemouth was the birthplace of this bloody business. Indisputable fact! You can't rewrite history, Charlie, just to snatch the largest portion of the pie.'

'There's no need to get hot under the collar, Mike,' Mountford implored, previously unaware of Lorenzo's potential volatility. 'This guy has an agenda. He's on a mapped-out killing spree. Firstly on your patch, now on mine. Where next? He knows, but we don't. See my point? There's nothing to indicate where he's based, where's the epicentre of all this.'

There was logic in Mountford's appraisal and Lorenzo mumbled a grudging apology. Tension defused.

On the ten-minute drive from the police station to the home of the Chapmans, Lorenzo kept his own counsel about the anomalies teasing him: the graphologist in Southampton was in no doubt that the author of the first note was left-handed; the CCTV footage showed Anne Chapman's attacker wielding a hammer in his right hand, and the pathologist who performed the PM on Mary Walker was equally adamant that the lethal cut had been made by a right-handed slayer. The contradictions seemed theoretically insoluble, unless two people were involved, which would have made it much easier for Anne Chapman to have been lifted over the fence at the garden of remembrance and carted to the open grave. Against that, there was no sign of an accomplice on the CCTV recording.

*

One of the community police officers opened the door for Lorenzo and Mountford.

'The family's GP has just left,' she said. 'Mr Chapman's been given a high-dose sedative-shot, so he'll soon be very drowsy. The window of opportunity for a lucid interview may be a brief one.'

'OK, I'll cut straight to the chase,' said Lorenzo.

Gary Chapman looked the shell-shocked wreck that he was; a forty-year-old who could have fooled anyone that he was entitled to a pension: eyes watery and red-rimmed; cheeks, grey and unshaven; hair, stringy and uncombed; face gaunt and stained with tears old and new. He was sitting on a plain sofa, head buried in shaky hands, the children being entertained in another room by distraught relatives, who were bravely behaving in the tradition of seasoned actors: the show had to go on, whatever the misfortune.

After Mountford had introduced Lorenzo, Mr Chapman looked at the detectives through the gaps between his fingers, like a prisoner on Death Row peering plaintively and pleadingly from the bars of a cell. He *was* a prisoner in his own private hell, from which there could never be escape while this side of the grave.

'I shall be as quick as possible and, if any questions are a repeat of what you've been asked already, please accept my apology in advance,' Lorenzo began swiftly, while Mr Chapman sat motionless, in a traumatized trance. 'Was your wife a local girl?'

'Sort of. She was born and raised in Corby; not far away up the road.' Voice vapid, expression vacuous. Lips quivering. 'Scottish roots, though. Grandfather came down from Glasgow after the war for a job in the steelworks, which were closed long ago. A ghost town now. He married a Corby girl whose parents had also moved south from Glasgow. In those days, Corby was known as either Little Scotland or Little Glasgow.'

'But your roots aren't Scottish?'

'No, I'm a genuine local lad. Family lineage has never crossed the county border.' No smile, not even in his voice.

'Has your wife ever lived in Bournemouth?'

Long pause, mental inertia, expression distant: on another planet. Finally, 'No, why?'

'There was a similar crime on my patch in Bournemouth and I'm trying to see if there's any dovetailing, however tenuous. How about you?'

'Pardon?'

'Have you lived or worked in the South, around Bournemouth, in the counties of Dorset, Hampshire or Wiltshire?'

'No, as I said, I was born here. Grew up here. Work here. Dull boy. Nothing dull about Annie, though. We have been to Bournemouth on holiday.'

'When?'

'Twice.'

'But when?' Lorenzo repeated himself patiently.

'The year after we married … I think. Then two years ago. Both times we stayed in the same boarding house. Friendly couple ran it. Can't recall their names. My brain's in such a muddle. Something like Wainwright or Bargate. It'll come to me, probably just after you've gone; usually the way, isn't it? We had fun.' He drew in breath, trying not to crack up.

Lorenzo pressed on, conscious of the heady drug in Chapman's bloodstream that would be flowing fast towards his brain. 'Did you make friends?'

'No, not really. We kept to ourselves. And on our second visit, we had the children, of course, so the holiday was tailored around them: beach all day, early evening meal, a bit of TV and bed; that was it. Except for one evening when we went to a show in the end-of-pier theatre. Lovely weather. Lovely holiday.' More tears now as nostalgia turned the screw, planting a lump in his throat.

'When you were in Bournemouth two years ago, did you fall out with anyone, have a row or unpleasant experience? Perhaps something that seemed very trivial at the time to you and your wife?'

'Good grief, no! We had a wonderful, friendly time, as I said. Annie got on with everyone, wherever we went. She wasn't the sort to get into squabbles. I reckon myself easy-going, too.'

'Can you remember the name of the boarding house, if not the people who own it?'

Mr Chapman thought for a moment. 'Yes, the High Rise on the West Cliff. Family-run. Very clean. Wholesome food. Our type of home-from-home place. No standing on ceremony. Children-friendly, too.'

'I don't wish to offend or embarrass you with this question...' Lorenzo obviously knew that he would, however much he gilded the build-up. 'But when you were on holiday in Bournemouth, did anyone pay undue attention to your wife?'

Puzzlement added more creases to Mr Chapman's already heavily furrowed forehead and cheeks. 'I'm not sure what you mean?'

Lorenzo's dance of diplomacy was merely taking him round in circles. There was no option left but the forthright approach. 'Did anyone try flirting with her?'

Lorenzo's directness at least had the merit of breathing new life and energy into Mr Chapman as incredulity and anger flared in his eyes and nostrils.

'Annie wasn't that sort of woman. Grief! Have you no respect?'

'Mr Chapman, I wasn't inferring any immodest behaviour by your wife. On the contrary, in fact: I was just wondering if she'd been pestered with unwelcome interest from another guest or even a stranger on the beach, perhaps? An incident that may have outraged her?'

Mr Chapman came off the boil. 'No, nothing like that occurred.'

'Had your wife *ever* complained to you of being stalked or threatened here, in Kettering?'

'No, I've already told Inspector Mountford that.' He looked appealingly to Mountford for this catechism to be curtailed.

'I've nearly finished,' said Lorenzo, seeing Chapman's eyes begin to fog over as the sedative landed its first blow to the brain. 'I don't suppose you'd know if there were any residents with a Bournemouth affiliation in the nursing home where your wife was matron?'

'I've already gone down that road,' Mountford intervened. 'Not with Mr Chapman, but with the proprietor of the nursing home.'

'And?'

'Of course it was impossible to be 100 per cent, but it seems not. There could be some unknown, tenuous connection, but nothing in the records, nothing that's ever been mentioned to staff or by visiting relatives. To be honest, that line of inquiry seems to me to be a non-starter.'

Lorenzo agreed. He'd merely been going through the motions, more box-ticking. The interview with Mr Chapman was over. The new widower was asleep, probably exchanging one nightmare for several others.

Lorenzo made arrangements to stay overnight, booking into the George Hotel, opposite the imposing Parish Church and ancient marketplace. He wanted to be on hand for the pathologist's report on the PM, which was due the following morning.

Before having a shower and going down to the hotel's oak-beamed restaurant, he spoke on the phone with Valentine. There had been no progress in Bournemouth, but Valentine had some 'encouraging' news to impart about the bane of both their lives, Chief Constable Helen Kingdom.

'Perversely, the second murder seems to have lifted her spirits.'

'And I can guess why,' said Lorenzo.

'That makes you smarter than the rest of us.'

'Hardly a revelation!' Lorenzo said facetiously. Humour on the phone could easily be misinterpreted, so he added, 'Only joking. The thing is, you see, she's now out of the eye of the storm. The murderer has moved on, like a cyclone. She no longer bears the cross alone of having to catch this maniac; responsibility is shared. Basically, she's insecure and that's why she's such a bloody pain.'

'She'd love you for saying that!'

'She's the kind of chief executive cop who wants a smoking-gun at the scene of every serious crime. She hates mysteries and tantalizing loose ends. She's never been a detective, you see. Never worked the streets undercover. She actually hates *us* because she's a uniform-freak. She has a military mind and would be better suited to the army, barking orders on the parade-ground, marching with her chest puffed out, inspecting boots and buttons. Whodunits irritate her. She cannot comprehend why suspects don't immediately confess the moment they're confronted by evidence she considers overwhelming. What's the point of Sherlock Holmes or Hercule Poirot when man invented the thumbscrew and rack – that's her philosophy.'

'Who's rattled your cage today?'

'*You*, Valentine, by mentioning the unmentionable!'

Subject was swiftly changed. Lorenzo reported on his day. Valentine whistled when Lorenzo disclosed that they had CCTV of the killer.

'As well as getting the PM in the morning, there may be news from the Land Rover manufacturer,' said Lorenzo. 'In any event, you can start compiling details of all known Land Rover owners in our region. It might not be such a big task as it at first sounds. When we have a list, it's then going to be a door-knocking job.'

'I assume the husband, Mr Chapman, is in the clear?'

'Definitely a non-runner.'

'And it's not a copycat?'

'Ninety-nine per cent sure it's not. I'll call you tomorrow soon as I have something worth sharing. Ciao.'

Next morning, Lorenzo was ready for breakfast the moment the restaurant opened. He'd just been shown to a table and was the only guest in the room, when his mobile became active.

'It's Tricia, I hope I haven't woken you.'

'If you had, I'd deserve a good kicking. I'm all ready for breakfast, washed, shaved, dressed, fresh and bushy-tailed. Still keeping the pledge, so no hangover.'

'If only you could get Luke to join the club!'

This was a conversation Lorenzo didn't want, so:

'What can I do for you so early?'

'Can you spare me a few minutes?'

'We're talking, aren't we?'

'Not on the phone. I'll pop round to you if you'd rather not come here while Luke's in.'

'I'm not at home, Tricia. I'm in Kettering, up in the East Midlands.'

'I should have realized that's where you'd be. I've been reading about the murder there. Extensive coverage on TV, too. That's what I need to talk to you about. Let me whet your appetite. I think I know what it's all about. In fact, I'm certain I do. And if I'm right, it'll not only help you catch the killer, but also possibly save other women from a similar fate.'

Lorenzo's appetite had indeed been whetted, but no longer for breakfast. Thanks to Tricia, his hunger for food had just been well and truly murdered.

10

Home Office pathologist Prof Graham Keller completed the PM by noon, concluding that the death of Anne Chapman was the result of the severing of her jugular by a knife with a one-sided cutting-edge. Prof. Keller was also 'reasonably certain' that the knifeman had been right-handed. But to confuse matters, the blow to the head had been delivered, 'most probably' by a left-hander, causing a skull fracture and 'slow drip' brain haemorrhage. Though the trauma injuries had not killed her, they probably would have done if the end hadn't been precipitated by the slitting of her throat. The time of death was estimated between 9.15 p.m. and 2 a.m. Not very helpful and probably of little consequence, thought Lorenzo.

'Looks like we have a double act,' said Mountford, as they drove from the hospital to the police station. 'The left-hander wields the hammer, the right-hander carves.'

'You could be right,' conceded Lorenzo, reserving judgment. Somehow a twosome didn't play right with him. He couldn't disprove Mountford's supposition, of course, so he didn't attempt to initiate a debate. All he had was an intuition that these killings were the work of a lunatic loner, maybe someone ambidextrous, who was exploiting his inherent skill to confuse.

By 2.00 pm, the detective assigned to learning all he could about the Land Rover on the CCTV footage had made steady headway. Certain aspects of the bonnet design and alloy wheels indicated that the model was three or four years old. The range had sold well, despite the growing hostility to four-wheel-drive gas-guzzlers, and there were thousands of these vehicles on UK roads, owned by town and city dwellers, as well as farming folk.

'Because of its age, it may not still be owned by the original purchaser,' observed Mountford.

'Nevertheless, it should have had at least one MOT, so there'll be a paper trail somewhere, even if the vehicle has been sold more than once.'

On blown-up photos of the vehicle, both Lorenzo and Mountford noticed a small dent just above the rear offside wheel.

'Perhaps it's been in an accident and suffered more extensive damage than a mere dent,' Lorenzo speculated, more with tepid hope than enthusiastic expectation. 'In which case, there might be a police file on it somewhere and a garage history of the repairs undertaken.'

Once again it was all a bit *might have been*, but the fingers-crossed exploration of these kinds of obscure avenues so often led to rainbow's end.

With nothing left for Lorenzo in Kettering, he prepared to head homewards. However, before he departed, the two detectives agreed that their respective teams would continue investigating independently, but all developments would be shared daily by email.

From his car, still at Kettering police station, Lorenzo played two-way catch-up with Valentine. The information-flow was 90 per cent one way: Valentine had little to tell his boss, except that the *headmistress* had been unusually benign and benevolent.

'Probably because I'm not around,' said Lorenzo, adding the warning, 'but if I were you, I'd treat it more as the calm before the storm than a climate change.'

It was after 6 pm by the time Lorenzo crossed the county border from Hampshire into Dorset, so he decided to steer for home, hoping for a meeting with Tricia. Rotating in his head, like a musical carousel with a mesmerizing motion, were the words: 'I think I know what it's all about. In fact, I'm certain I do.'

As he manoeuvred into his private parking-space, he looked for Luke's car. Because he worked from home, he'd normally be around at this time of day, even though his nightly excursions to the nearest pub were starting progressively early. Some days he played golf, leaving home in the morning and not returning until gone midnight. The nineteenth hole could be a real test of stamina.

Tricia heard Lorenzo's car and hurried to greet him. Her welcome was warm.

'I knew it couldn't be Luke returning. He left for the pub with one of his golfing cronies only half an hour ago. We should have at least six hours to ourselves.' Her eyes conveyed much more than her mouth.

'You've had me intrigued all day,' said Lorenzo, pocketing his car-keys. Their bodies kept brushing unnecessarily as they walked towards Tricia's house.

'I've been itching to explain,' said Tricia, hardly able to contain her euphoria.

There were three clauses to the pledge Lorenzo had made to himself: no more binge-drinking, no more gambling and no more womanizing married women. He had always known that the third part would be the hardest for him to heed. He was at an age when most single women were either too young or too old for him; bored and restless housewives had long been his Achilles' heel. He didn't set out to seduce, but gravitation would take over; he'd always been a slave to nature and its impulses. He accepted that his defence was pathetic: *I'm sorry, M'Lord, I didn't mean to help myself to what was not mine to take, but I couldn't resist it.*

How many times had he heard that in court from thieves? And what had always been his reaction? A contemptuous snigger. Yet here he was, about to pick and taste fruit that wasn't his to savour, but for weeks he had known that this would come. The passage to Tricia's bed had been inexorable; from empiric experience, Lorenzo knew that the moment the Rubicon was crossed, from friendship to fornication, the relationship would be changed irrevocably; once toothpaste was out, it could never be returned to the tube. The same applied to semen. He was aware of all this. He knew the end would be traumatic, tearful and recriminatory, but man would always be made an idiot by his testosterone. The breaching of the contract with his self was virtually predestined, so he would not fight fate. But being the consummate professional, nosiness had to precede pleasure, so the kitchen came before the bedroom.

As soon as they were armed with mugs of coffee and seated opposite one another on stools at the table, Lorenzo said, 'OK, let's hear it.'

Now that the moment had at last arrived for which Tricia had been waiting eagerly all day something akin to stage-fright froze her.

'Well?' Lorenzo prompted.

'I hope you're not going to think I'm crazy,' she started tentatively, tantamount to dipping a toe in water to test the temperature.

'I'm hunting a madman, Tricia, so the madder your theory, the more likely it is to be near the mark.'

Confidence now lit up Tricia like electricity returning after a blackout. 'How *au fait* are you with the Jack the Ripper murders?'

Now a wry smile washed over Lorenzo and settled. 'Is this a wind-up?' he said, amusement in voice and eyes.

'No, Mike, the question's a serious one.'

'OK, I'll play along,' he said indulgently. 'I know the basic story. A few years ago I watched a TV documentary on the subject; one of those that tried to unravel the mystery of the Ripper's identity. But I've never read one of the hundreds of books that have been published about those Victorian crimes. To be honest, I can't understand the fascination; perhaps it's because the Ripper was never caught and so everyone can play armchair detective, and no theory, however outrageous, such as pointing the finger of suspicion at royalty, can ever be disproved. It's not as if Jack the Ripper was the trailblazer of serial killing, though I suppose it could be argued that he's the high priest.'

'Do you know the dates of the murders?'

'Only that they were in the 1880s, I believe.'

'Forget the year, Mike. Although, for the record, it was 1888.'

'I'm getting a feeling that you must be a Jack the Ripper aficionado.'

'Ever since I was a callow student of criminology. But, as I said, forget the year and concentrate on the day and months. Jack's first murder was on August 31st. The second was on the night of September 8th/9th. See where I'm heading?'

Lorenzo was no longer smiling. He was computing with mental jet-propulsion. 'Mary Walker was murdered on September 1st.'

'But the note apologized for the wrong date, blaming "circumstances beyond my control". The killer could have been lying in wait for her to return home on the evening of August 31st, but she didn't get back from town until after midnight, skewing the date. Can you recall the name of the Ripper's second victim, who was slain on September 8th/9th, 1888?'

'No, I can't, Tricia.'

'It was Annie Chapman.'

Blanching, Lorenzo was now riveted.

'What time was *your* Chapman killed?' said Tricia.

'Uncertain. According to the pathologist, it could have been any time between the abduction and 2 a.m.'

'Your man, Mike, is not only doing it by the calendar, but also by the name. He's matching name and date, reincarnating Jack the Ripper.'

'You're over-reaching,' said Lorenzo, almost triumphantly. 'One thing I do remember is that the Ripper's first victim was Mary Nichols.'

'Right and wrong, Mike. Your man has been wickedly devious, delaying your chances of catching on to the agenda – and the timetable of *events* to come.'

'How come?'

'Because Mary Nichols' maiden name was Walker! Mary Walker! Too much of a coincidence, Mike; the names, the dates, the slit throats, and the notes alluding to the significance of the timing. But the clincher for me was the line in the first note: *Think about dear John.* We thought he might be hinting at revenge for a romantic betrayal, but it's nothing like that, if I'm right. People named John are frequently known to friends as Jack. President John Kennedy was Jack to his clan. Here the killer is telling you to revere his beloved *Dear John.*'

'Simple code for his *dear Jack.* Jack the Ripper,' intoned Lorenzo.

'Exactly.'

Tricia had it figured and Lorenzo was hooked. Carnality had gone to the back-burner.

11

Lorenzo was woken by a cold, metallic tickle to his sweaty forehead.

One eye blinked, then the other.

The room was filled with darkness, except for shafts of pale slivers from the moon that sneaked like a peeping tom around the edges of the curtains.

Lorenzo was disorientated; *Where am I? This isn't my bed.*

The vibes were alien; so, too, the silence. Then he remembered in a flash-flood of mental, self-flagellating replay.

But the heavy, stressed breathing wasn't coming from Tricia, who, still naked and damp with perspiration, a by-product of their recent physical activity, lay peacefully asleep beside him. Someone else was in the room. Someone hovering, like a restless poltergeist with malevolent intent.

There was no mistaking the menacing feel of gun-metal, which conveyed a unique, unnerving message.

The silhouetted figure at Lorenzo's side of the bed loomed large and sinister.

Lorenzo tried to lift his head from the pillow but was forced down by pressure from the metal, which he now recognized as the twin barrels of a shotgun.

'Don't you dare move, you bastard!'

Luke Lockwood's voice was as instantly identifiable as the gun-metal had been.

Tricia stirred, her husband's pent-up anger, a subliminal intrusion, breaking through the shroud of blissful sleep that had cocooned her. She curled towards Lorenzo, snuggling into him foetus-fashion, a hand feeling for his lips.

With her eyes still closed, she murmured dreamily, 'What time is it, Mike?' She was still oblivious to the reason for her slumber being abruptly interrupted.

'It's time for your comeuppance, you two-timing whore!'

Now Tricia sprang up with the action of a coiled spring suddenly released.

'Yes, it's your dear, devoted, loyal husband!' Luke sneered, his rage white-hot. 'I suspected something like this was going on behind my back.' Then mirthlessly to Lorenzo, 'What you'd call a fair cop, wouldn't you say?'

Tricia now made out the gun in her husband's trembling hands, tremulous with fury, not fear.

Intrepidly emboldened, Tricia switched on a bedside lamp. 'Have you lost leave of your senses? Put that thing down before you do damage, you bloody fool!'

Lorenzo winced mentally. He wanted to caution Tricia. Luke was drunk. Alcoholic madness lurked behind his glazed, murky eyes. Reasoning with a man in this deranged condition would be impossible. But Lorenzo feared that anything he said would only exacerbate the situation.

'You're in no position to try giving orders, bitch!' Luke eyed his wife with a poisonous combination of hate and disgust. 'You didn't expect me home so soon, did you? You gambled your lives on habit, my routine. Well, you've been well and truly outsmarted. Do you know how foolish you both look? Exposed by the naked truth!' He laughed evilly at his derisive rhetoric.

'I said put down that gun!' Tricia continued to seethe.

Lorenzo admired her bravery, but feared the consequences, especially as he saw the finger on the triggers start to squeeze as Luke's face became contorted with demented wrath.

'You don't get it, do you?' Luke said to his wife, not shouting; in fact, his voice was quieter than normal now as his emotions turned to ice; a very dangerous signal that Lorenzo recognized as tantamount to the withdrawal of a hand-grenade pin, just prior to the explosive being thrown. 'I'm the one calling the shots.' He faked a laugh. 'Appropriate pun, don't you think? You're both going to pay. I'm going to blow you away. Are you really so dim that that hasn't sunk in?'

Only now did Tricia begin to appreciate the danger she and Lorenzo were in. Luke had crossed a line: he couldn't back down; neither could the status quo be maintained. And the only way forward was for Luke to go through with the threat, something which Lorenzo had already come to terms with. He was cursing himself for having drifted sightlessly into this hapless plight. After sex, he and Tricia had remained entwined, cooling off, before sleepily continuing the conversation they'd had downstairs about the possibility of the double killer being 'Jack's Heir'.

'Luke won't be home for hours,' Tricia had said complacently. 'Let's lie together for a while. There's no rush.' Lorenzo had never been a successful gambler, now harshly confirmed.

'This isn't going to solve anything,' said Lorenzo, wide awake now, his brain slipping seamlessly into cop-mode; hostage-scene negotiator.

'Shut up, arsehole!' Luke boomed, as if the metaphorical hand-grenade had exploded.

'That's it! I've had enough of this crap!' fumed Tricia, kicking back the duvet.

Drink had dulled Luke's reflexes and he responded with bovine inertia, taking a split-second too long to compute what was happening. His momentary vacillation provided just the chance Lorenzo had been hoping for, recognizing that it was *now* or *never*.

As the barrels of the shotgun angled away from Lorenzo towards Tricia, he lunged for the firearm. While gripping the gun a few inches from the muzzle, tilting it upwards, it fired, blowing a gaping, ragged hole in the ceiling, plaster sprinkling down like sand in an egg-timer.

Tricia screamed, while the force of the shotgun's kick-back knocked Luke off balance and before he could use the smoking gun as a cudgel, Lorenzo wrenched it from his grasp and tossed it in one fluid movement to Tricia, who, despite her shakiness, caught the weapon with the aplomb of an ace slip-fielder.

The two men rolled off the bed, crashing on to the floor in a tangled heap, but Luke was no match for Lorenzo in unarmed combat. A sharp knee-jerk to the groin and snappy punches to the solar plexus and chin ended the contest abruptly. Luke wasn't unconscious, but he was a spent cartridge, doubled up in agony and weeping, not so much from the pain as the humiliation of abject failure.

This was the moment that Tricia became hysterical.

'He tried to kill us! I want him gaoled, locked away forever. He's crazy! I'll never be safe unless he's taken out of circulation permanently. I want a divorce. I want him out of here. For God's sake, arrest him, Mike! Look at the ceiling. But for the grace of God, those holes would have been in our heads!' She paced as she ranted, shivering as she sweated, bathed in hot and cold shock.

'Put something on,' Lorenzo said, softly but firmly.

Tricia stopped as she saw herself in the dressing-table mirror; a naked apparition as white as a ghost, holding a shotgun, which she held on to as tightly as if it was a crucifix to ward off a demon.

'Give me that,' said Lorenzo, trying to ease the gun from her grasp, but her fingers were as stiff as if a form of living rigor mortis had set in. 'Come on, Tricia, everything's going to be fine now.'

But her eyes were blank.

'It's me, Tricia,' he said, flicking his fingers, like a hypnotist waking his sleeper. 'Let go. I'll see that no one harms you again.'

Her fingers finally loosened their grip and suddenly she, too, was crying. Husband and wife weeping; one broken by shock, the other dismantled by Lorenzo's fists. The three of them were in for a long night, Lorenzo knew. Whatever sleep they'd already had that night would be the last for many hours.

Almost sleepwalking, Tricia went to her wardrobe, took out a silky, pink housecoat and wrapped herself in it, as if insulating herself from all terrors of the night.

'Have you any brandy?' said Lorenzo, slipping into his shirt and trousers.

'We should have, unless that drunken bastard's finished it off,' Tricia retorted, pointing towards her husband and preparing to aim a kick towards his genitals, which Lorenzo adroitly thwarted.

'Find the brandy – or whisky – and make three black coffees.'

'Not for *him*, I won't. Are you nuts, Mike?'

'Just do it, *please*, Tricia. Pop some brandy in yours and mine, but obviously not in Luke's.'

'We have plenty of weedkiller; that'll do nicely for him.'

Lorenzo now appreciated more than ever why police officers dreaded dealing with domestic disturbances, but never could he have imagined being so intimately enmeshed in one; tangled in a web very much of his own making.

Before Tricia exited the bedroom, Lorenzo asked her, holding up the shotgun, 'Does he have a licence for this?'

'Yes. But not for shooting people!'

There was blood on the carpet from Luke's mouth. An incisor had been dislodged and was being held by Luke almost endearingly, as if he intended putting it under his pillow in the hope of a visit from the Tooth Fairy.

'OK, we've some talking to do – and fast,' said Lorenzo, keeping possession of the firearm, even though it was now empty of ammo.

Luke was sobering up swiftly. His headache came courtesy of Lorenzo's fists. The hangover would come later, leaving him with a double head-banger. The *real* hangover, however, would be the long-term consequences.

'What is there to talk about?' fumed Tricia, shaking her head in frustration. She'd been on her way to the kitchen to do as Lorenzo beseeched but had scampered back to the bedroom in lathered exasperation on hearing Lorenzo call for a pow-wow, amounting to a truce, it seemed to her. 'He's a violent, armed criminal. The only fit place for him is in gaol.'

'Please calm down,' implored Lorenzo, referee-style. He was

now thinking only of himself, of self-preservation. Of course he was aware that he should already have handcuffed Luke, read him his rights, and called for back-up. He was equally aware that to have pursued the correct procedure would have been tantamount to professional suicide. Chief Constable Kingdom would shred him.

He flinched at the mental vision of potential newspaper headlines: *Top Detective in Shotgun Romance with Married Landlady.... Naked Murder Case Detective in Bedroom Romp and Gun Battle.*

He would be suspended and instantly discharged from his current high-profile investigation. His long-term prospects would be equally bleak. Even if he survived a misconduct charge and internal inquiry, he was sure to be demoted at least, sacked from the CID, and transferred to another force, probably somewhere remote and inhospitable, such as the Outer Hebrides.

This imbroglio had to be sorted within these four walls. There was no doubt in his mind that he could handle Luke, who was bereft of bargaining power; Tricia would be the problem. She was lusting for her pound of flesh. Not only was she outraged, she quite rightly feared for her life. Drink had deranged Luke. Tricia would never again feel safe in a house with him. Whenever he drank in the future, he would be likely to erupt into a jealous rage, tipping him over the edge. For her own peace of mind, she required her husband behind bars, plus a restraining order, denying him any form of access to her, once he was released.

Lorenzo understood all this, but out of self-interest he had to manipulate Tricia into agreeing to a private settlement. He had to be Machiavellian, exploiting their intimacy, purporting to love Tricia and highlighting that a public scandal would trash their privacy and fracture, possibly irrevocably, their emotional bond. In essence, he would use their relationship as a weapon.

'How do you expect me to be calm when all you want to do is *talk* to this bastard? This can't be covered up, Mike. This is too big for some cosy arrangement. What would you do if anyone in the street, for example, pulled a gun on you?'

'Different altogether,' croaked Luke, finding his voice and spitting blood. 'He wouldn't be in bed with another man's wife. Stuffing her like a Christmas turkey.'

'I thought I told you to keep your filthy, drunken mouth shut!' Tricia shouted, once more preparing to kick Luke and having to be restrained by Lorenzo.

'You really aren't making things any easier for yourself,' said Lorenzo, addressing Luke. And then to Tricia, 'Please fetch those coffees.' Whispering in her ear, he continued, 'I'm thinking of us. I want what's best for you and me. Sod him! I'd love to see him banged up and rot in Hell, but we've got to think this through rationally, so that we're not the ones who get hurt most.' He was playing her now, finding a rhythm, making his pitch.

'I'll be as quick as I can,' she said, no longer taut and trembling, some colour returning to her cheeks.

As soon as Tricia was out of the room, Lorenzo said, 'You're a bloody fool, Luke.'

'I know. I should have blown you both away without bothering to say a word. If I hadn't been drunk, I'd have done a proper job. You'd be dead; so would she. And I wouldn't be in this mess, but I wanted to see you both squirm.'

'No, Luke, you'd be in a far bigger hole, spending at least the next thirty years incarcerated.'

'It would have been worth it.'

'Wrong. It never is. The truth is, you're feeling sorry for yourself. Here's the reality: no one stole Tricia from you, Luke; you threw her away. When she needed you, where were you? At the pub. Getting legless. Or getting your leg over, as far as Tricia knew.'

'*I'm* not the unfaithful one.'

'There are many different versions of betrayal; yours was neglect, nightly desertion.'

'What do you know?'

'Enough.'

'All from pillow-talk, eh?'

'No, Luke, from witnessing the result of your physical abuse, from seeing the hours Tricia was left alone while you were drinking yourself senseless with other people; shutting your wife out of your social life. You're a loser, Luke. The question now is whether you're prepared to cut your losses.'

Now Luke gazed up forlornly from the floor at Lorenzo. Self-pity was telegraphed from his watery eyes and sagging mouth, which had been partially assisted into that sad shape by Lorenzo's punches.

'Are you proposing a deal?' he said, leering now, like a crafty Fagin.

'If I am, it's not from a position of weakness, Luke, so don't start getting uppity.'

'Why aren't you doing what Tricia's been urging, then? Scared of the outcome? Scared *you*, not *me*, will end up the vilified villain?'

'Don't try playing poker with me, Luke; I was weaned on it. If any shit is going to hit a fan, it's going to be all yours, believe me.'

Luke's smugness quickly evaporated. 'So what *is* the proposition?'

'Your marriage is dead,' said Lorenzo, in the manner of a definitive statement. 'Now you must be prepared to bury it. Tricia gets the house and you vacate *immediately*.'

'I work here.'

'Tough. So does Tricia.'

'The riding school's just a hobby.'

'I shouldn't repeat that in front of Tricia. You won't work from here if you go to prison and that's the only alternative.'

Luke sulked. 'I want painkillers,' he said, like a child in a tantrum. 'I hurt all over.'

'Are there any in the house?'

'In the bathroom. Surely you know where everything is by now, considering the amount of time you must have spent in here – and *in* my wife!'

Lorenzo wasn't tempted by the bait. 'Tricia mightn't be disposed to get them for you.'

'Oh, I'm sure she will if *you* ask her.'

Lorenzo heard the kettle boiling. There wasn't much time left before Tricia would return, so Lorenzo continued to resist being sidetracked.

'Not only will you leave the house forthwith, you'll also go straight in rehab.'

'Paid for by whom?'

'You, of course.'

'What kind of rehab? I don't do drugs. I'm no sexaholic, not like some people I know.'

'You're an alcoholic, Luke. You have a serious drink problem. There's no time for denial. You need to dry out. But it's not only your liver that needs sorting urgently.'

'What else, then, doc?'

'Your head.'

'Since when did you qualify as a shrink?'

'This isn't open for discussion, Luke. I'm laying down the terms. There's no guarantee that Tricia will agree to them, but if *you* don't, you're finished.'

'You too.'

'Perhaps. Perhaps not. But if I am *finished*, it'll only be temporary, whereas yours will be permanent.'

Luke's burdensome sigh was that of a broken man, reluctantly resigning himself to his unpalatable fate.

'I'll have a solicitor draw up a sworn affidavit for you to swear and sign, in which you'll admit to your criminal actions of this evening; a confession that could be used to prosecute you at any future date should you renege on the conditions of the agreement.'

'Who will the solicitor be – *if* I play along?'

'A good one.'

'You mean a shyster?'

'On the contrary; one who has acted for the police in prosecutions at magistrates' court. Someone honourable and reliable. Not your type, Luke.'

'What else am I expected to do?'

'You'll fork out for repairs to the ceiling. You won't contest the divorce. You'll agree never to return to this property. You'll also promise never to try to make contact with Tricia or to harass or stalk her by any method known to obsessive man – or beast. Not that I'm accusing you of being either, of course.'

'Do you realize that this estate, with "The Barn" and stables, is worth much more than a million.'

'The market value's irrelevant, Luke. Tricia gets it and that's final. She may still demand more.'

'Fuck her! Fuck you! She's not getting any of my hard-earned money; not a penny. And *that's* final.'

'I wasn't thinking of money.'

'What then?'

'Your freedom. Taking that from you may be more important than anything else for Tricia. Your destiny's in her hands.'

'And your smooth tongue.'

'Don't knock it, Luke; it could be your lifeline.'

The door opened. Tricia entered bearing three mugs of black coffees on a tray.

'Luke requests painkillers from the bathroom,' Lorenzo said derisively.

'If you'd hit him harder he'd still be out cold and free from pain.'

During the night, seemingly the longest so far of Lorenzo's life, he succinctly outlined the proposals he'd put to Luke.

Tricia's initial reaction was to recoil in horror from the arrangement, steaming, 'He gets off scot-free? Like hell he does!'

'Since when has losing everything been getting off free?' Luke countered.

At one point, Lorenzo took Tricia outside the door, where quietly he explained, 'A scandal could kill off your riding school. The value of the estate would plummet. Both of us could end up pariahs, because there's no predicting how the media would run with it. For all we know, Luke could be the one milking all public sympathy. But this way, we control everything.'

'How do you control someone who was ready to blast off both our heads?'

'You drain the drink from his system because that's what he was running on. No fuel, no fire. If you like, I'll move in with you so that, at least at night, you have a resident bodyguard.'

'I like,' she smiled.

Lorenzo had swung it.

Valentine was shaving when Lorenzo called him at 6 a.m.

'Hold the fort for me until lunchtime,' said Lorenzo; no pleasantries. 'I've got an important appointment first-thing. Set up a case-conference for 2 pm, with the main players in the team. A completely new dimension's been added to the investigation. See you at two, if not earlier. No problems to report?'

'No, but....'

'Till two, then.'

Of the three of them in the Lockwoods' house at dawn, Luke was by far the most distressed. Slumped in the living-room on a settee, tears still coming and passing like April showers, he seemed as harmless as a dismantled Second World War bomb.

Taking Tricia aside again, Lorenzo said, 'This is the plan: within the hour I'm going to drive him to the Autumn Shades Sanctuary, an award-winning rehab clinic in the New Forest.'

'How do you know they'll take him?'

'They will, trust me. They owe me. I'll call you from there to reassure you he's in.'

Tricia nodded her tacit approval.

'From the clinic, I'll also call Cherie Signore, the solicitor I talked about.'

'And how do you know she'll be available?'

'She will be for me.' Not the best of lines to shoot to Tricia in the circumstances, and to his credit he instantly acknowledged his gaucheness. 'She needs work to keep landing on her desk from the police, so she'll drop other things to do me a favour.'

If Tricia had been more awake and alert, she might have

regarded the explanation as compounding the original indiscretion, rather than a mitigating factor.

'I'll stress the importance of her joining me and Luke at the clinic this morning, so that the whole deal is packaged before I leave.'

'Is it really possible to complete all that in such a tight timescale?'

'Should be. I'll update you. Take my word, I won't leave Luke until he's been fully processed.' Police-speak seemed to comfort Tricia. 'I'll make staff aware that he must be supervised around-the-clock.'

Tricia relaxed visibly.

'I don't know how I'm going to get through today,' she said, her tiredness seeming to proliferate. 'I've got so many riders booked in and it wouldn't be fair or make business sense to cancel at such short notice. Kylie will be here soon. It's going to be hard keeping my feelings from her; she's a bright kid.'

'Switch on to auto-pilot, it's the only way; adrenaline will keep you from crashing.'

She smiled weakly. 'I assume your meeting at two is to *sell* the Jack the Ripper angle?'

'It shouldn't take much selling.'

'You haven't asked me the most obvious follow-up questions.'

'Which are?'

'For starters, how much time you have.'

Lorenzo frowned. A night without sleep and all the accompanying stress and dramatic pyrotechnics had brought out the Neanderthal in him.

'The date of the third Jack the Ripper murder and the name he'll be targeting, dummy!'

Lorenzo rolled his head in disbelief at his mental sluggishness.

'Please, please, don't tell me it's today or tomorrow!' he said, in the manner of divine supplication.

'It's not that bad. You have well over two weeks to make

preparations and hammer home warnings to the public. However, there's a nasty sting in the tail.'

Lorenzo braced himself. 'I know by now that every silver lining is just another booby-trap.'

Tricia smiled sympathetically. 'On September 30th, 1888 there were TWO victims in the one night: Liz Stride and Catherine Eddowes. Will Jack's heir be able to fit in two with the appropriate names, or will he settle for just one? And if just one, which? And where? Quite a conundrum, even with the time you have available, don't you think?'

Suddenly Lorenzo's headache was worse than Luke's.

12

At a little after 1 a.m., Lorenzo and Cherie Signore postured combatively on the sweeping steps at the imposing, colonial-styled entrance to the Autumn Shades Sanctuary.

'Another fine mess you've got yourself into,' said Signore impishly, her eyes wolfish, her smile sardonic, but not argumentative.

'And again you've dug me out of it.'

'You hope.'

'At the very least you've bought me time.'

'Time to hang yourself.'

'Ever the optimist. Some things never change.'

'Especially dick-led males.'

'There speaks a woman of experience! Thanks, anyhow. Oh, incidentally, bill Luke Lockwood, not me.'

While Signore sashayed away towards her Porsche, crunching gravel with her dagger-heels, Lorenzo leaned against a mock Roman column and fired off a text to Tricia:

Deed done. Affidavit sworn and signed. Luke bedded down for the foreseeable. Situation secured. Deciding how to sign off delayed him a couple of beats. Finally, he settled for the simple, *Mike x.*

He was pleasantly surprised by how uncomplicated the technicalities had been, mainly because of the cool efficiency of Signore. The second generation British Italian had the looks and figure of Sophia Loren and also a Latin temperament, should anyone have the temerity to put a flame to her gunpowder.

Tricia phoned soon after receiving Lorenzo's text, but he

didn't answer, deciding it was best to play dead and allow her to leave a voicemail message. She would assume he was driving, which he was a couple of minutes later.

Valentine and the rest of the frontline team were eager to hear about the *new dimension* to the investigation.

Lorenzo had the floor in the briefing-room and soon incredulity was etched across the gallery of faces in front of him during his presentation. However, the mood became electrically animated as the indisputable pattern sank in.

Of course there were one or two sceptics, the usual suspects.

'Jack the Ripper disembowelled his victims and buggered off with the viscera,' stated Detective Constable Pete Marlowe, a twenty-five-year veteran who'd joined the CID because he thought it would give him an excuse to remain scruffy.

'Not in the first killing,' Valentine corrected the dissenter.

'The symbolism is sufficient,' Lorenzo maintained, eliciting a round of nods from 99 per cent of his audience. 'Slit throats, matching names and dates; it's all there.'

'Agreed,' said Valentine, weighing-in with his boss and speaking for the large majority, who could see the bedrock of logic underpinning Lorenzo's premise.

'OK, so we know what he's doing, but how do we stop him?' Marlowe continued to probe, with the instinct of a back-row, political heckler.

'We unmask him,' said Lorenzo. 'Stop to think for a moment: if we're right about this scenario, and I'm convinced of it, then in one step we have covered a mile towards nailing him. Quite a leap.'

'How so?' Marlowe said stubbornly, not an easy convert.

'We already know the name – or names – of his next victim. We also know the date on which he intends to strike.'

'But not where,' said Marlowe.

'You want it on a plate?' said Valentine.

'That would be nice and obliging,' Marlowe retorted, beginning to bore. 'What I don't get is the motive.'

'What was Jack the Ripper's motive?' said Valentine. 'He was nuts; nothing more, nothing less. There's no point trying to get inside the head of a nutter. All serial killers are deranged, by definition. If you attempt to rationalize their barmy behaviour, you'll become as moonstruck as they are. Just accept it.'

'Jack collected human organs, perhaps for medical research,' Marlowe argued. 'He could even have been a collector for a medical school.'

'More likely he was merely collecting trophies for himself,' said Lorenzo. 'We'll never know, but in any event, it's irrelevant. All serial killers murder for a reason that makes sense to them, however much we're revolted by it. Many of them are waging a war against whores. They believe they've been chosen as God's warriors. Religious crusaders on the march to sanitize our streets.'

'Not all,' Marlowe balked.

'No, of course not all,' said Lorenzo. 'I was just giving one example. A woman teacher may have refused to allow a boy to go to the toilet during a lesson and he pissed his pants. Twenty years later, he starts chopping up teachers, hacking out their bladders. Attempting to identify motives with serial killers is a futile exercise because they're on a different planet. The motive matters only after an arrest; it will rarely help in unravelling the mystery. Let's look at this operationally; we have more than two weeks to work this and every reason to be confident of bringing about a successful closure before the deadline.'

'How so?' Marlowe hadn't been silenced for long.

'Well, for starters, he's obviously obsessed with the Ripper murders. Is anyone here familiar with the recent FBI profile of Jack the Ripper?'

'I am,' said Valentine.

Bemusement was headlined across the faces of most of the others.

'Are you telling me the FBI has nothing better to do than investigate unsolved cases of well over a century ago and not even on their own continent?' said Marlowe, embellishing his contrived astonishment. 'Now that really is cold-case exhumation with an exclamation!'

This time Marlowe drew a ripple of restrained mirth.

'Not a bad publicity stunt, though,' said Valentine.

'Whatever, the FBI's behavioural science experts concluded that the infamous Jack was aged twenty-five to thirty-five and was riddled with syphilis, contracted from rag-and-bone prostitutes,' said Lorenzo. 'Now, it's plausible that our copycat Jack has been a regular prostitutes' punter and, as a consequence, suffers from a venereal disease.'

'So we look for someone with the clap?' Marlowe said derisively. 'Medical records are confidential. There's no way of accessing that kind of data without getting arrested! We'd soon be reported to the police!' He looked for applause, but by now his peers had decided that their resident comedian was beyond a joke.

'Forget medical records,' Lorenzo said flatly, ignoring the sniping. 'We check *our* records, *our* databases.'

'Looking for what?' asked an intense female detective, her question genuine.

'Punters who've been prosecuted over the last couple of years for kerb-crawling and propositioning in our red-light districts. One of them in his statements may have complained about catching a dose, which he'd passed on to his wife and she'd walked out on him as a result; something of that nature. Someone left in a simmering rage. I'll leave Valentine to assign that beat.'

'Assaults on prostitutes could be worth looking into,' Valentine suggested. 'Serial killers usually get their *exalted status* by increments, starting with lesser violent, sex-related crimes.'

'Constructive thinking,' Lorenzo praised his partner, always generous with encouragement, especially when it was self-serving. 'Also bear in mind the possibility of his being ambidextrous; won't be many of those among the old lags. But there are many other directions for us to explore.'

'Such as?' There was no keeping Marlowe muted.

'As I've already stressed, our man is obviously a Jack the Ripper buff. He's probably been reading every book that's ever been published on the subject. He can't get enough of it. He salivates over what, in his grotesque psyche, are the *juicy bits.*'

'So we look for someone who's been borrowing Ripper books from public libraries on our patch,' said Valentine, falling in with Lorenzo's reasoning.

'Yes, but because of the economic climate and financial cutbacks in the public sector, libraries keep only a limited selection on any one topic,' said Lorenzo. 'So if they don't keep a particular book on their shelves, it has to be ordered by a subscriber and a computer-search is made to locate which libraries elsewhere have it; perhaps out of our region. If someone has been requesting a whole series of Jack the Ripper books, the electronic trail should be a doddle to follow, giving us a name, address, and even a phone number.'

'So we can phone our suspects and ask them if they've read any good gory books recently,' said Marlow, chuffed with himself.

'I think it's more likely he's been buying books,' said Valentine, warming to the mindset that was coming out of this brainstorming session. 'Buffs like to own a collection – to have, to hold and cherish.'

'Like taking a wife, then discovering everything about her belonged on the fiction shelves; make-believe that failed to suspend disbelief,' Marlowe mocked.

'Certainly like *possessing* a loved one,' said Valentine. 'He wouldn't want to have to give back the books. He'd want them on hand permanently.'

'To refer to them whenever his memory needs refreshing?' said Lorenzo.

'Exactly,' said Valentine.

'I think you could be right on that score,' said Lorenzo. 'So we visit the big chains, Waterstones and W.H. Smith.'

'Amazon is probably an even better bet,' Valentine suggested. 'The bookshops are more likely to stock only recently published books. Amazon will have a much bigger selection.'

'Any other thoughts?' Lorenzo asked, looking around and jotting notes.

'If this *is* the right way to be going, our man is likely to be spending hours trawling the Internet for every snippet of info on Jack the Ripper and similar serial head-bangers,' said Marlowe, at last making a serious contribution. 'There's probably an Internet chat-room where these weirdoes meet to toss-off on their conspiracy theories; a sort of Jack the Ripper old boys' club. Is it possible to identify someone through the number of hits on a site? I'm a devout Luddite when it comes to computer technology; I'd much prefer still to be filling in paper forms, even in triplicate.'

'I'll have someone talk with our techno boffins,' promised Lorenzo, deciding that this particular theme had been exhausted for the time being. 'The next issue to consider is victim-selection: how's he doing it?'

'Easy-peasy these days,' opined Valentine. 'Electoral rolls are online. He no longer has to go into the reference section of libraries, ask for the electoral rolls, and then scroll through them, page after page, street by street, house by house, until finally chancing upon a name he's hunting for, which would be unbelievably labour-intensive. He could pore through the entire electoral roll of a whole town by the old-fashioned method and be unlucky. Now all he has to do is pull up the electoral roll online of a town or city, tap in a name, and press "search". Hey presto!'

'That's a worry,' said Lorenzo, ruminating.

Valentine and the others waited for Lorenzo to elaborate.

'All the time I've been assuming that *our* Jack is local,' Lorenzo explained. 'But he could have been sitting in Edinburgh or Alaska googling the name "Mary Walker" and then "Annie Chapman". However, my gut feeling remains that *here*, this region, is the epicentre, the genesis of these crimes.'

'No doubt in my mind, either,' said Valentine. 'And the fact that *our* Jack knew that the maiden name of the original Ripper's first victim, Mary Ann Nichols, née Walker, clinches for me that he's a rabid student of his progenitor.'

'What's good for the goose is equally good for the gander: if *our* Jack can exploit the Internet to access electoral rolls for relevant names, then so can we,' said Lorenzo, finding a positive from a negative. 'If he's really adventurous enough to contemplate a "double delivery" on September 30th, he'll have to be looking at the residents of our largest cities, because they'll represent the only chance of his finding an Elizabeth Stride and a Catherine Eddowes within easy reach of one another.'

'Realistically, I can't envisage his punting for the double,' said Valentine. 'The logistics are mind-boggling. He'd have to juggle a surveillance on the two. Document their routines. Timing will be crucial for a double "big event". All that preparation in just a couple of weeks? No, he'll go for one.'

'Probably, but we can't afford to take any chances,' said Lorenzo. 'We also have to try to cover all bases because there's no telling which name he'll plump for: Stride or Eddowes.'

The most testing question came from the intense female detective, Susan Washington.

'Are you going public on all this, sir?'

Lorenzo massaged his unshaven chin. 'I don't see how we can morally and strategically avoid it,' he said unenthusiastically.

'The media will feast on the fodder we distribute,' Marlowe prophesied, somewhat gleefully.

'The killer will know immediately that we've pieced it all together,' Valentine pointed out the obvious.

'Makes no difference,' said Lorenzo. 'He can't cover his tracks and he has to go on, regardless.'

'Why?' said Washington. 'He could just stop, cut and run, surely?'

'Not this fella,' Lorenzo said emphatically. 'He's committed. He's made a pact with the Devil. He's on a mission and he's going to see this through. What Jack the Ripper did, he can do better. In his twisted mind, he's upstaging the original, finessing, adding trimmings, such as the notes, the cryptic clues, the *Dear John* teaser. He'd expect us to catch on eventually. For him, from this point, the *game* becomes more stimulating. On reflection, it's now more a *race* than a *game*, and he's well ahead. We've no idea how many women there are in the UK with the names Elizabeth Stride and Catherine Eddowes, but *he'll* know already. His research would have been completed before he kicked off.'

'And no doubt he'll have already chosen which one gets the cut – a Stride or an Eddowes,' Valentine surmised.

'Oh, yes, that's given,' said Lorenzo. 'And there could be thousands of each name.'

'So what's the game-plan?' said Marlowe, a sneer creeping across his foxy face. 'We tell them all to lock and bolt themselves indoors throughout the whole of September 30th?'

'I could think of a lot worse ideas,' said Valentine.

'But the best idea of all is to have *our* Jack bolted behind bars before that date,' said Lorenzo. '*That* must be our goal.'

'You realize we're going to be accused of causing panic, don't you?' warned Washington.

'I'd rather be accused of scaremongering than jeopardizing the safety and welfare of women,' said Lorenzo. 'I accept we're in something of a Catch-22 hole. Damned if we open our books to the media and damned if we don't.'

'A choice between two evils,' said Marlowe.

'No, it's a choice between two ways of *eliminating* evil,' said Lorenzo. 'We're going to work day and night. The clock is ticking. The countdown has begun.'

From the briefing-room, Lorenzo hurried to his office to update Chief Constable Helen Kingdom.

'A fanciful hypothesis,' she said haughtily. 'All your own brainchild, is it?'

'No, as a matter of fact the brainchild is ex-FBI.'

'I didn't imagine such vivid inspiration could have originated from you,' she said, barbed as ever.

Lorenzo responded with a one-fingered salute, merely for his own gratification because there were fifteen miles between Bournemouth and county HQ at Winfrith.

Kingdom was a snob. FBI, CIA, Interpol and Scotland Yard

impressed her. Lorenzo had her figured. Her imperiousness was a camouflage for an inferiority complex. Basically, she was small-time. She'd risen through the ranks in the leafy, sleepy shires. Snaring poachers had been her forte, her claim to fame. She was besotted by national and international law-enforcement agencies, yet resented Lorenzo's Scotland Yard credentials, rather than embracing them. Very Freudian.

Kingdom conceded that an 'upfront policy' with the media was 'essential', but quickly adjoined, 'As before, leave that to me. You've got more than enough on your plate, so steer clear of reporters. There's bound to be requests for interviews, especially from TV, and I'll handle those. It'll carry so much more weight coming from the top, from someone in authority.'

Always having to subjugate others was an integral part of her nature, underpinning her insecurity.

I'd better tip-off Mountford before the news breaks,' said Lorenzo, as an afterthought.

'Mountford? Who's he? An undertaker friend of yours? Giving him a job for the 30th?'

If Lorenzo had said that, Kingdom would have called him 'sick'.

'DI Mountford's at Kettering; lead detective in the Anne Chapman murder.'

'Mrs Chapman may have died a hundred and fifty miles away but, as far as I'm concerned, we're *leading* the investigation. Understood?'

'Yes, ma'am.' He understood far more than she did.

'Good. However, yes, out of courtesy, by all means put him in the picture, but don't let go of the reins.'

'I'll do as you say.'

She snorted, unconvinced. At least she was right about that.

Lorenzo devoted the remainder of the day to assigning tasks and programming a structured operation, the admin side of his job that he hated.

Early evening, a letter was delivered to Lorenzo by a member of the civilian clerical staff. The letter, addressed to Lorenzo and marked 'Personal' on the envelope, had been received at headquarters and re-directed, with other documents, on a police vehicle.

The moment the letter landed on his desk, Lorenzo recognized the handwriting. A first-class stamp had been used and it had been posted in Bournemouth the previous day.

Lorenzo's heart began beating like a drum-roll. A suffusion of sweat acted as an adhesive to his clothes, especially the collar of his shirt. His fingers twitched, but his brain remained cool and steady.

Despite his tiredness from a night without sleep and all the violent and emotion-sapping drama, including the more recent hard-bargaining at the rehab clinic, leaving him with panda bear eyes, Lorenzo's brain was functioning at its high-octane optimum. Almost certainly many people had handled the envelope during its journey, but most likely only the writer's fingerprints would be on the contents; possibly breakthrough evidence, so it was imperative that contamination should be avoided at all costs.

Before slicing open the letter, he pulled on a pair of latex gloves, taken from his briefcase. In his impatience, he dropped the weighty letter-opener on to his foot and swore aloud, kicking it petulantly to one side.

Carefully, he eased the single A4 folio, folded in three, from the slim, white envelope. The undated missive on plain white paper was short and pithy. Lorenzo read in tomb-like silence.

> Dear Humble, Parochial Detective,
> The knife has been sharpened,
> The hammer-head has been polished,
> And in the idiom of US prison-speak,
> Dead-woman is walking (big clue there!),
> But not for long.
> Happy hunting (for me, not you),
> Dear John

13

Midnight was ancient history by the time Lorenzo arrived 'home'. A new dawn was nibbling at the black edges of night. The turbulent events of 24 hours ago seemed like a hazy, fragmented nightmare. Perhaps even someone else's nightmare.

Lorenzo, in the manner of a programmed robot, at first made towards 'The Barn' from his car. Then, in a jolting flash, everything flooded back, catching him unawares, like an ambush. Total recall could be a nasty shock.

Tricia was nervously peeking around the curtains of her bedroom, having heard Lorenzo's car. By the time he reached the front door, she was there to let him in.

'Sorry, I forgot to give you a spare door key,' she said. 'You must be bombed; I know I am. I waited up until about one; dead on my feet. But when I got to bed, I was too tired to read and too restless to sleep. I began to think you'd had second thoughts and wouldn't be coming.'

They were in the hallway now and she looked at him uneasily for reassurance, something desperate in her eyes that could have been those of a fugitive.

'I'm drained dry,' he said, wriggling out of his crumpled jacket. 'So much has been crushed into such a small capsule of time, I'm dizzy. Brain blitzed.'

'I'm glad you're back.' The anguish and tension were still there.

Lorenzo knew what was gnawing away inside her head, like rats in the rafters: *Why didn't you call me when you must have known what I was going through? You must have had at least one spare minute when you could have punched my number, just to ensure that I was coping, that I was safe.*

After just one day he was already feeling emotionally trapped, a prisoner of domesticity, the kind of straightjacket from which he'd always had to break free. He could never live the life of a caged bird.

'I kept meaning to call you, but each time something else turned up and I was sidetracked,' he said, believing appeasement was necessary. 'You know, from your own professional experience, what it's like. Things are moving fast now, except for Luke, who's well and truly immobilized, so relax.'

Tricia *did* relax.

'I'm grateful and I *do* understand how your job can be a runaway train and there's no way off; you just have to go with it. Can I get you a drink?'

'No, thanks, I just want to sink into the sack.'

'Me, too. I know I'll sleep now you're home. Will you be able to lie in?'

''Fraid not. Must be in the office by seven, latest.'

'God, Mike, you'll kill yourself at this rate! You won't be getting more than two or three hours' sleep total in two nights.'

'It's what I'm underpaid for.'

Tricia was worried about him, but accepted that this wasn't the time for a lecture on health issues – about *anything*, in fact. But at the FBI she'd witnessed so many men – and women – who were washed up, beached flotsam, in their thirties, reduced to mental wrecks by the pressure of the job, and most of it self-imposed: over-dedicated people who were ground to dust on the treadmill. Agents who could never switch off until the overload blew a fuse. And what thanks did they get? Shown the door! Simply dismissed for not being made of the right stuff. Inadequate. Lacking steel. Pensioned off. Some collected by men in white coats and carted unceremoniously to funny farms.

Despite Lorenzo's overwhelming exhaustion, he was unable to unwind. Lying in bed, his body was inert but his brain rotated like a vortex, blown round and round by thoughts of the letter. This was something he would like to explore with Tricia, exploiting her expertise, but that would have to wait; she was already where Lorenzo longed to be. His brain finally closed up shop only shortly before opening time.

Wilfred Graham was bemused by the visit from two detectives – Lorenzo and Valentine.

'What on earth is this all about?' he said, shaking his head, as he led the detectives into his compact, tidy living-room.

'Probably nothing at all for you to be alarmed about,' Lorenzo said disarmingly. 'Mind if we sit?'

'Oh, no, of course not. Please, wherever you like. I didn't mean to be discourteous.'

The detectives opted for the chintzy armchairs around the plain fireplace. Graham squatted opposite on the edge of the matching settee, its pattern a little faded.

'Well?' said the house-owner, his eye anxiously shuttling between the detectives. 'I hope you're not harbingers of bad news about a relative of mine.'

'No, nothing like that,' said Lorenzo. 'I understand you have placed an order with a local bookshop for six hardback books about Jack the Ripper?'

'Is that a crime now?' Graham said, no barbs to his sarcasm, but bewildered.

'I realize my question must sound very strange,' Lorenzo said, insincerely apologetic.

'Rather more than that! You really *are* police officers? I'm not being set up for something crass like that old *Candid Camera* programme?'

Both detectives simultaneously handed over their ID perfunctorily for inspection.

Graham was in his mid-thirties. He had a bookish appearance: sturdy-rimmed glasses, pallid and pinched face, myopic eyes that had probably been subjected to too much close-up reading in poor light; straight dark hair that was prematurely thinning, frizzy greyish sideburns, and neglected teeth. In stature, he was tall and gangling. His speech was measured and confident, with no significant regional accent.

Satisfied with the credentials, Graham returned them, more bemused than ever, a ghost of a grin sticking. The suspected Jack the Ripper link with the murders had not yet been released to the press.

'You may have read a few days ago about the murder in Bournemouth of a Mary Walker,' said Lorenzo, his eyes as fixed on Graham's puzzled face as those of a mongoose confronting a venomous reptile.

'I don't read the local newspaper, but I heard about it on the TV regional news. But, once again, what has that to do with the books I'm buying?' he said, eyeing the detectives owlishly.

'These inquiries are purely routine. Like doctors investigating a patient's illness, we rely on a process of plodding elimination, so please rid yourself of any thoughts that you're a suspect.'

'In that case, what....'

Lorenzo cut him short. 'We have reason to believe that the person we're looking for is an obsessive crime-reading buff – of a particular period. Not of fiction. The true-crime genre. Especially of Ripper-style murders. All very vague and woolly, I know. However, ordering six books on the subject of one notorious ripper murderer struck us as worth following up, though I'm sure the explanation will send us on our way very quickly.' Lorenzo was only too aware that his storyline must have come across as pathetically threadbare.

Graham sat forward, dry-skinned hands clasped between his legs, and guffawed, his belly-laugh seeming out of tune with his bony body.

'How amazing!'

'What is?'

'That something as mundane could lead to a visit from the investigators of a real-life gruesome murder.'

'You know the saying about big oaks coming from little acorns; that's how most serious crimes are solved.'

'Well, I'm afraid you're going to be disappointed here.'

'I'm sure you're going to get around to answering my question,' said Lorenzo, his voice and eyes hardening, almost indiscernibly though.

Graham's slightly condescending smile vanished, as spontaneously as an electric-light being switched off.

'I'm a supply teacher. My specialist subject is history. Like so many people, I'm an addict of the Victorian era; everything about it. Nowadays in teaching we're always looking for innovative ways of whetting students' appetites for learning. Historically – excuse the pun – children have been turned off by history. "It's so boring" is what you hear repeatedly. "Just dates of wars, kings and queens; corn laws and industrial revolutions". But when you introduce Victorian crime into a lesson – Oliver, Fagin, infamous poisoners, and Jack the Ripper, they're suddenly hooked. They can't get enough of it. So the trick is to teach history subliminally. You wrap the Victorians around the nefarious underbelly of the times. Naturally, it's the boys who are hungriest for every *juicy* morsel about Jack the Ripper. Who do I think he was? Could he really have been a member of the Royal Household? They crave for so much detail and it's not something you study in depth for a History degree.'

'So you're swotting up?'

'Taking my own crash course and paying for it, yes. Forking out almost £120 just for those six books.'

'Are you currently teaching?'

Graham paused and his eyes rolled, like spinning wheels. He wasn't unsettled, but there was a definite change to his rhythm, like a runner stepping into a pothole and losing his stride.

'No, but I'm preparing.'

'Have you been offered a contract?'

He hesitated again. 'No. Sometimes I'll be taken on for a term or even a full year. More often, though, I fill in on a daily basis, when someone's ill, attending a course, or on maternity leave.'

'So when did you last teach?'

'In June or July. During the summer term.'

'At one school or several?'

'Several.'

For some reason he didn't appear to be so comfortable and forthcoming now.

'Have you *ever* had a full-time teaching job?'

'Oh, yes, from leaving university until the last couple of years.'

'So what made you go part-time?'

Now Graham began stroking his bare arms, as if soothing his self. His shirt-sleeves were rolled up and Lorenzo could see his pulse pumping in his wrist and neck.

'I went through a bad patch.'

It was obvious to the detectives that Graham had been preparing to say more, but censored himself.

'It happens to us all,' Lorenzo said glibly, trying to empathize. 'Was it a health problem?'

Another hiatus. 'No, domestic.'

The answers were becoming more economic, more heavily edited.

'Are you married, Mr Graham?'

'I was.' His eyes ducked and dived.

Lorenzo could almost taste the bitterness.

'So two years ago your marriage broke up?'

Graham avoided eye-contact, a fist pressed to his mouth. Turning to face Lorenzo again, he said, 'Is it really necessary to go into this? I've explained to you about the books. My matrimonial affairs of yesterday are unrelated, surely? This is just opening up old running sores for no useful purpose.'

'I appreciate your feelings,' said Lorenzo, undeterred. 'Are you divorced?'

'Yes.' This was snapped; Graham's mood had darkened. A depression was setting in.

'And you kept the house?'

'Yes; in that respect justice was done.'

'She walked out on you, did she?'

Graham stared at Lorenzo as if preparing to stamp on a

maggot. For almost a minute no one spoke. When it came to stand-offs, Lorenzo was never the one to be intimidated. In fact, he relished them, being reminded of his misspent poker days.

Graham was first to blink. 'I changed the locks. I made sure she couldn't get back in – ever. She went to court, but I had right on my side. She was a Jezebel! The queen bee of harlots!' His voice climbed almost to a crescendo and there was a raging bull in his distorted features.

'Do you have children?'

'Thank God, no!' He was a shade calmer now.

'Had your marriage been deteriorating over a period of time or was there a watershed moment, a breaking point?'

'I was happy. I thought we had a great marriage.'

'But your wife thought differently?'

'Not that she showed it. We did all the things that happily married couples do. But she was a cockroach.'

'Strong words, Mr Graham.'

'Not strong enough. We taught at the same school. After lessons one afternoon, I went looking for her and poked my head around the gym-door. I'd found her. Her bum was pressed against the climbing-frame, her skirt up to her chest, knickers around her knees, and the chairman of the PTA was working up a full head of steam, going for a record high jump. What words would *you* use to describe a wife like that?'

'I'm divorced, too,' said Lorenzo, eschewing the question but building a bridge.

'Only the night before we'd made love in bed and she'd said she might be pregnant. She wanted to know how I felt about it.'

'And how *did* you feel, Mr Graham?'

'Overjoyed. I didn't realize, though, that the child most probably had nothing to do with me; she left out the fact that it was almost certainly a bastard!'

'*Was* she pregnant?'

'I don't know. I don't care.'

'If she was, you *could* be the father.'

'She probably had an abortion.'

'But you don't know?'

'As I said, I don't care.'

'It would be understandable if the legacy you inherited after such an experience was a hatred of women.'

Graham was shrewd enough to see where Lorenzo was heading.

'No, Inspector. I hate my ex-wife, not all women. Despite my loathing for her, I'd never kill her, because I'd be the loser. I'd go to gaol and ruin what's left of my life. By letting her live, I know she'll end up in penury and purgatory, and that's something I want to live to savour, but not from behind bars.'

'Just a few more questions, Mr Graham. Where were you on the evening of Mary Walker's murder?'

Graham was suddenly deflated, all mental strength evaporated.

'How should I know? I can't even remember when it happened.'

Valentine reminded him.

'It still doesn't mean much to me. I rarely go out at nights. I spend most evenings at home, reading and listening to music. *That* Friday night would have been the same. One day is very much the same as any other for me.'

'Might you have had friends or relatives in?'

'Definitely not.'

'What vehicle do you drive?'

'An old jalopy.'

'What sort of *old jalopy*?'

'A twelve-year-old Toyota saloon. Four-door. It's a rust-heap. See for yourself, it's in the garage.'

'Take a look,' Lorenzo said to Valentine.

'Do any of your relatives or friends own a Land Rover?' Lorenzo continued with the catechism, while Valentine went to examine Graham's car.

'I've absolutely no idea.'

'Have *you* driven a Land Rover recently, maybe a rental one?'

'I've no need for such a vehicle.'

'That wasn't the question.'

'No, I've *never* driven a Land Rover or any similar anti-social fuel-gannet.'

Valentine returned and simply nodded to Lorenzo.

'As a teacher, you must have lots of examples of your hand-writing in the house.'

'Of course. Why do you ask?'

'I'd like to have a look, please.'

'Isn't this all rather OTT?' Graham again protested.

'It would be better for you and us to get this matter sorted in one sweep, rather than dragging it through instalments.'

'Oh, very well if it'll get you out of my hair. I've been working on a thesis, doing a rough draft by hand before committing it to a file on my computer. I'll fetch it for you.'

'What's the subject?'

'Jack the Ripper. Of course.'

As soon as they were in their car, Valentine driving, hands dancing animatedly on the wheel, Lorenzo said, 'Well, what's your verdict?'

'I think he's a good fit, except he doesn't own a Land Rover and does own a rust-heap. How about you?'

'His handwriting is similar to the perp's, but not a spot-on match, not to me, anyhow. His writing seemed to be left-handed but, equally, he could be ambidextrous, so that doesn't help us. I'm hedging my bets until we've spoken to a few people.'

'Such as?'

'Someone in authority at the county education department.'

'Shall I drive to Dorchester now?'

'Yes, but go via Winfrith. We'll drop off our little booty at HQ for analysis.'

The *booty* comprised Graham's thesis, a knife lifted from the kitchen with a blade similar to the one that had ended the lives of Mary Walker, and a hammer that had been kept in a tool-box.

Dean Rogers was the chief education officer at County Hall.

'Oh, yes, Mr Graham is well-known to us. There's no need for me to refer to our records.'

'I believe there was an incident a couple of years ago that resulted in his leaving full-time teaching?' said Lorenzo.

'I'd call it a *scandal* rather than an *incident*. Fortunately, we were able to contain it.'

'How do you define *contain*?'

'We kept it out of the newspapers and off TV.'

'So what's the official version?'

'The head of the school walked into Mr Graham's classroom late one afternoon, when all the children had gone home, and found him...' His voice trailed away as he searched for a suitable continuation.

'Yes?' Lorenzo prompted.

'Having sex with the religious education teacher, who was married to a rather prominent clergyman. There! That's it in a nutshell. I'm afraid there's no way of sanitizing it.'

'But...' Lorenzo started, for once struggling for words.

'Wasn't Mr Graham's wife a teacher at the same school?' said Valentine, helping out his boss.

'Oh, yes. She was devastated, of course. Graham and the RE teacher were suspended instantly and finally, after due process, dismissed for industrial misconduct. Neither has ever taught since.'

'Not even as a supply teacher? I'm referring specifically to Mr Graham.'

'We couldn't dare allow him in a classroom again.'

'To say I'm confused is a gross understatement,' said Lorenzo. 'It's our understanding that it was Mr Graham who caught his wife in flagrante delicto and divorced her, getting the house in settlement.'

'In addition to many other things, Inspector, I think you'll discover that Mr Graham is a fantasist. There was no divorce. He kept the house because his wife, so distraught and humiliated, ran away and committed suicide,' explained Rogers.

'How did she kill herself?'

'Horribly. She cut her throat.'

14

Dean Rogers had more to relate about Wilfred Graham.

'I'm not divulging confidential information by telling you that Mr Graham has been in and out of numerous psychiatric clinics. Of course he knew he was to blame for his wife's violent death, but, like so many people in those situations, he dived into denial. He hid in a make-believe world, turning truth on its head, making his wife the villain and him the victim. After a time, he really believed the lie and he lived it. I suppose it was his only way of surviving, but it caused him no end of grief and mental problems. He was on all kinds of drugs, including Prozac.'

'Let's get this clear: he's *not* a teacher?' said Lorenzo.

'Not now.'

'Not since his wife took her own life?' Lorenzo probed further for definitive clarity.

'Correct.'

'So he couldn't now legitimately be preparing for taking history lessons?'

'Only in his own delusional mind.'

'Was history his specialist subject?'

'Oh, yes, and he had a very good degree from Oxbridge. I do hope he's not in more trouble. He must have been living on the edge these last couple of years. Anything else and he'll be at breaking-point.'

'I'll bear that in mind,' said Lorenzo.

*

Half an hour later, Lorenzo and Valentine were at their desks in Bournemouth, having driven somewhat dazed from Dorchester, Dorset's historic county town.

While Valentine checked with the DVLA Swansea to verify Graham's claim that he owned only one vehicle, Lorenzo gambled on the national criminal records' database lottery, hoping to hit the jackpot there. No such luck, however. Graham had no criminal convictions. Neither was he on the Sex Offenders' Register, something that should have been obvious to Lorenzo. If Graham didn't have a criminal record, he couldn't possibly be listed as a known sex offender, but Lorenzo knew only too well that mistakes were made; human error sometimes resulted in records being inaccurate. Just a few months earlier, a Home Office minister had admitted that mistakes by the Criminal Records Bureau (CRB) were having a 'devastating' impact. Serious errors had risen by 20 per cent on the previous year.

'According to Swansea, Graham owns only one vehicle,' Valentine reported, popping his head around the door to Lorenzo's office.

'The rust-heap?' said Lorenzo.

'Afraid so.'

'Come in and park your bum, Matt.'

Valentine pulled up one of the two chairs on the visitors' side of the desk.

'Are we writing off Graham?' Valentine said despondently, as he shuffled his chair closer to his boss.

'No, we put him on hold.'

'How about mounting a peeping tom job on him?'

Lorenzo reclined, a finger and thumb pinching his lower lip.

'We could do worse.'

'I'll take that as a yes, then.'

'You'll go far, Detective!' Lorenzo's sarcasm was good-natured. 'How are we doing with a list of Land Rover owners in our region?'

'Complete, according to Craddock.'

Detective Rosemary Craddock, one of the most experienced and long-serving members of the CID team, had been delegated the brain-numbing Land Rover task.

'How many do we have?'

'Around four hundred, so I believe.'

'Let's prune.'

'How, without questioning all the owners?'

'By asking Swansea to email us personal details. The important factor for inclusion on the shortlist will be sex – male, of course – and age. The profilers reckon our man is likely to be aged 25 to 35, but that's only an estimated guideline, too narrow for my liking and not to be relied upon. So let's broaden the criteria. I think 25 is about right for the bottom end.'

'How about the top end?'

'Add twenty years. Make it 55. Any news on the handwriting front?'

All tip-offs of handwriting resembling the killer's notes were being investigated.

'A slow slog,' said Valentine. 'Nothing so far to pump the pulse. Except that Graham appears off the hook.'

'As I feared. It would have been all too easy for our man to have fallen into our lap just like that, with the first hit. Oh, well!'

'Yet in so many respects, he's a profiler's dream for a suspect serial killer.'

'Two bodies hardly amount to a serial corpse-count.'

'But *he's* on his way.'

'Did you really have to remind me of that?'

Valentine grinned apologetically.

'I'm going out alone,' Lorenzo announced abruptly.

'You should be safe, boss. It's not yet dark.' Valentine was becoming brave and even imaginative with his new-found humour. 'Anything I should know about?'

'Not yet. While I'm gone, get Craddock to chase up Swansea for those ages. I'm hoping we can settle for a shortlist of eighty, tops.'

'Still quite a long shortlist for the limited time we have.'

The allusion to the countdown to September 30th automatically steered Lorenzo's eyes to the calendar on his desk.

'All the more reason why we shouldn't squander any more time here gassing.'

Tricia was in the tack-room polishing saddles and bridles. The riding schedule for the day was over. Now came the hard work; cleaning up, grooming and feeding the horses, plus preparing for tomorrow's riding programme. Kylie had already gone home.

Apprehension aged her face the moment Lorenzo appeared, with the impact of an apparition; a ghost of the recent past and a foreboding premonition of the future.

'It's OK, *he* hasn't done a runner,' Lorenzo reassured, hoping his greeting would calm as effectively as valium.

'Are you ill?' The real question was: *what are you doing home so early? Has something gone awry with the Luke deal?*

'No, I'm fine. I haven't finished for the day. It's a business call, hoping again to tap into that FBI brain of yours.'

Now Tricia was fully at ease.

'Let's go indoors. I could do with a drink.'

When they were around the kitchen-table, Lorenzo produced a copy of the letter that had been mailed to him:

> Dear Humble, Parochial Detective,
> The knife has been sharpened,
> The hammer-head has been polished,
> My imagination is sharp as ever,
> And in the idiom of US prison-speak,
> Dead-woman is walking (big clue there!),
> But not for long,
> Happy hunting,
> Dear John

'It's now become very personal,' said Lorenzo.
Tricia frowned. I don't understand. Why?'

'Because this was addressed to me by name. He's making it a duel, a contest. Me against him.'

'That's only because you're lead detective, which he's gleaned from press reports.'

'Nevertheless, it *has* become personal; that's the way *he* wants it, obviously.'

'Gives him an extra buzz,' Tricia guessed.

'That's the way I see it. But what I want from you is your take on *this*.' He prodded the copy of the note with a finger. 'Particularly these two lines:

"And in the idiom of US prison-speak,
Dead-woman is walking (big clue there!)"'

'This is the bit where he's having fun with me.'

'I'd even go as far as suggesting he's *getting off* on it,' Tricia said distastefully.

'But do you *really* think it's a clue, a carrot, he's feeding me?'

'Oh, yes, I'm convinced of it.'

'That's what I feared.'

'*Feared?*'

'Yes, because I'm not on his wavelength, nowhere near. Any thoughts?'

'Not many. It could be that he's already kidnapped a Liz Stride or a Catherine Eddowes and he's keeping her as a prisoner, tied and gagged in a cellar, attic or shed. Keeping her until the date of execution, September 30th. So, symbolically, she's already dead-woman walking.'

'But, as far as I'm aware, there's been no missing report logged of a Stride or Eddowes.'

'Maybe she lives alone and wouldn't be known to be missing. She could be living a long way from here, in the Midlands, up North, or even in Wales or Scotland. There's been no publicity so far about the Jack the Ripper connection and the probable name of the next scheduled victim.'

'So if a Stride or Eddowes is missing elsewhere, there'd be no reason for that police force to treat it as a big deal – not so soon, anyhow.'

'Quite. If this theory is right, it tells you something else about the killer.'

'Which is?'

'He's a loner. Living alone, yet buying provisions for two. He'll have to be feeding his prisoner and providing her with fluids, keeping her healthy for execution, the way it's done in US gaols.'

'And how it used to be here, until hanging was abolished,' said Lorenzo. 'A doctor had to declare the condemned prisoner fit and healthy enough to die. But I'm not going to assume he's a loner, not yet. He could have an accomplice, maybe a woman.'

'A *woman.*'

'A wife or a lover. It wouldn't be unknown, far from it. Think Ian Brady and Myra Hindley, Fred and Rose West.'

Tricia pulled a face that translated to, *you got me there!*

The flashing signal on Lorenzo's computer-screen advised him of an urgent internal email, which he opened immediately, even before looping his jacket around his chair.

The electronic missive was from Craddock.

Swansea had moved fast and had provided a list of Land Rover owners, men aged upwards of 25 but not above 55, in the Dorset and west Hampshire region: 243 in all. A much bigger shortlist than Lorenzo had envisaged.

He was about to lash out with a foot in a tantrum at any available object within reach, when he remembered something that would help to refine the search; the Land Rover manufacturer had identified the model on the CCTV footage as a limited edition. This hadn't been factored into the request to Swansea.

Back to the drawing-board, Lorenzo instructed himself. Time to shout for Valentine or Craddock.

By midnight, the shortlist had been trimmed to a manageable 81.

'Tomorrow we start door-knocking,' Lorenzo told Valentine. 'By *we*, I mean mob-handed. Bring in the Blues. I'll negotiate with the headmistress.'

'Cap in hand?' said Valentine.
'Better than head on the block.'

Next morning, Lorenzo awoke to national mayhem. The tabloids were awash with garish headlines, such as, The Second Coming of Jack the Ripper ... Jack the Ripper Rises from the Grave ... Lock up your Wives and Daughters ... September 30th is D-Day.
Of course, D now stood for death.

15

Dan Miller worked as a nightclub bouncer. He was 38 years old and built like a fortress. As a 21-year-old, he'd served in the Royal Marines with distinction, until beating up a prostitute in Plymouth on a drunken night out. The whore had demanded payment in advance; Miller said he never paid for any service until he'd tested and tasted for quality. Her reaction was to order him out of her flat. His response had been to give her the payment he considered she deserved. As a consequence, she spent the next week in hospital and Miller spent the next year in prison, before being booted out of the Navy.

Miller had been brought up in Bournemouth and, on release from prison, he returned there, moving in with his parents again; nothing to do with the pull of the womb, just a matter of convenience. He earned a living labouring on building sites, but the work wasn't regular.

The chance to become a beach lifeguard was too good an opportunity to miss. Although the job provided only seasonal employment, for Miller it was divine pleasure rather than a chore. From dawn until dusk, he manned an ocean-side eyrie, ogling through binoculars all the gambolling bare flesh and bikinis. A legal peeper – and paid for it! Over pints in pubs, he would regale his mates with anecdotes about 'the best job in the world. I just stand there and watch all those creamers parade in front of me. I ache all day, without moving a limb or muscle.'

He soon tired of dossing with his staid, slippers-and-armchairs parents, but to afford his own place he needed a full-time, *proper* job. His background in an elite military outfit made him an ideal candidate for a gym instructor. It also brought him even closer to glistening female flesh than as a life-guard. And it was in the gym that he flirted with a young woman who was to become his wife. Angela Runcorn was lithe, blonde and shapely. She was also impressionable and fell for his embellished yarns of derring-do in faraway places with strange sounding names, where he rescued innocent victims held in captivity by cut-throat rebels. The roistering stories were always sufficiently vague to defy outright refutation and, of course, he omitted the fact that he'd been gaoled and ignominiously thrown out of the Royal Marines.

They had a beach-wedding, a two-night honeymoon on the island of Jersey, and set up home in the flat Angela already rented. She was working as a solicitor's secretary and earned reasonable money. She had expected Dan to contribute at least half the rent money, but he had different ideas; she should continue paying the lot, because the flat was still contracted in her name only and he would continue spending his wages on nights out with the lads.

The marriage lasted six turbulent months. She changed the locks one day while he was at the gym and dumped all his clothes and other belongings in the meagre front garden. Obsessed with revenge, he stalked her for months. She began dating the manager of a shop and the two were soon living together in Angela's flat, Miller's former home. One night, he waited until Angela and her lover were in bed together, then torched the flat. The couple escaped unscathed, but the building was gutted; three other couples were also made homeless.

Miller was back in prison, this time for eight years.

Now he was married again, with a woman who, apparently, knew very little of the truth of his past; only a repeat of the lies that had duped Angela.

But the reason that Lorenzo and Valentine were on Miller's doorstep was the fact that he owned a black Land Rover that matched the Limited Edition model on the CCTV footage.

Equally importantly, the nightclub that employed him as a doorman was the Rambo, the same establishment where Mary Walker's partner had worked part-time.

Police officers, uniformed and detectives, were working in pairs, visiting the 81 men on the shortlist. The three *favourites* would be interviewed by Lorenzo and Valentine: *favourites* because they appeared on the Criminal Records database.

7am wasn't a welcome time for a nightclub employee to have visitors, the reason why the detectives were there. Miller could have been in bed no longer than two hours; he would be just entering the deep-sleep zone and be at his lowest ebb. Just perfect, from Lorenzo's perspective, for putting Miller under pressure.

Lorenzo kept his thumb on the bell non-stop for almost five minutes before the door was suddenly thrown open, as if being used as a guillotine. The door-frame was filled by a barefooted hulk, swathed in a white bath-robe. A glowering face fronted a boulder-shaped head; Dan Miller, a bouncer stereotype, was in attack-mode.

'What the fuck!' Then, through bleary, rheumy eyes he saw enough of Lorenzo's ID to defuse his aggression.

'You were saying?' Lorenzo said challengingly.

'Look, I work nights. Seemed like I'd been in bed only five minutes when the bell rang. And rang. You were doing my head in. I thought you must be a cold-call salesman. Lucky for you that you'd already pulled your ID.'

Lorenzo sniggered derisively, implying, *lucky for you, more like.* 'You *are* Dan Miller?'

'That's me. *All* of me.' He patted his beer-belly, more convivial now, although his voice was that of a habitual smoker, his throat clogged with phlegm.

'We have some questions for you.'

'What about?'

'A couple of murders,' Lorenzo said starkly.

Any jauntiness quickly faded. 'Did you say *murder*?'

'No, I said *murders*. Plural. This isn't something we can do on your doorstep.'

'Christ! I don't know anything about murders. You'd better come in. Do I need a solicitor?'

'I don't know, Mr Miller. You tell us. Do you?'

By now they were inside the rabbit-hutch of a house, passing a poky kitchen that resembled a bomb-site. The main downstairs room was no tidier and scarcely larger.

'Sit anywhere you can find space,' said Miller, as he ferreted for cigarettes, finding a squashed packet under the cushion of a tatty armchair.

'Shove that stuff on the floor,' Miller continued, putting a lighter-flame to a cigarette before pointing to a two-seater settee, wedged against a wall. The *stuff* was washed clothes waiting to be ironed.

The plasma-screen of a TV was smeared with fingerprints, as if someone had wiped a hand on it while eating fish and chips or a pizza. Through a solitary, grimy window, the detectives saw a fenced back garden, the stunted lawn overgrown and peppered with weeds. Miller's home was part of a social housing estate near the railway station and about three-quarters of a mile from where Mary Walker lived and died.

'Is that your Land Rover out front?' Lorenzo enquired, nothing circuitous about his approach.

'You know it is,' Miller answered slyly. 'You blokes never ask questions like those without already knowing the bleeding answer. Now, what murders are you here about, because I know nothing about anything like that.'

'You must have read about the murder in Boscombe of Mary Walker.'

'Of course. Her fella worked part-time at the club where I'm a security official.'

Security official was posh spin for doorman.

'Did you know Ms Walker?'

'Nah. Never met her in my life. We were all questioned about what time her partner left the club that night; you must know that. You pulling my tail?'

'When were you last in Kettering?' A quick change of direction without warning, comparable to tossing a pebble in a pond and watching where the ripples went.

'Where?' Miller's brown, marble eyes travelled fast and furiously between the detectives.

'Kettering. In Northamptonshire.'

'Never heard of it. Never been there in my life, unless I passed through without knowing, like on a train going north.'

'If you've never heard of the place, how do you know it's north of here?'

Gotcha! thought Valentine.

Miller scratched his shaved head, an ugly grin becoming set in stone.

'Because we're on the south coast. Because everywhere gotta be north of here. That's a no-brainer.'

'Could be east or west,' said Lorenzo.

'Well, I just assumed,' Miller said sulkily. 'Anyhow, what's that place – Kettering, you say – got to do with Mary Walker? And me, for that matter?'

'Nothing and everything. Murder number two was committed there.'

'So I can't help you. I've never been to that place, whether it be north, east or west of here.'

'Is your wife about?' Another swift, disorientating digression.

'How do you know I'm married?'

'As you've already pointed out, Mr Miller, we know all the answers in advance of the questions.'

'Smart fart, aren't you?'

'I'll take that as a compliment.'

Valentine was thinking that his boss was capable of triggering a punch-up in a nunnery.

'She's at work,' said Miller. 'Starts at 7am on a supermarket checkout treadmill. Leaves home at 6.30.'

'Where were you on the night of Friday, August 31st?'

'That the night the Walker tart got topped?'

'It was the night that the very respectable Ms Walker had her life taken from her, yes.'

'Well, the answer to your question is another that you already know.'

'Just for the record, repeat it, please.'

Miller sighed theatrically. 'I was at the club, eight 'til four.'

'That's 8pm on the Friday until 4am on Saturday?'

'That's what I just said, isn't it? Listen, that's my shift seven/seven, except Christmas Day and if ever I get a holiday or take a well-earned sickie. If you don't believe me, check again with the guv'nor. You can also take a gander at the CCTV footage. We have two sneaky glass eyes at the entrance. You'll see I was never away from my patch for more than a couple of minutes when I had pee-breaks.'

'Nevertheless, we're going to have to impound your Land Rover.'

'You what!'

'I'm sure you're telling the truth, but the only way we can cross you off our list is by having Forensics go over your vehicle.'

'What the fuck for?'

'DNA clues.'

'Whose DNA?'

'Anne Chapman's.'

'And who the effing hell might she be?'

'Don't you *really* know, Mr Miller, or are you just sodding around with us? Don't you read newspapers? Don't you follow news on TV?'

'I read the sports pages, especially the horseracing, but Anne Chapman means bugger all to me. I'm sure she's not a jockey, so she might as well be the Wizard of Oz.'

'Mrs Chapman was murdered in Kettering. Similar MO to the Boscombe crime.'

'Nothing to do with me and I need my car for work.'

'Walk. The exercise will do you good.'

'You've no right.'

'Don't worry, I'll get the *right* … in less than half an hour.'

'Why is it that all Old Bill are bastards?'

'Because that's the way we were born, I guess.'

*

After showing themselves out, Lorenzo said to Valentine, 'You guard the Land Rover while I get the paperwork done and arrange for the vehicle to be towed away.'

'He doesn't look the right candidate to me, unfortunately,' Valentine said dismally.

Lorenzo grimaced. 'After Mary Walker's murder, we were interested only in her partner's alibi when talking to the club's manager. The rest of the staff weren't on our radar; no reason for them to be, then.'

'By not *looking* right, I'm talking about Miller's physique. He's nothing like, in stature, the guy caught on CCTV attacking Anne Chapman outside the nursing home. Also I can't see a dent in the Land Rover, though he could have had a swift repair job done.'

'We'll see what the experts say,' Lorenzo said mulishly.

'You didn't even ask for a sample of his handwriting.'

'That's because I doubt he's ever learned to write words with more than four letters,' Lorenzo explained sullenly.

'So why bother to put him through the wringer?'

'So we're seen to be thorough. No box left unticked; all that admin crap. Mainly, though, just to be bloody awkward, to piss him off and make him sweat, which is still a lot less than he deserves.'

16

Tom Bellinger, who had a desirable address opposite an undulating, landscaped golf course in the millionaires' belt of Bournemouth's Queen's Park, was number two on Lorenzo's hitlist.

The house was everything you'd expect in such a salubrious area. Lorenzo suspected that the pretentious name, 'The White House', gave him an insight into the character of its occupants. The solid, formidable façade was indeed white. But which came first: the colour or the name? Lorenzo half-expected to find a tradesmen's entrance around the side, with the front door reserved for relatives, friends, invited guests, and local royalty.

'The White House' was spread generously on sloping ground that rose steeply from a tree-lined avenue. A gravel driveway curled around a rockery garden to a double garage. A white Mini Cooper was parked at the colonnade entrance. The garage-door was raised and there was no vehicle inside. All windows at the front were louvered. A couple of sprinklers hissed as they rotated, spraying the drive as well as the garden, and by the time Lorenzo reached the front door, he looked and felt as if he'd wet himself.

Lorenzo imagined the door being opened by a haughty butler. He was disappointed to be greeted by a friendly, female face. Disappointed because he'd always wanted the chance to be rude to a starched and pompous flunky: *And who shall I say wishes the pleasure of an audience with the master? Old Bill, you stuffed shirt! A pig with no respect.*

'Yes?' she said sweetly.

'I'm looking for Mr Bellinger.'

'Well, you've found his house.'

'But not him.'

'Do I *look* like him?'

'I wouldn't know. I've never met him.'

It took a second or two for it to dawn on Lorenzo that this woman was almost flirting with him, a dangerous thing for anyone to do with a stranger on the doorstep.

'Are you here on business?' she said, still sociable, nothing officious about her manner.

'Yes, police business.'

'Oh!' The skittishness evaporated like a dark cloud eclipsing the sun. Then, with some levity restored, 'I suppose this is the moment when I should ask to see some form of identification?'

After the formality of proving his authenticity, the woman said, 'Well, I'm Mary Bellinger, Tom's wife.' She proffered a hand for shaking. Her grip was firm and confident. 'I'm afraid Tom's not in; he's gone for a round of golf with one of his cronies. Only across the road, though. You probably saw the course when you pulled up. Oh, how stupid of me! You're local?'

'Yes, I am.'

'Then you don't need my telling you where the golf courses are in this area. What a chump I am! Would you care to wait?'

'If you've no objection....'

'Of course not. Do come in; nice to have some company. He shouldn't be too much longer. If you're in a hurry, I can always get him on his mobile.'

'Don't do that. I wouldn't like you to catch him in mid-swing. Could cause a nasty accident.'

She laughed openly as they crossed a mosaic-floored vestibule into a very masculine lounge, with black leather furniture, dark-wood panelling, volumes of leather-bound books stacked spine-to-spine along rows of shelves, a mahogany table beside the windows, and ceiling-to-floor drapes, the colour of red burgundy wine.

'May I get you something to drink while you're waiting, Inspector?'

'No, I'm fine, but thank you,' said Lorenzo, raising a hand in the halting manner of a Blue directing traffic.

'I do hope my husband's not in any trouble?' said Mrs Bellinger, as they simultaneously sat next to one another on the four-seater settee. Her question really was a polite way of saying: *Now what's this all about?*

'I'm sure we can sort everything very quickly,' Lorenzo replied circumspectly, his discretion not appreciated, causing alarm rather than serving as a salve. 'I noticed the Mini outside....'

'That's mine. Are you here about a driving matter?'

'Indirectly,' he said obliquely. 'What does your husband drive?'

'A Land Rover. Expensive to run, but it's useful for carting all our golfing and tennis equipment around. I suppose you could call us a sporting pair; that's what brought us together. We met at a local tennis club, playing mixed doubles. My girlfriend's partner let her down and Tom stood in for him. The rest is ancient history, along with Adam and Eve.'

'And you play golf?'

'Better than Tom, but don't tell him I said so.' A ghost of a grin didn't stay long.

'But not today?'

'No, it's a boring business round for him today. You know the maxim about more deals sealed on the fairways and nineteenth hole than at lunches or in the boardroom; well, it's certainly true for Tom.'

'What's his line of business?'

'Haulage. That doesn't sound very exciting and I don't suppose it is. But it's no one-man-and-a-van operation. Tom owns a fleet of lorries that deliver and collect cargo all over the Continent, as far east as Turkey and into the most outer regions of the old Soviet Union.'

Lorenzo gauged Mrs Bellinger's age as in the mid-forties. She was dressed casually – jeans, white blouse and sandals – but there was an air of elegance and sophistication about her. She had a full figure, and a sagacious and piquant face that required little makeup to accentuate its striking highlights. Everything about her could be summed up as decorous and head-turning.

'Business must be good,' commented Lorenzo, his vacuuming-eyes taking in everything. There was nothing idle about his questions or observations; they all had a tendentious purpose.

'Tom inherited this house from his parents,' she said, second-guessing him. 'They died in a motorway car crash. That was long before I knew him. He was an only child, so he got the lot. No sibling jealousy and rivalry to contend with over the will.'

'How long have you been married?' This was a testing question.

'Only three years. Seems a lot longer, though.'

She giggled disarmingly and somewhat girlishly, which was at odds with her urbane maturity.

So she's probably ignorant of her husband's conviction eight years ago for people-smuggling. He'd been imprisoned for seven years, but had served only half of that because of good behaviour.

'So many books!' said Lorenzo; another launch-pad question.

'All came with the house. All classics or encyclopaedias. Never get read, only dusted.'

'Don't you enjoy a good read?'

'Oh, yes, but a *good read* for me is a paperback; historical fiction, preferably. Near enough to truth to suspend disbelief.'

'Not crime?'

'No, that's Tom's genre.'

'Fiction or true crime?'

'Oh, fiction. American mainly. You should see the floor his side of our bed! The complete collection of everything ever written by Michael Connolly. Have you read any of his books?'

'A few. His procedural knowledge is faultless, I'll grant him that. So there aren't any books in the house on Jack the Ripper?'

'I should doubt it,' she said, squinting. 'Why is it I get the distinct impression that you're not just making random conversation?'

'Because you're astute,' said Lorenzo, manufacturing a facsimile of a smile.

'Patronizing me won't work, Inspector.' Now she eyed him coldly. 'This hasn't anything to do with what we've read in our newspaper this morning?'

'Depends what you've been reading, Mrs Bellinger.'

'About those murders. Those horrible current Jack the Ripper murders.'

'Only because your husband owns a black Land Rover. There's nothing more to it than that; I give you my word. I'm going through the necessary motions. Despite all the new, state-of-the-art technology and DNA science, we still plod.'

Her mood was now mirthless and intense. 'There was nothing in our paper about a black Land Rover.'

'Well, we know that the killer was driving such a vehicle on the night of the second killing.'

'So you're here to ask Tom about his movements on the relevant dates?'

'In a nutshell.'

She brightened again marginally, relief visible. 'Well, that shouldn't be a problem. Tom keeps two diaries, one for business and the other for social engagements. He maintains precise records; he's meticulous, in fact.'

'Does he work from home?'

'Oh, no. He has an office at the depot in Boscombe, where there are two giant warehouses and parking bays for the trucks, some of them juggernauts, absolute monsters. When he's not there, the show's run by his despatcher.'

'And where does he keep the diaries?'

'With him. In his office, when he's at work, and at home when he's not.'

'So they're here now?'

'I imagine so, but don't ask me to find them for you; that would be out of order. Tom would never forgive me.'

At that moment they both heard a key turning the lock of the front door.

'That'll be Tom now,' said Mrs Bellinger, getting up briskly. 'I'll let him know you're here.'

Giving him a few seconds to compose himself and arrange things in his head, Lorenzo was thinking, but not uncharitably. *Smart lady!*

Tom Bellinger was the kind of person who dominated a room with his sheer dynamic chemistry.

'Inspector!' he greeted Lorenzo effusively, as if reunited with an old friend. 'I hope you haven't been kept waiting too long. Mary could always have reeled me in by mobile-phone.'

'I offered,' Mary said informatively, not defensively.

'There's no urgency, just routine,' Lorenzo lied, rising to shake hands.

'You've no drink!' said Mr Bellinger, aghast, as if ashamed by such inhospitality in his fiefdom.

'I declined,' said Lorenzo, not the least hoodwinked by this shallow showmanship.

Lorenzo's first impression of Bellinger was that his physical stature matched the man who was captured on camera attacking and abducting Anne Chapman. There was latent power in his handshake and, although he was fifty years of age, he didn't appear to have lost any of his black, wavy hair and the only sign of grey was in the truncated sideburns. Lorenzo visualized Bellinger as strikingly handsome twenty years ago, but too many gin and tonics at the nineteenth hole had blemished his skin and inflamed the whites of his eyes. Still, he packed charm and affability by the bucket-load, and Lorenzo could see how he must have bewitched Mary.

'I think I should make myself scarce,' said Mary, heading hurriedly for the door. 'Nice to have met you, Inspector.'

'Well, Inspector,' said Bellinger, hands in the pockets of his fawn, lightweight golfing slacks, 'I understand you're here about my Land Rover and the possibility that I might have been driving around the country doing unspeakable damage to young women.' He conjured up amusement in his clipped voice, but this wasn't reflected in his warrior-eyes.

'Right on both counts,' said Lorenzo, choosing the enigmatic approach.

Raising a flared eyebrow, Bellinger said, 'So this is a serious matter?'

'The subject matter is serious, but that's not to say you're a serious contender. Your wife tells me you keep a couple of well-documented diaries.'

'That's true.'

'They should be useful in shortening my visit. I'm here, you see, to quiz you about your movements on the evening of two specific dates, which might well be resolved by your diaries.'

'I hope so. I'll fetch them for you; they're in my study. And you're sure I can't fix you a drink, not even tea or coffee?'

'Quite sure.'

When Bellinger returned, he was carrying a large glass of red wine, in addition to the bulky, business-styled diaries.

'Good for the heart, apparently,' he said, hoisting the glass. 'We owe the medical world a debt of gratitude for giving us a medical excuse for drinking red wine.'

'I'm more interested in the diaries,' said Lorenzo, feeling it necessary to take Bellinger out of his comfort-zone.

'Of course. Here, take them. You know the all-important dates. Look for yourself.'

There was no sapping confidence from this man. But was he really as sang-froid as he seemed? His slightly portly belly was moving like a jittery pulse under his smart, white woollen T-shirt, with a pair of red and blue golf clubs embroidered on the chest.

While Lorenzo trawled through both diaries to the two relevant dates, Bellinger postured nonchalantly against bookshelves, wine-glass to his lips; not a care in the world.

'On the night that Mary Walker was killed, there's no engagement listed in your social diary,' Lorenzo observed.

'That would be because I didn't have one; simple as that.' If irony was intended, it was adeptly veiled.

'It appears from your business diary that you had a busy work-schedule, culminating with a management meeting at 7pm.'

'We do that once a week.'

'What does it entail?'

'Four of us sitting in my office, tippling wine or beer, and analysing the previous month's profit or loss. Mostly loss these days. When the economy is flat or downhill, as it is currently, we're hit as hard as anyone else. Fuel prices keep hiking, but we can't pass it on to customers infinitely. And because of the recession, our clients are in retrenchment. It's a vicious circle.'

'But you still have time for golf on a weekday?'

'Better than dwelling on doomsday and sinking into a suicidal depression.'

'Back to that management meeting: what time did it finish?'

'About nine. Ten latest.'

'Then what?'

'We dispersed, went our separate ways. I'd have come home. Had a late dinner. Mary would have waited to eat with me. We make a habit of dining together each evening. At weekends, we'll pop out for a meal. On Saturdays our favourite haunt is an Italian beach-bistro. On Sundays we lunch at one of the cliff-top hotels, most frequently the Carlton.'

'You have expensive tastes, despite the recession.'

'For some of us it's necessary to keep up appearances.'

This was the cue Lorenzo had been silently begging for: the ideal opportunity for delivering a metaphorical boot below the belt.

'How many people for whom you keep up appearances know that you're an ex-con?'

Bellinger's demeanour mimicked that of a jumbo jet shot down at high altitude by a sniper's ground-to-air missile. His lips quivered; his fuselage shuddered. His eyes were ablaze with hatred, while his body-language exuded impotent anger. But all he could muster in retaliation was the pathetic cliché, 'That was a cheap shot, Inspector.'

'Not at all, Mr Bellinger. People-smuggling is a pretty loath-some crime. You made a load of money from poor, desperate people. If your affluent lifestyle was threatened by the recession, might you not be tempted again by the spoils of low-life crime?'

'No, I wouldn't be!' Now he approached Lorenzo tiger-like, a beast about to pounce on its snared prey. 'I've paid my price. I did wrong, but now I do everything right. I've built a new life. Now, why are you *really* here? Are the murders just a smoke-screen for something else?'

'I'm here to ask questions, Mr Bellinger.' Keeping him guessing wasn't such a bad idea. 'Does your wife know about your criminal past?'

'Damn you, no! And don't you dare go telling tales.'

'I'll give you the benefit of any doubt and not take that as a threat. These diaries don't help you with an alibi for the night that Anne Chapman died. There isn't a single entry in either diary for that date.'

'Since when did I *need* an alibi? If I had been involved in those crimes, don't you think I would have concocted something in the diaries to have excluded me from your inquiries?'

'That would have been a dangerous game to play, Mr Bellinger. If we established it as a bogus entry, then you'd immediately be a prime suspect.'

'This is ridiculous! I'm calling my solicitor. I'm not answering any more of your questions and you can get out.'

'Very well, but you're playing this very badly.'

'Out!'

After overseeing the impounding of Dan Miller's vehicle, Valentine returned to the nerve-centre of the investigation, liaising with the other pairs as they went and came from their door-knocking rounds.

Lorenzo phoned Valentine from outside the Bellingers' residence after his abrupt eviction. After regaling Valentine with an account of his abrasive encounter with Tom Bellinger, Lorenzo told his partner to organize another legal hijack: 'Land Rover *and* two diaries this time.'

'Any dent in *his* vehicle?'

'How is it you have a knack for spoiling my day, Valentine? The answer to your question is no damage that I can see.'

'Sorry I asked.' Then breezily, 'Briefing the car-snatchers good as done. What next?'

'Something to eat. I'm coming in.'

'Is Bellinger hot?'

'Under the collar, definitely!'

Valentine laughed, camaraderie-fashion. 'Sounds like you've got the cockroaches scuttling.'

'Trouble is, cockroaches are the world's best survivors.'

It was mid-afternoon by the time Lorenzo and Valentine were teamed-up in the canteen for a late snack-lunch.

'The heavy mob should be at the Bellingers by now with their tow-away gear,' Valentine reported gleefully.

'I wish I'd stayed. Tom Bellinger will be hopping around, tearing out his hair, like a madman.'

'Only *like* a madman? You don't think he *is* a madman, as in the self-conceived resurrection of Victorian Jack?'

'He could be. I'm hopeful. Certainly can't rule him out until we get feedback from Forensics. But we'll need an airtight case because he's a slippery shit and you can bet your life he'll have a tight-arsed charlatan of a lawyer.'

'Didn't do him much good when he went down for seven years.'

'True.'

They ate and drank some more tea before Valentine said, 'What did you make of his wife?'

'Far too good for him.'

'I did some more electronic doodling while you were on the way back. There's not a hint of Bellinger getting up to mischief since he did time for people-smuggling.'

'Perhaps he learned his lesson.'

'So you reckon his business is legit now?'

'I didn't mean that. By *learned his lesson,* I meant he'd found a way to outsmart us.'

'Did his wife tell you she's into amateur dramatics?'

'No. Where you get that from?'

'Googling. No rocket science. You'll be intrigued, as much as I was.'

'Go on, you big tease, you've got me salivating, so you'd better not disappoint.'

'In January, her performing company put on a stage version of *Hands of the Ripper.* Originally, in 1971, it was a Hammer horror movie. Mary Bellinger took the part that was played in the film by the late Angharad Rees.'

'And what role was that?' Lorenzo said numbly.

'The murderous daughter of Jack the Ripper.'

17

Next morning, two letters, one considerably more significant than the other, were delivered several miles apart. One was addressed to Tricia Lockwood; the other to Lorenzo at Bournemouth central police station:

Dear Lady Macbeth,
I've been reading in the newspapers about the born-again Jack the Ripper. I note that, for the storyline to maintain its credibility, the next victim, on September 30th, will be a Liz Stride or a Catherine Eddowes.

I am hoping, nay praying, that he makes a mistake. Not a bad mistake, but a virtuous one. Are you beginning to get my drift? I think you probably are. You may be very foolish, but you're not dense.

Yes, I'm thinking about you, more so than ever since reading these delicious stories. Drooling over the concept of that madman's blade bringing the Red Sea to your throat!

Oh, for such a poetic mistake! Poetic justice it would be, indeed! Getting it wrong for him and the plot would be getting it so right for me!

These sentiments come directly from my heart, and aimed directly at your jugular.

This may be the rambling of a broken man, but at least it has the merit of sincerity.

With all my sincerest contempt,
Your ever-loathing,
Luke (May you RIP – Rest In Pieces)

Letter number two:

Dear Detective Inspector Lorenzo,

At last you are in tune with the plot! Hooray!

I had you fooled with the first one, didn't I? But I didn't anticipate your being quite so obtuse and slow to catch on. Or perhaps you have deliberately delayed making the public aware? It doesn't matter because the outcome will be the same: you'll lose, I'll win! The truth is, you're out of your depth. Drowning. (Not a clue, incidentally!)

Now to the upbeat news: number three has already been selected. Nothing can save her. Spoilt for choice, I was. The die is cast! Neat pun, yes?

All your warnings to the public will go unheeded. Women never listen, especially to a man! I have every confidence in their arrogance and blind faith in their indestructibility. All those in the firing-line – once again not a clue – won't believe it could happen to them. This sort of thing happens only to others. People always think that, don't they?

Don't forget your dates. November 8th will be quite a challenge for me because Mary Kelly, as you will know by now, bowed out of this world very bloodily in her own home. Can I repeat it? Oh, yes, trust the Devil always to find a way. Put your money on Jack!

By November 9th it will be all over and Jack the Ripper, Mark 2, will disappear into the ether, as mysteriously as Mark 1. But my achievement will count for so much more. Detective science was in its infancy in the 1880s. Now you have everything in your favour, especially with DNA profiling, but still I'm not even on your radar, that I bet. I am sleeping like a babe, not a worry in the world.

I shall go down in history as the better of the Jacks. A legend in my own knifetime!

How impotent you are! I know the feeling only too well.

Yours truly,

Jack, the master of his trade

Tricia opened her letter at 10.02. By 10.05, she was on the phone to Lorenzo.

'I've got to speak to you, Mike.'

'Fine, speak.'

'In person. In private.'

'Tonight?'

'Before then. Now, if possible.'

'Haven't you got rides scheduled?'

'Yes, but I'm cancelling them. I'm shutting up shop.'

Lorenzo's muscles tensed and alarm-bells boomed in his head. *Only one possibility*, he thought.

'Luke hasn't reneged on the deal and done a bunk? He's not *there*, with you?'

'No, but he might as well be.'

Now Lorenzo was as confused as well as being uneasy. 'Can you be here within half an hour?'

'Less than that.'

Tricia had the letter in her hand when she was escorted, by a female Blue, breathlessly into Lorenzo's cubicle, ridiculously called an office. Valentine was perched on the edge of the desk.

'Give us a few minutes alone, Matt,' Lorenzo said, winking.

Without a word, but granting Tricia the courtesy of a nod, Valentine exited the office with the uniformed officer.

As soon as the door was closed, Tricia thrust the letter on the desk in front of Lorenzo.

'This came in the post,' she said, flustered. 'Read it! *He* must be completely off his rocker. Raving – in every sense! It's so hateful, so toxic.'

'Let me read,' said Lorenzo, a polite way of saying, *just shut up for a minute!*

Tricia ran fingers through her uncombed hair as she ambulated. Tears flooded her feral eyes but did not fall. 'The calculated cruelty of the bastard!'

'OK, I've read it,' said Lorenzo reclining, hands threaded behind his head. His inclination was to loop an arm around

Tricia and pull her into a bear-hug embrace, an intimate gesture of reassurance and solidarity, but they were in a goldfish-bowl, with only a glass panel between them and the main detectives' pool.

'Well?' She ceased pacing and stood facing him, arms spread apart, shaky hands gripping the edge of the desk. 'Say something, for God's sake!'

'Did you keep the envelope?'

'Is that the best you can do?' Then, suddenly more equable, 'Yes, here.' She ferreted in her leather shoulder-handbag and produced the envelope, which she'd screwed up in temper.

Lorenzo dispassionately examined the post-mark. 'Mailed in the New Forest.'

'I *can* read,' she said testily. 'One of the first – and obvious – things I looked for.'

'Have you called the clinic?'

'God, no! Why should I do that?'

'Just to make certain that Luke's still there. I'll do it. I'm sure he is. One of us would have heard by now if he'd gone over the wall or tunnelled out!'

'It's not funny, Mike.'

'I know it's not and I'm not treating it as such. I'm just trying to help you get this in perspective and proportion.'

'Why should we have heard? He's not a prisoner. He's there voluntarily. The clinic staff don't know the circumstances, the terms of the deal, unless Luke's been rabbiting. It could be a week or more before we get to hear. I could be dead long before then.'

Lorenzo vacated his chair and edged as close to Tricia as discretion would allow. 'There's no threat in this letter, Tricia.'

'No *threat!*' She threw up her arms. 'He wishes me dead. Not just dead, but flensed. Look *here*.' She prodded the letter. 'He's drooling over the prospect of all my spilt blood. It's there in black and white.' Now the tears did flow.

Lorenzo fished a handkerchief from his pocket. He was about to dab her eyes when he noticed the mounting interest the other side of the glass, so he tucked the handkerchief into her hand.

'I realize this must have come as a shock, but he's willing someone else to harm you. There's no suggestion that he's recruiting anyone to damage you or planning to do it himself. It's fanciful, violent imagery, a distasteful wind-up. He's still raging inside.'

'Exactly! And when someone's like that, there's no telling what he might do,' she said, dabbing her eyes. 'He'll be lying awake at night, plotting revenge, aroused by his murderous machinations. Remember, I know more than you do about the workings of the deranged human brain.'

'I'll make that call to the clinic now.'

'I'm grateful, but it won't change anything.'

'Meaning?'

'I'm sure you're right, that he *is* still there, but it doesn't guarantee he will be tomorrow or the day after. When I said I'm "shutting up shop", I didn't mean just for today. I can't stay there any longer, Mike. Not with things as they are. Not with this cloud of uncertainty hanging over me.' She reclaimed the letter and shook it, her grip on it as tight as if she had the author by the throat.

'Where will you go? Not back to the States?'

'No. I have friends in London. An American couple. They're employed at the US embassy. I have an open invite. I'll take them up on it. Time to cash in my chips. Chill out.'

'But what about your business here? You can't just walk out on it; you have commitments and a lot of money tied up in your riding school and estate, surely? You're doing well. You've established a regular gang of followers.'

'Suddenly all that is inconsequential.'

'Is it your intention to sell up?'

Tricia closed her eyes. Still the tears escaped, seeping beneath the lids like dripping taps.

'I need time to give it plenty of thought – in isolation, away from the emotional heat. Despite everything, Luke's winning, don't you see? He's driving me out. He's running the show; I'm the puppet on a string. *His* string.' Now she waved the letter as if it were a white flag of surrender. 'This is the first shot in the psychological war.'

'And the last, it would seem, if you walk away from it.' He almost said *run away* instead of *walk away*, but did some quick editing.

'No one can stop him writing to me.'

'Oh, we can, if it amounts to harassment.'

'One letter hardly constitutes harassment. Anyhow, to get a restraining order, we'd have to bring up all the grubby history and hang our dirty washing on the public line. But if he's not curbed, he'll rack up the pressure and start texting and phoning me. Catch-22.'

'You don't have to open his letters; you'll identify his writing on the envelope.'

'And if he calls or texts?'

'You hang up or delete, you change your mobile number, and then psychological warfare backfires on him.'

'Making him madder than ever; leaving me wondering what he'll get up to next. It's all so much hassle. No, my mind's made up.'

'At least let me make that call.'

'Don't bother; it's not going to make any difference.'

'When will you go?'

'Today. I can be packed by this afternoon.'

'What about Kylie?'

'I'll make up a story about a sick relative. I can't possibly leave her to run things. It wouldn't be fair. Too much responsibility for her age. I'll treat her fairly; give her a couple of months pay and a glowing reference.'

'How long will you stay with your friends?'

'Depends how far the elastic of hospitality will stretch.'

'If I were you, I'd contact Cherie Signore before you leave. Take her into your confidence. She's a stalwart.'

'I intend to give her power of attorney.'

'Wise move. See what she thinks. Ensure that by walking out you're not jeopardizing your legal rights over the property, despite the signed agreement with Luke. Just cover yourself.'

'I can always say I'm going on an extended vacation, which isn't a lie. I want time to think and take stock ... in a vacuum. To be able to tread water and not be swept along by the swell and undercurrents.'

Lorenzo understood. He was also secretly pleased. The hiatus would bring a natural resolution to their ill-conceived affair. A short-circuit would enable it to fizzle out free from the customary fireworks that crackle and explode around break-ups. From the beginning it had been an affair of convenience on quicksand, without any prospect of a long-term future.

Lorenzo had always been bad at relationships. His marriage had been a Titanic disaster. So, too, all his other emotional and physical couplings. Even after such a short time with Tricia, he was already beginning to suffer from claustrophobia and the urge for freedom, to roam alone, to belong nowhere and to belong to nobody. Most one-night stands were even too long for him. He had the instinct of a vampire; all lust died at dawn. He thrived on the chase, but as soon as the quarry was snared, he couldn't resist the compulsion to move on; the reason he was such an accomplished cop – he was restless, always chasing, never settling, never resting on his laurels.

Now he'd re-settle in 'The Barn', while looking for somewhere else to rent, though that would probably have to wait until the riddle of *Jack* was solved.

'What will *you* do?' said Tricia solicitously, as if privy to his musing.

'Return to 'The Barn', if that's OK with you?'

'Of course it is,' she said gently, about to take hold of his hand, then remembering where they were.

'Now you can have a look at *my* letter! You're not the only person to have a pen-pal.'

Startled, she said, 'Luke hasn't written to you, too?'

'No, no, it's my old chum, *Jack*.' Funereal humour seemed

appropriate. He extracted a photocopy from a buff folder next to his computer. 'How's that for fan mail?' he said, with a wry smile, flicking the copy across to Tricia, as if dusting his desk of crumbs.

Tricia was grateful for the distraction.

'He really is a loathsome, cocky bastard,' she said, as she finished.

'Becoming overconfident, you reckon?'

'Without a doubt, but how much that will help you is debatable.'

'Is he bluffing, about the third victim already earmarked?'

'Definitely not. This guy's for real; that he's already proved.'

'Any clues this time?'

'A very big one, I'd say. *How impotent you are! I know the feeling only too well.*'

'You think that should be interpreted literally?'

'Don't you? Incrementally, we're getting a clearer understanding of your *Jack*. He's someone who has habitually associated with prostitutes.'

'And contracted a venereal disease that has rendered him impotent, something we've already speculated upon.'

'But now, in my view, you have it underscored. How's the elimination process coming along?'

He treated her to a précis of his confrontations with Dan Miller and the Bellingers.

'Miller just doesn't seem a fit to me,' she said pensively. 'The author of those notes – or letters, call them what you will – has something of a dramatic style . A sort of stage-sense. The words and phrases are chosen carefully; suspenseful. Not what I'd envisage from the pen of a nightclub bouncer.'

'We're in agreement there,' said Lorenzo, disgruntled.

'But Mrs Bellinger's thespian activities are interesting, though; very interesting, especially in view of my previous comments.'

'And why didn't she volunteer to me about her role in a Jack the Ripper play last winter? I gave her every opportunity. I specifically brought up the subject, asking if there were any Jack the Ripper books in the house.'

'And she said no?'

'Categorically. Said her husband read crime fiction, addicted to Michael Connolly, while she was a fan of historical novels.'

'Jack the Ripper is an ingredient of Victorian folklore; that's historical.'

'But not fiction!'

'Maybe you should have *her* handwriting scrutinized, as well as her husband's.'

'You think she might have written *this*?' said Lorenzo, retrieving the photocopy from Tricia.

'Well, she's the theatrical one of the pair. We talked previously about the possibility of a double act, a twosome. She'll alibi her husband and vice versa.'

'He's a crook, but....'

'What?'

'I just can't see her involved in this grotty business.'

'Too *nice*, is she? Too middle-class? Too well-mannered? Too well-bred? Too urbane? I can't believe you're gullible enough to be duped by any of that stereotyped hogwash. It wouldn't be the first time that a demon masqueraded as an angel.'

Lorenzo laughed at himself. 'She certainly put on an angelic show.'

'Have they kids?'

'Apparently not.'

'Maybe he's not up to the job.'

'Because of dabbling with diseased goods?'

'Fits the viable script, doesn't it?' said Tricia.

'If I get a positive feedback from Forensics on Bellinger's Land Rover, I'll have them both in. Get samples of *her* handwriting and demand answers over the *Hands of the Ripper* deception.'

'For your sake, I hope *Jack* is in the system because, if he's not, you're in trouble, Mike. Big trouble.'

Lorenzo knew exactly what Tricia meant. Just a few days ago, it seemed that time was on his side. Now there had been a

seismic shift and, once again, time was as much the enemy as
Jack.

With every tick of the clock, the new deadline would be
drawing hauntingly and inexorably ever closer.

18

Valentine joined Lorenzo for the third showdown. Firstly, there had been Dan Miller, then Tom Bellinger, and now Peter Lawson, a freelance insurance broker from a hamlet near the tiny town of Ringwood, just across the county border in Hampshire. Lawson was an ex-teacher and both detectives were mentally making the comparison with fabulist Wilfred Graham, the other former pedagogue, as they approached Lawson's home, an eighteenth-century thatched cottage beside the sluggish River Stour. A stout and sturdy Norman church, flying the patriotic flag of St George, towered above a droopy platoon of willows the other side of a nearby motorway.

Valentine pulled up directly behind Lawson's black Land Rover, which was parked on the grass verge, alongside a picket fence, in front of the picture-postcard cottage. A man in a grey suit was propped against the near-side bonnet of the Land Rover, talking into a mobile-phone. His conversation continued after the detectives had alighted from their Ford pool car. From the grass mound, Lorenzo could see that the lawn at the rear of the cottage sloped gracefully to the sleepy river; this was trout and teacakes countryside.

'Seems like I've got visitors,' said the man on the mobile, his voice veneered, concealing a rougher surface. 'I'll have the policy drawn up and bring it round to you in a couple of days, when you can comb through it at leisure. OK? Good, see you then.'

With the mobile silenced, Grey Suit swaggered curiously towards the detectives.

'You here to see me?'

'If you're Mr Peter Lawson, then yes,' said Lorenzo, hands buried in trouser-pockets.'

'And you are?'

The time had come for the ritual flash of ID, which was always a party-pooper.

'I was just on my way out. Is this going to take long?'

'Maybe half an hour,' said Lorenzo, shrugging phlegmatically. 'Much depends on your answers.'

'Any chance of your coming back another time?'

'No chance.'

Lawson's face soured. 'Do we need to go indoors?'

'Preferable to standing here at the roadside, I'd say, but the choice is yours. We could do it in your garden, if that suits.'

'Let's do that,' said Lawson, holding open a small gate in the fence. 'Take the path round the side of the cottage. I'll follow. There's a wooden table with bench-seats on the lawn.'

As they assembled at the table, Lawson made a meal of looking at his chunky, imitation Rolex, a non-subtle gesture of impatience.

In view of Lawson's aloof and dismissive demeanour, Lorenzo decided to immediately take the sledgehammer approach. Sometimes a sledgehammer was just the tool for cracking a nut, especially a demented one.

'Relax, Mr Lawson, we're not here to harangue you about your predilection for young, underage girls.'

Even Valentine flinched.

Lawson blanched, deflated, all pomposity punctured with one prick into the tender loin of his ego.

Lawson's shifty eyes shifted faster than ever. 'I've paid for my stupidity.'

'And you've never misbehaved since?'

'Never.'

'Our records show you're no longer a teacher.'

'I left teaching fifteen years ago.'

'Not your choice, though, was it? You were kicked out, after doing time for taking advantage of one of your teenage, female pupils. How long was it you got? Two years? Three? Five?'

'You know damn well! Two and a half. I was out on parole in under a year. Marriage broken. Career in tatters. Disowned by my two kids. But I've survived. I've never felt sorry for myself. I picked myself up, brushed myself down, and reinvented myself. I've never lived off state benefits. I've always paid my way. Now, why are you making me regurgitate the vomit of my past?'

Seeing that Lawson was sufficiently contrite and softened up, Lorenzo tried civility.

'It's your Land Rover that interests us.'

'My Land Rover? So this is a motoring matter?' His relief was evident.

'Not exactly.'

Two pairs of eyes drilled into Lawson.

'What then?' he said, mystified.

Lorenzo was in no rush to enlighten Lawson. He counted slowly to five in his head before answering in a flat tone, no cadence, not a scintilla of emotion, as cold and unswerving as his eyes, 'A Land Rover like yours was used in a murder.'

'What murder? You don't think....' Beads of sweat had broken out like blisters across his expansive forehead. He was thickset, around 5'11" in height, with a pendulous, hangdog face and fake brown hair, blow-dried to conceal the bald patch at the rear of the prominent dome.

'Anne Chapman.'

Lawson's eyes disappeared into their puffy shells, like a jumpy crustacean scared into taking shelter.

'I don't know any such person,' he said, almost gibbering.

'You read newspapers, don't you? Watch TV? Listen to the radio?'

Lawson's face had been turned into a blank canvas, all definition erased.

'Anne Chapman was abducted from a nursing home in Kettering, driven to a cemetery in a Land Rover, executed with a knife, and dumped in a grave that had been dug for somebody else; a cuckoo in the nest.'

Some thoughts brought a flicker of life to Lawson's eyes and twitching cheeks. A pulse pumped furiously in his bull-neck.

'You mean the new Jack the Ripper murder? The second one?'

'You got it! You read and listen, after all. You are indeed a member of the living world. Welcome!'

'But why me?' he blurted.

'Why *you?* Why *you,* what?' Lorenzo pretended not to comprehend.

'I can't help you, that's what I mean. Just because I drive a Land Rover.... Do you have a registration number? Thousands of people own Land Rovers.'

'But they don't all live in this region and they don't all have criminal convictions, especially for sexual offences,' Lorenzo said mercilessly, as if driving a stake into Lawson's heart.

'Was that really necessary?' Lawson said meekly.

'Not necessary, but reasonable,' Lorenzo continued remorselessly.

'But that Chapman woman was killed in Northamptonshire, more than a hundred miles away, isn't it?'

Lorenzo had no intention of allowing Lawson to dictate the direction of the interview.

'Do you live alone?'

'Yes. I've already told you I'm divorced.'

'You could have remarried. You could have a partner, woman or man.'

Anger restored some colour to Lawson's blood-drained cheeks.

'Have you ever been to Kettering?'

'Several times, as a matter of fact,' he said haltingly.

'What for?'

'As a child, I was brought up in a neighbouring county, Bedfordshire. We used to go to Kettering on outings to a pleasure park that had a boating-lake, miniature railway, a tunnel, restaurants, golf and tennis courts, plus a vast playground. Everything a kid could ever want when it came to play.' Nostalgia choreographed his expressions.

'I'm not concerned with your childhood. Have you been in that area recently?'

'Not for a year or more.'

'And why were you there then?'

'On business. Selling a medical insurance package to a relatively small company that specializes in educational books for schools and colleges. Several of its employees travel overseas frequently. The insurance cover also enables any of the sales team to get private treatment should they be taken ill while on their business travels in this country.'

Lorenzo wanted to prevent Lawson from striking a comfortable rhythm.

'So where were you between 8 p.m. on September 8th and, let's say, 2 a.m. on the 9th?'

Lawson hesitated and coughed affectedly into the back of a hand.

'I can't possibly give you an accurate answer without consulting my diary, but I can tell you that I'd have been in bed well before 2am, whatever I'd been doing earlier.'

'OK, so where's your diary?'

'In my car, in the glove-compartment.'

'Fine. Let's take a look.'

'I'll fetch it.'

Lawson swung his legs off the bench-seat and started towards his Land Rover.

'You two stay there, I'll only be a minute.'

Neither Lorenzo nor Valentine had attempted to move. Now however, the suspicions of both detectives were instinctively kindled.

'We'll come with you, keep you company,' said Lorenzo.

'There's no need, really. I'm not going to run off. I've nothing to be afraid of.'

'We'll just stretch our legs, take in the lovely view,' Valentine said disarmingly.

A new suffusion of sweat descended from Lawson's hairline like a visor, to cover his face. Trying to appear bewildered, he patted his jacket and hips.

'I can't believe it, I don't know where I've put my car-keys.'

'I don't believe it, either!' Lorenzo said meaningfully. 'Try your pockets. And if you don't produce them, I'll have a go.'

'Oh, yes, here we are,' said Lawson, suddenly eliciting the keys from a jacket-pocket and hurrying towards the car.

Lorenzo broke into a trot to catch up.

'I don't know what all the fuss is about, I'm only fetching a diary, for God's sake!' said Lawson, becoming increasingly agitated.

'I'll tell you what, you give me the keys and I'll collect the diary.'

'I'd rather you didn't,' Lawson demurred feebly, panicking overtly.

'Fait accompli now,' said Lorenzo, snatching the keys and tossing them to Valentine.

'You can't do that!' Lawson protested.

'Just did,' said Lorenzo.

As Valentine unlocked the driver's door, Lawson slumped, head in hands.

Valentine leaned across to the front passenger-seat and snapped-open the glove-compartment.

'Well, well, what have we here?' said Valentine, as he emerged from the Land Rover, smiling triumphantly.

In one hand he held a black diary. Dangling from his other hand, was a garment, matching the diary in colour but not in material. Valentine's expression was that of a fisherman who had just bagged a big one.

The garment was a pair of women's lace knickers.

19

'**W**ell, Mr Lawson, no wonder you didn't want me or Detective Valentine to look into the glove-compartment of your vehicle,' Lorenzo said wryly. 'One pair of black lace knickers, apparently soiled.'

He held them with disposable latex gloves above the table in the sparse interview-room, before dropping the underwear disdainfully into a transparent evidence-bag. Then, sardonically, 'I don't suppose you're going to claim that they're yours, Mr Lawson? Or maybe you are? Have to reckon with all sorts these days.'

Valentine, sitting next to Lorenzo, snickered on cue.

'I behaved the way I did because I was embarrassed,' said Lawson, looking from one detective to the other, hoping to forge some kind of kinship.

Lorenzo was unmoved. 'You know what's going to happen next?' The question was rhetorical. 'These are going to Forensics. They'll be subjected to every conceivable test for DNA clues and other forensic evidence, such as fibres, human hairs, and body-fluids. Doesn't that worry you, Mr Lawson?'

No underwear had been removed by the killer from Anne Chapman or Mary Walker. This was the hole in the potential case against Lawson, a flaw of which the police were only too well aware. So whose knickers were they? Was there another victim Lorenzo didn't yet know about? Or was there an innocent explanation? *Innocent* as in a shag in the Land Rover between two consenting adults.

As usual, Lorenzo conducted the inquisition, while Valentine took notes and prompted, when necessary.

'I assume these were being kept as a trophy?' said Lorenzo, hoisting the evidence-bag, exaggerating a sneer as a means of intimidating. He had to bluff as much as possible out of Lawson, before the suspect demanded a lawyer. But if Lawson was the killer of Mary Walker and Anne Chapman, he'd know that these knickers couldn't possibly incriminate him for either crime. The fact that Lawson clearly was a worried man was, perversely, a worry also for Lorenzo.

'I intended getting rid of them,' said Lawson candidly but discomfited, head hung.

'Because they'll sink you?' Lorenzo gambled. 'Because they'll establish your guilt?'

'But not of murder!' Lawson countered heatedly, almost shouting.

'Your diary shows you have no alibi for the nights on which the two murders were committed.'

'So what? That doesn't mean I'm responsible for those crimes. Thousands of people won't be able to account for their movements on those nights. Can you?'

'But I don't own a black Land Rover with a pair of women's knickers stashed away secretively in the glove-compartment!'

Cue for another smirk alongside Lorenzo.

'If there is an innocuous explanation, why weren't you going to return the underwear to its owner? Why were you going to destroy the knickers?'

Lorenzo had a long wait for an answer, but he had an instinctive sense of momentum when it came to interviews with a suspect. Like an iconic athlete, he knew when to make the running and when to lay off the pace.

'You know something of my history, Inspector. I don't kill women. I love them.'

'No, Mr Lawson, you love deflowering young girls.'

Valentine had never before heard a cop use the word *deflowering*, but it had the effect of jolting Lawson; there was something archaic about its ring, a trademark of historical romance, but it packed more punch than contemporary police parlance. Lorenzo scored a bullseye.

'I thought I'd got it out of my system. The truth is, I need help, Inspector. Medical help.'

'Are you about to make some kind of confession? If so, you're entitled to have a solicitor present.' Lorenzo played it by the book now. He'd seen too many watertight cases lost on legal technicalities.

'I'm so ashamed. Frankly, I don't want anyone else to hear what I have to say.'

He must have known that what he was about to disclose would enter the public domain if presented in court, but fool's paradise was an irresistible allure, helping him to hoodwink himself into believing that the day of exposure might never come.

'You're fully aware that this interview is being electronically recorded and filmed?' Lorenzo was anxious to plug all possible legal loopholes.

'Yes, you told me all that at the beginning. Let's get this out the way: the knickers belonged to Jennifer Flanders.'

'*Jennifer Flanders,*' Lorenzo repeated contemptuously. 'And where shall we find her, among the living or the dead?'

Continuing to eschew all eye-contact, Lawson said, 'She hasn't been harmed.' Shaking, he added quickly, 'Certainly not by me.'

'You're ducking my question: where is she?'

Lawson looked everywhere except into the eyes of the detectives.

'She lives in Duckingford.'

Duckingford was a village about six miles away, towards the small cathedral city of Salisbury.

'You're not being very forthcoming, Mr Lawson. Do I have to siphon from you every drop of information?'

'You ask the questions and I'll answer them honestly,' he pledged.

'Fair enough. Are the two of you in a relationship?'

Despite his promise, Lawson stalled at the first opportunity to be candid.

'Not exactly.'

'Yet a pair of her knickers were left in your vehicle. Who removed them, you or her?'

Lawson fidgeted and hyperventilated some more.

'I think I must have done.'

'And when did this happen?'

'A couple of evenings ago.'

'And what occurred between the two of you was with her consent?'

'No force or coercion of any kind was used.'

'And you kept the knickers, not as a trophy but as a souvenir, in remembrance of a memorable shag?'

'That's offensive!' Lawson balked.

'OK, so what spin would you put on it?'

'We made love.'

'But you're not in a relationship with her, you say. Is she married?'

'No, good gracious, no; nothing like that.' A wistful, evanescent smile brought moisture to his secretive eyes.

'How long have you known this woman?'

Lawson faltered. Markedly flustered, he replied, 'I've known Jennifer for several months.'

This was the moment when everything on this issue fell into place for Lorenzo.

'When you had sex with her two nights ago, was that the first time?'

'Yes.'

'Does she live alone?'

'Oh, no.'

'Has she ever invited you home, to her place?'

'No, never.'

'Has she ever been here?'

'Yes, just the once, two days ago, when we made love.'

'You had sex indoors?'

'Yes, in my bedroom.'

'Yet the knickers are in your car.'

Lawson blushed so fiercely that Lorenzo thought his skin might start peeling due to the heat his body was generating.

'I wanted them out of the house. They made me feel guilty. I was going to bin or burn them.'

'Why feel guilty? This Jennifer of yours isn't married. Could it be that she isn't a woman? Is she a child? Are you up to your old tricks, Mr Lawson, despite all your assurances to the contrary?'

It was head-in-hands time again. Lawson sobbed in spasms. Lorenzo could have wept, too – because Lawson was slipping away from him as a realistic suspect for the murders.

'You must help me,' Lawson pleaded pathetically.

'That won't be up to us,' said Lorenzo, unable to camouflage his disgust. 'We do our utmost to make Humpty Dumpty fall. We don't try putting him back together again. How old is this girl?'

'Fifteen, I'd guess,' Lawson stammered, speaking through the gaps between his fingers, which were splayed over his desperate face.

'How did you first meet?'

'I was driving through Duckingford mid-afternoon and she'd just come out of school. She was in uniform, wearing a very short skirt. She was walking with a friend. She seemed so mature and had such style.' He talked now as if in a trance. 'She walked with a catwalk-sashay, all movement centred on her swaying hips. I pulled up about two hundred yards along the road, after overtaking them. I watched them through the driving-mirror coming towards me. Jennifer was a head taller than her friend and her deportment was that of a fashion-model. As they passed my car, Jennifer gave me a long, tantalizing smile, then winked. She knew exactly what she was doing. She was very aware, a real vamp.'

'Are you trying to blame her, the child?'

Valentine feared that Lorenzo was about to lose control of

himself and erupt into attack-mode. Lorenzo was a father. He had a daughter. From empiric experience, he knew only too well that the parents of daughters, he very much included, would happily castrate all Peter Lawsons. But he was also such a consummate professional that he would never allow his feelings to compromise his work.

'No, I'm not blaming Jennifer, but she knew how to tease and turn male heads. She was fully ripe, unlike her friend who was just a kid in all respects.'

'Did you follow them?'

'No. But over the next few days I couldn't get Jennifer out of my head. I told myself to get over it, that she was a gaol-bait temptress. She was as grown-up as any twenty-year-old. I counselled myself that I shouldn't take a chance because of my inherent weakness. But in the end, I couldn't kick temptation. A week later, I returned to Duckingford, a little earlier this time, and parked where I'd stopped before. I didn't have to wait long before I saw her approaching. I was watching her again through the mirror and I could tell from her expression that she instantly recognized my car.'

'Was she with her friend, the same girl as before?'

'No, she was alone, though there were lots of other girls around in similar uniform. It was a little after 3.30p.m.'

'What happened this time?'

Lawson vacillated, as if uncertain how to proceed.

'Did she treat you to another wink as she walked by?' said Lorenzo, helping to keep the narrative moving.

'No. She didn't pass. She stopped alongside my car and stooped to look at me through the front passenger-window, which I lowered. The windows operate electronically, so I didn't have to lean across. "Are you waiting for someone?" she said confidently, not a hint of shyness. She was wearing bright red lipstick and her voice was fruity and slightly husky, which seemed contrived. I was the nervous one.'

'What was your answer to her question?'

'The truth. No, I wasn't there to collect anyone. She'd taken me by surprise. I hadn't expected her to take the initiative. She made all the running. "I saw you here a few days ago," she went on, just as if she were talking to someone she'd known all her life. "I thought you must be the dad of one of the other girls. I do like your car. I've always fancied a bit of fun in a four-wheel drive job." She was leading me on to the punchline.'

'Which was?'

'"Would you like me to drive you home?"'

'I assume that her answer was "yes, please"?'

'It was saucier than that: "I thought you'd never get around to it. You're very coy for a man of your years. I find that sexy, though. Kind of Hollywood retro. Manners maketh man stuff."'

'So she hopped in?'

'Like a shot. She placed her schoolbooks between her legs, making her skirt lift. Other girls were passing and they gave us odd looks, which seemed to please Jennifer. I soon learned she enjoyed being noticed and being in the spotlight.'

'Didn't it bother you that you were observed by so many of her peers?'

'It should have done, but I couldn't help myself. *In for a penny, in for a pound.* Also, I had no intention of harming her.'

'But, Mr Lawson, you could have been blindly blundering into a honeytrap. You were already compromised, over the rubicon. Did you drive her home?'

'She asked to be dropped at the corner of her road. Just before she got out, she touched my thigh and said, "Shall I see you again?"'

'To which you replied?'

'"Same time next week?" "Lovely," she said. "Look forward to it."'

'Had you touched her?'

'No. We just talked. And that's how it was for weeks, honestly. I'd drive her into the country, usually a clearing, by a pond, in the forest. We began kissing. She was so experienced at French kissing; talk about Deep Throat, *she* almost choked *me!*'

'But it wasn't until recently that you had sex with her?'

'That's right. She was growing tired of just talking and petting. She said, "Is this all we're ever going to do. Don't you want to do the *real* thing with me?" I asked her if she was really sure she wanted to do it and she said, "Of course, stupid! I'm gagging for it. Where've you been all your life, in a monastery?"'

'Did you at any point seek to establish her age?'

'No.'

'Why not?'

'I was afraid of the answer. I know I was a fool, but it's easy to brainwash oneself into believing in something you desire. As I've said, she looked twenty and I wanted to believe it, to deceive myself. Unless something's done, I'll never change.'

'Did she go voluntarily into your home?'

'Absolutely.'

'And into the bedroom?'

Lawson nodded, shame-faced.

'You undressed her?'

'Do we have to go into such salacious detail?'

'Most definitely.'

'There was a natural progression, a fusion. We sort of undressed each other. The frisson for me was indescribable.'

'And at no time did she ask you to stop?'

'Grief, no! She was all over me and on top, pinning me down, so predatory! I couldn't keep pace with her. She wanted it two or three times in the space of half an hour.'

'How you must have suffered!' Lorenzo said coldly. 'Did you wear a condom?'

'I wanted to. In fact, I put one on, but she ripped it off. She said something about being addicted to bareback riding, bronco-style. It was surreal. "Live dangerously for once in your life," she panted. This from a teenager!'

'But it turned you on?'

'God, I'm such an idiot!' he ridiculed himself again.

'How long were you in the bedroom together?'

'In total, about three-quarters of an hour.'

'What was said between the two of you as you both dressed?'

'Nothing much. Mostly the usual awkward talk. She did say at one point, "Wow! That was good. Hopefully, next time it'll be great."'

'And that massaged your ego, eh?'

'No, Inspector, I was clobbered by the banality of it all. One thing I can tell you assuredly, she was no virgin.'

'Obviously! You've just admitted having sex with her two or three times in one session, so she waved goodbye to virginity with you that afternoon, if not before.'

'It was *before*, believe me.'

'Did you drive her straight home afterwards?'

'Yes.'

'And did you arrange to see her again?'

'Yes, today,' he said sheepishly.

'Well, you're going to stand her up, I'm delighted to say. A bad day for both of you. Did you ask to keep her knickers as a keepsake?'

'No, she offered them to me in the bedroom. Said I could have them in bed at night, like a comforter, in loving memory of her.'

'You realize she will have to be interviewed?'

'Yes,' he said, so softly he could scarcely be heard; head bowed.

'Then her parents. Details of her age will be crucial. You might be lucky. She might have turned sixteen.'

'I doubt it.'

'What makes you say that?'

'I saw her schoolbooks. I was once a teacher, remember? I could work-out which grade she was in.'

Lawson was incriminating himself, as if in an act of self-flagellation, wanting to hurt and purge himself. Hanging himself with every offering. Hell-bent on suicide.

'No doubt her parents will demand their daughter has a pregnancy test.' Lorenzo's salt to Lawson's wounds was added only to intensify the suffering, and not as a healing catalyst.

*

Jennifer's parents were distraught, of course. They would not countenance that their 'bashful, blushing child' would have gone to bed of her own volition with a middle-aged man.

'She must have been raped,' declared Mrs Maureen Flanders, horrified. 'He must be a dangerous sicko. Jenny's a sweetheart – and innocent! Well, she was until mauled by that monster!' She confirmed that her daughter, their only child, was a shade over three months short of her sixteenth birthday.

Jennifer's story conflicted with Lawson's, naturally. Interviewed in the presence of her mother, she claimed Lawson had pursued her relentlessly with a sob story that he was so lonely living alone, 'friendless and without a relative in the world'. She added, 'He more or less stalked me.'

'Why did you get in his car on the first occasion, when he was a stranger?' Lorenzo asked, non-judgmental in tone.

'Because I thought he was being kind and considerate. He looked harmless. You know, like a smiley uncle.'

'Later, why did you go to his home and then to his bedroom?'

'Because he paid me £50. I'd never seen that much money before. I thought of all the lovely clothes I could buy.'

'What are you saying, Jenny?' her mother trilled hysterically. 'You've always had everything you wanted. You couldn't have been provided for better. All the other girls are jealous of your fashionable, designer clothes. You've been spoilt, Jenny. How could you do this to us?'

Overwrought and weeping, Mrs Flanders said to the detectives, 'He must have drugged her. She'd never voluntarily sell herself for money. She's only fifteen! She's been brought up properly, God-fearing.' Then to Jennifer, 'Tell the truth now, has he been plying you with drugs?'

'When we were at his cottage he did give me a soft drink. I suppose he could have slipped in something when I wasn't looking.'

'There you are!' Mrs Flanders said triumphantly, as if everything were resolved. 'I knew it! He doped her. She wasn't thinking straight; still isn't. That's the only way he could get her to do such a thing. The dirty old basket!'

Lorenzo had no doubt that the truth lay somewhere towards the middle of the two versions. He was equally confident that Jennifer hadn't been drugged and purity wasn't one of her vices.

Without diminishing the seriousness of Lawson's offence, Lorenzo would become galvanized only if there was a connection with the murders; if there wasn't, he was squandering more valuable time. Other officers could process Lawson if the only charge against him was unlawful sex with a minor.

Lawson's Land Rover was the third vehicle of its kind to be impounded for forensic scrutiny, all of which was time-consuming and labour-intensive for the science detectives. While awaiting the results, so much of the investigation inevitably had to be put on hold, jacking up Lorenzo's frustration levels. The handwriting in Lawson's diary was also being evaluated by experts, but Lorenzo didn't anticipate a breakthrough there. The very fact that the killer left handwritten notes indicated that he was confident of not being trapped down that route.

While Lawson was detained in custody, Lorenzo spoke that evening on the phone with Tricia.

'How's London?'

'Fine. Manic as ever. Keeps the cobwebs of boredom away.'

'You settled in?'

'Yes, but still edgy.'

'No cause any more, trust me. No contact on your phone from Luke?'

'Not so far.'

'If you do change your number, don't forget to tell me.'

'Of course. Are you missing me?'

'What do you think?'

Evasiveness wasn't recommended against someone FBI-trained, but Tricia allowed it to ride.

'Any progress your end?'

Concisely, he summarized the Lawson scenario.

'Forget him,' she said peremptorily. 'He's not your man. He fucks, your killer flenses. Your *Jack* is flaccid between the legs, not a hard man.'

Dark humour helped to lighten the burden of dead-end baggage.

20

September 30th approached.

Autumn smacked of winter-dampness. Decay was in the air; malodorous rotting. The rain had none of the sweet freshness of a summer shower. Sodden leaves on pavements and roads were a prelude to slippery ice. The sky was bloated with foreboding, mirroring the mood of Lorenzo and his snappy hounds.

Painstaking work by the forensic detectives so far hadn't produced any positive results, though the tests and analyses were still ongoing. Chief Constable Helen Kingdom was twitchier than ever. The press was ratchetting up the media-choreographed drama of the macabre countdown. The Home Secretary had even intervened, demanding to be apprised daily of the latest feedback from Forensics. Amid the mounting tension and ghoulish expectancy, Lorenzo concentrated on being a calming and upbeat influence.

On the morning of the 29th, Kingdom summoned Lorenzo to her lair for a final briefing about preparations that were in place. The bird of prey had morphed into a quarry with the hunted eyes of an animal on the run. She couldn't stand still. She circled her desk a dozen times, as if strapped on a treadmill. If she wasn't vertiginous, Lorenzo most certainly was, just from being a spectator. She picked up folders for no apparent reason and put them down without even opening them; stress was shredding her.

'Outline the game plan,' she said finally, collapsing raggedly into her executive leather-throne, almost disappearing into the sumptuous upholstery, like a stick insect gobbled up by a lizard.

'As you know, we have three in the frame,' Lorenzo said perfunctorily.

'But not exactly likely lads, right?' Kingdom said sourly.

'I could be wrong.'

'Yes, it has been known,' she retorted spontaneously, heavy with undertow.

'Let's hope I am yet again,' said Lorenzo, equilibrium still on an even keel. 'Peter Lawson's in custody, so we don't have to concern ourselves with him.'

'And then there were two...' said Kingdom, alluding to the Ten Green Bottles ditty.

'The others – Dan Miller and Tom Bellinger – are under 24-hour surveillance. Come tomorrow, I'll have two teams, each forty-strong, shadowing them. If they enter a public toilet, one of our men will be pissing with them. As soon as Miller or Bellinger is mobile, the relevant team will roll too.'

'And if you lose them?'

'That isn't an option; it doesn't enter the equation.'

'I'm glad to hear that, Inspector. If there is a cock-up, it's your debacle. You'll face the firing-squad.'

Lorenzo didn't bother to joust with her kindergarten rhetoric.

'If there is no murder of a Liz Stride or a Catherine Eddowes, we'll know that one of *our three* is probably *Jack*.'

'Only *probably*?'

'Well, there would be another possibility ... that we've scared him off with all the public bulletins. But I wouldn't buy into that, certainly not in advance.'

'I'm sure you realize that should this pitiful self-proclaimed *Jack* manage to strike again, we'll be trashed worldwide as Keystone Cops. We'll both be history. But you, first. Understood?'

'We've done all that's humanly possible.' Lorenzo knew that he sounded plaintive and that irked him.

'Immaterial, Inspector. Nothing counts except the result. As in

football, being a lucky winning team is preferred to playing styl-
ishly but losing.'

'I didn't know you were a follower of football.'

'I'm not, but I follow sackings that make the headlines, which
are almost as interesting as my favourite reading – the obituary
columns.'

Lorenzo didn't sleep. He didn't even go to bed. Neither did
Kingdom. At 4 a.m., Lorenzo returned to his office. Valentine
was in the detectives' squad-room, mixing with the other night-
owls on the graveyard shift.

As soon as he saw Lorenzo, Valentine peeled off from the
others to join his boss.

'Can I get you a coffee?'

'A barrelful, very black and very sweet.'

A few minutes later, both with feet on the desk, were
preparing mentally for the longest day of their lives.

'No sleep?' said Valentine.

'I didn't even try.'

'Me neither.'

'Are the teams in place?'

'Since midnight. All lights in Bellinger's palace went out
between 12.30am and 1am.'

'How about Miller?'

'He arrived home half an hour ago on foot. Presumably he'd
being doing his shift at the nightclub. His wife's vehicle is
parked outside their place. All we can do now is sit it out.'

Lorenzo grimaced. 'I wish we could have got to all male Land
Rover owners in our region,' he remarked ruefully.

'It's been a thankless slog for everyone. We had to cherry-pick.
Something like two-thirds of the owners have been interviewed.
Not bad, really – and still more doors will be knocked today. So
don't beat yourself up, Mike. You couldn't have done more.'

'Yet all the stone-turning has uncovered zilch apart from our
three rogues,' Lorenzo said irritably. 'And still nothing definitive from Forensics on Bellinger's and Miller's Land Rovers.'

A Liz Stride and a Catherine Eddowes were on the sofa of breakfast TV programmes.

'Are you scared?' Liz Stride was asked.

'Not the least.'

'Aren't you going to heed police advice to stay indoors tonight?'

'No need. I have a boyfriend. We'll be together.'

'What's your recommendation for all other women with the same – or similar – name as yours?'

'Just be sensible. Take precautions, but don't panic. Don't let one weirdo disrupt your life.'

On another channel, a Catherine Eddowes faced similar probing.

'Of course I'm petrified. I'm a single mum with a young family, but we're staying with my parents for a few days until all the fuss is over. We'll be safe there. We'll have all doors locked and bolted by eight this evening. This nutcase won't know where my parents live, even if he has me in his sights. Anyhow, my dad was in the Army. I could never be afraid when he's around. He's a trained killer in unarmed combat. He'd snap that runt into twenty little pieces and feed him to foxes.'

'All good publicity,' opined Valentine. They were watching TV in the canteen as they passed an hour putting away breakfasts, the sight of which would have given a dietician a heart-attack.

Valentine's phone bleeped. While chewing, he read the text. 'Miller's on the move,' he said, almost choking on the coarse skin of a sausage.

'Where to?'

'Dunno.'

'Walking?'

'Dunno.'

'Then find out, for fuck sake!'

'That's exactly what I'm doing,' Valentine said equably, sticky fingers tapping the keyboard of his Blackberry.

Nerves were already frayed – and the only action so far had been eating a cholesterol-charged breakfast.

'What's he up to?' Lorenzo murmured, more to himself than another question for Valentine, his bloodshot eyes glazed in reverie.

'He's currently in the Boscombe area,' said Valentine, reading a text from the screen of his mobile. 'He hopped a bus.'

'But he's just finished an eight-hour night-shift at the Rambo club. He should be in bed.'

Valentine's mobile played a cacophonous jingle. 'Yep,' he said into his mobile-phone. 'Hold on. I'll consult.'

Lorenzo cocked his head, eyes screaming for a running commentary.

'He's off the bus and now in Bowling Green Road.'

'What's he doing there? Just loafing?'

'No, he's gone to a block of flats. Pressed one of the intercom buttons and entered. No one let him in. The door must be remote-operated. They couldn't see which button he pressed. Intercom was mostly hidden by his bulk. Should they see if there are names against the buttons?'

'Tell them to stay back for the time being,' said Lorenzo. 'I want to give this some thought.'

Valentine passed on the instructions. 'Maintain a watching brief until hearing to the contrary,' he added.

'This has thrown me,' said Lorenzo. 'I didn't expect action this early in the day.'

'Maybe there isn't any *action*,' Valentine said levelly, boldly taking the initiative, maturing fast. 'I think it's essential we know as quickly as possible the names of the occupants of those flats.'

Like a chess grandmaster, Lorenzo was appraising all possible continuations.

'If there's a Stride or Eddowes living there, we can't afford to wait,' Valentine pressed. 'If he kills right under our noses, while our team just sit on their bums, we'll be dog-meat.'

'You ran an electoral-roll check for all Strides and Eddowes on our patch, didn't you?'

'You know I did,' Valentine said, affronted.

'And you had no hits in Bowling Green Road?'

'No, but that means zilch. Bowling Green Road's plumb centre of the red light district. It's a revolving-door population there, changing every day, every night; a transient ants' nest. Dossers – and they're the cream. Many of them don't register to vote, trying to avoid paying council tax.'

'Then they're not likely to give away the game by advertising themselves with their name up front beside the door.'

'Still, we ought to cover ourselves, don't you think?' said Valentine, less flurried.

'Sod self-protection! Doing the job right is all I care about,' Lorenzo snapped irascibly.

Although chastened, Valentine didn't brood and was subdued only temporarily.

'Ask how far they are from the block of flats?' said Lorenzo.

Valentine went back on line. Lorenzo supped coffee while his young turk talked.

'About a hundred yards,' Valentine reported, covering the mouthpiece with a hand.

'Any chance of seeing the intercom-panel through binoculars?'

'I'll ask.'

Lorenzo waited for the response.

'They've already tried that, but the angle's all wrong.'

'OK, one of them had better saunter past the building, purporting to be looking for an address, like he's a little bit lost. If he's close to the wall, he shouldn't be visible from any window above on the same side of the street. It ought to be possible for him to read the names beside the buttons, without stopping. He must keep walking; go round the block, buy a newspaper or something, and return to the vehicle from the other end of the street.'

Valentine passed on the message.

Breakfast was over. Indigestion was next on the menu.

A Scotland Yard commander had been liaising daily with provincial and other metropolitan forces. Now loudspeaker

187

warnings boomed from police vans in towns and cities throughout the country. Never before had there been such a nationally-orchestrated police operation, with regular updated bulletins issued to the Home Office.

Although Lorenzo had suspects, large question marks hung over all three. And even if Miller or Bellinger was the perp, it was doubtful that the next target would be in the Bournemouth area; but nothing could be taken for granted. Lightning often *did* strike twice in the same place. Maybe there was a Stride or Eddowes living in Bowling Green Road, Boscombe, just a few streets from where Mary Walker had lived. Perhaps Miller was already fulfilling the barbarous promise.

There was another possibility, of course: Miller could be collecting his partner in crime; the twosome theory had always been near the top of the guess-list. She might have a car, which would give him the transport he'd need if the crime was to be committed outside the town.

Twenty minutes elapsed before the next call from the Bowling Green Road unit, by which time Lorenzo and Valentine were boosting morale with turbo tub-thumping sermons in the detectives' squad-room.

An update came in from the Boscombe brigade.

'Four buttons beside the intercom, only two names – Russell and Milo,' said Valentine.

'Run the address through the electoral roll. I'll be in my office.'

Less than five minutes later, Valentine had the list of occupants.

'Four flats, two couples and two singles.' He read from his flip-over notebook. 'Sally and Dean Russell, Tony Milo, Greg and Sheila Martin, Joan Townsend.'

'So which flat is your money on, Matt? Who's he with?'

'One of two – Tony Milo or Joan Townsend.'

'Milo could be his killing partner,' Lorenzo speculated. 'The composer of the notes, the reason why there's been no handwriting match.'

'And if he's with Joan Townsend?'

'He's probably flirting with adultery.'

'Or unless Townsend's maiden name was Stride or Eddowes, and whose other first names are Liz or Catherine,' said Lorenzo, sharpening the focus. 'He's already pulled that trick.'

Miller emerged furtively, shortly after 9 a.m., walked stealthily to the main drag, and caught a bus home, where the surveillance squad had earlier reported Miller's wife leaving on schedule for work at a supermarket.

Meanwhile, Bellinger made an appearance mid-morning, leaving his residence dressed for golf. After hoisting his golfing gear into his wife's Mini, he motored the short distance to the clubhouse. From a safe distance, he was trailed around the eighteen undulating holes of the landscaped course. Back in the clubhouse, he stayed until late afternoon, emerging with a handsome, middle-aged woman, not his wife. They held hands and kissed surreptitiously near his vehicle. One of the officers, a trained lip-reader, watched the couple through high-powered Army binoculars and translated the conversation for Valentine.

Bellinger: *A shame that all good things must come to an end.*

Woman: *What are you saying ? Is this goodbye?*

Bellinger: *No, not at all. I meant that time together passes so fast.*

Woman: *I enjoyed it too. Thanks for a lovely lunch.*

Bellinger: *Sorry I gave you such a hard time on the links.*

Woman: *That's OK, I made you pay for it in the bar and restaurant.*

Bellinger: *True. Mind you, revenge will be sweet.*

Woman: *Shall I see you tomorrow? My husband flies out early in the morning to Brussels on a two-day business trip – allegedly! You could come to my place and we could forget the golf.*

Bellinger: *An offer no self-respecting, hot-blooded male could possibly refuse. I'll tell my wife I'm seeing a very important client who needs my services.*

Woman: *And the beauty of that, my love, is every word will be true.*

Bellinger: *Till tomorrow, then.*

He blew her a kiss.

Bellinger: *What time?*

Woman: *Any time after 8 a.m. I'll ensure I'm suitably dressed to please.*

From the golf course, Bellinger drove home, not to be seen in public again that day.

Miller was next spotted at 7.43 p.m., when he was tailed on foot to the Rambo nightclub and was observed on door-duty until almost 4 a.m.

Lorenzo and Valentine were still at the police station when dawn crept in. Lorenzo had deployed his arms as a pillow on his desk. Slumped in his chair, head and trunk sprawled across his desk, he'd totalled about 45 minutes' sleep.

Valentine's sleep had come in five-minute power-naps, a misnomer because he was left as blitzed as his boss. Both brain-dead. Numb from the neck upwards and not much use below, either.

During the night, there had been a gangland slaying in London, fatal shootings in Nottingham and Manchester, count-less rapes and drug-busts, but nowhere had there been a murder of a Liz Stride or a Catherine Eddowes. Indeed, no report nation-wide of any woman having her throat cut. No jeering message attached to a corpse.

Chief Constable Kingdom created history by smiling.

'Playing it loud and very public paid off,' she gloated on the steps of county police HQ to a forest of microphones and reporters' tape-recorders. 'We either frightened *him* off or ensured that he was not in a position to harm anyone.' She would have liked to have used the metaphoric phrase, *Jack the Ripper, Mark 2, has been castrated,* but that would have been more Lorenzo's style than hers. She preferred to preserve the public persona of a *lady*.

Of course she was asked to explain the last sentence of her statement.

'Well, it could be that we already have the Jack the Ripper copycat in custody.'

She threw the press crumbs, but no meat, refusing to elaborate, leaving them hungrier than before she began.

That night, Lorenzo was almost at peace with the world. For the first time in weeks he slept without demons for bed-fellows and he woke reasonably refreshed.

But just after noon, he took a transatlantic call from a Lieutenant Sam Ravello, of the New York City Police Department. 'We have a homicide,' Ravello began, not bothering to bat shoptalk.

Isn't that one of the daily attractions of the Big Apple?

Wisely, Lorenzo kept this random observation to himself.

'Something strange about it, even for this city, so I didn't waste any time processing it through ViCAP.'

Lorenzo knew that ViCAP stood for Violent Criminal Apprehension Program, a US national registry of violent crimes, initiated in 1985 by the FBI, and available to all authorized law enforcement agencies.

'In no time at all I came upon a commonality with something you're apparently working.'

Lorenzo's antenna was suddenly as active as a jumpy nerve.

'The vic is a young woman. Throat cut. Body found only in the last couple of hours, but the medical examiner reckons she died yesterday. Just identified as a Liz Stride. Thing is, there was a message, scrawled in blood-red lipstick on the vic's mirror of her white art deco dressing-table.

It said: *This Jack is the master of his trade, just like his mentor. Thank the Victorians for teaching us so much.*'

21

Jack had gone international.

Jack was laughing.

Jack had planned everything down to the last meticulous detail. He hadn't been just one step ahead of the police; he'd been a mile in front – out of sight. He'd foreseen the precautions that would be taken; the warnings, the media feeding-frenzy, the lock-up-your-wives-and-daughters hysteria. And while Lorenzo and his regiment of investigators toiled ceaselessly, popping pills to stay awake, popping pills to sleep, popping pills to remain sane and keep blood-pressure low enough to avoid a gusher, *Jack* was leisurely plotting a diabolically devious twist to the itinerary in the reincarnation of the Whitechapel icon of horror.

He had deployed time constructively, going about his research methodically, drawing up his own shortlist for Death Row, and finally plumping for the transatlantic option to achieve maximum impact. So much had been written over the years in the US about Jack the Ripper, who was seen as their prototype serial killer, the rogue gene that had spawned Bundy, the Boston Strangler and Son of Sam; to name but a few of America's celebrity monsters.

Liz Stride was born 26 years ago in south Philadelphia on the downside of the social tracks. Her family represented an over-loaded, all-stops-to-nowhere loco. She came somewhere towards the middle of four brothers and five sisters; a third generation Italian/American family that rarely stopped anywhere long enough to be known by anyone in the neighbourhood, other than the pawnbroker, the catholic priest and a few debt-collectors. Her parents had confused birth-control with conception, an easy mistake when your education came from street mythology. Her father had ambition, but lost it every morning when he woke with a pile-driver hangover. All her brothers went to the only higher education college for which they were qualified – gaol. Her father turned petty thief – petty everything, really – and died from alcoholic poisoning; cheap alcohol, so at least he didn't add too much to the family's debt as he checked out, leaving the tab for others.

The booze that killed him had been stolen, evidence that there was some moral justice in social anarchy. Two of her sisters married when they were sixteen and pregnant; both were divorced within a year, after entering a women's refuge – and that was the high point of their lives. Her other sisters did drugs from the age of twelve or thirteen and were street-corner hookers before they were fifteen, controlled by pimps, beaten by pimps, abused by punters, but destroyed by themselves; self-immolation, overdosing on self-ingested immorality.

Liz Stride was determined not to tread the same devil's road as the rest of her siblings. She had class, intelligence and style – and knew it, because it had been consciously crafted. Proud and confident, she became an escort; an envied breed in the world of whoredom. She even had her own erotic website. But one very pertinent factor has so far been omitted.

Liz's family name was Perlo. She grew up as Liz Perlo, which wasn't right for a New York escort. A new *professional* name was required. So she wrote a list. Rolled them off her tongue. Discarded most of them. Pruned them to two or three. She was taking all challenges in her stride. *Stride* defined her: that was the name to shape her future, she decided. And it did, though not in the way she had dreamed.

Liz Stride died horribly. Liz Perlo would have lived to read about the unfortunate brutal demise of some other Liz Stride. In the tradition of her family, she'd made a really bad career-decision.

Liz Stride had been killed on the evening of September 30th and certainly before midnight. She was naked, except for bra, pants, stockings, suspenders, stilettoes and 1920s high society evening-wear gloves that covered her slender arms as far as her elbows. She was discovered between 9 and 9.30 the following morning by her cleaner, who was employed to tidy Stride's Manhattan apartment three days a week. Stride was on the floor at the foot of her water bed, a black whip nearby, as if it had just been released from her grip. The trademark slit throat had resulted in blood matting a large area of the thick-piled, cream carpet.

'What I don't get is it's nothing like your standard sex-motivated homicide,' said Ravello, his puzzlement transparent from a distance of three thousand miles. 'No rape. The medical examiner couldn't even find a trace of semen on, or in, the vic. Not on the black silk sheets or on the carpet. All of which, of course, points to the perp being the vic's first client of the night. Yet he didn't fuck her, or get off on the sight of the gore, of which he was the architect. No evidence either of robbery.

'She kept a diary, which the killer didn't lift, even though all her appointments were listed, recording not only the fee charged but also the johns' requirements. Three were booked for the night of the 30th. The first was a Jack Legend. In brackets she'd written, *Role-play requested. $500 for one hour agreed.* Now get this: five 100 dollar bills were on top of the dressing-table.'

'So you believe *Jack Legend* paid up front, honouring the agreement, killed her, but didn't retrieve the cash?'

'Exactly! And to me that's even weirder than the actual slaying and the cryptic lipstick epitaph.'

'So what about the other two booked punters?' said Lorenzo.

'Seems obvious that this Jack Legend – clearly bogus – was the killer and had fled the crime-scene before anyone else showed. The others would have rung the bell and gotten no reply. Hookers are notoriously unreliable, so they'd have just sworn and made other arrangements. There's more than enough female flesh for sale to go around in New York City. But I have to tell you, I can't get my head around this one; he pays his bucks, she undresses, all prepared for showtime, but he doesn't take what he's coughed up for. Instead, he gives her the ultimate goodnight kiss and leaves his big bucks as a tip for those who have to clean up the mess. Nice one!'

'No used condom?' said Lorenzo, remaining strictly focused.

'Nothing to suggest sex took place; no spent cartridges, as in rubbers: not the sorts of things a punter's likely to stick into his pocket, even if he's running from murder.'

'Any idea where *Legend* phoned from to make his booking?'

'Not yet. But from what I've gleaned, it seems to me that all the answers lay your end.'

Lorenzo knew that it would be only a few hours before the media caught on and caught up – and then someone's fan would be hit by the proverbial. His fan, of course; not Kingdom's.

He called an impromptu case-conference.

'Get one thing out of your heads: this isn't a cock-up,' he began, no humour intended, going on the offensive. 'Nothing and no one could have prevented this third murder. Any Liz Stride could have been targeted anywhere in the world. There was no forewarning that *he* was contemplating going international. Most importantly, this is a breakthrough, not a setback. Anything you might read to the contrary is garbage.'

A collective doubt was sketched on the sea of sceptical faces: *he's finally flipped, failure has broken him, send for the men in white coats, next stop funny farm.*

'How come?' demanded one intrepid veteran.

'I was just coming to that,' said Lorenzo, determined to swiftly turn an apparent gloomy negative into a glowing positive. 'Forget that Liz Stride, recently deceased, was an American and was killed in New York. Those details are irrelevancies, red-herrings. The facts to embrace are that *Jack* is a Brit, his home is over here, probably in or near Bournemouth, he drives a Land Rover, and almost certainly we have him somewhere already in the system.'

'So he simply went on a killing vacation, a sort of busman's holiday,' said the jaded vet.

Lorenzo welcomed the spiky interventions because they helped to repair ragged nerves.

'Our public awareness operation was so successful that we forced him to foul on someone else's doorstep. Now we move fast. We take him out of circulation before November, before a Mary Kelly somewhere in this wide world is unfairly bequeathed a premature funeral. An educated guess tells me that he's already back in the UK, back here, probably within a few miles of us. And there's a trail leading to him that's impossible for him to erase. He'll have booked a return flight; name on his ticket would have to correspond with that in his passport. There'll be a record of his entry into the US and his exit.'

'Like looking for a pin in a haystack,' Vet scorned.

'Oh, no it's not,' Lorenzo retaliated, as buoyed as if just reborn. 'We'll be looking for a name and address that's already on our list of Land Rover owners. Make a match and we have our man.'

'Match-making for a date with a murderer!' chimed Valentine, getting into the high-five mood.

'All his planning would have been undertaken this end, so he probably didn't fly out much before the 29th,' said Lorenzo 'And I think he'd have wanted out of New York ASAP, possibly on the first flight to Heathrow or Gatwick on the morning following the deed, obligingly narrowing our field of search.'

'He obviously loves playing cat-and-mouse with us, so don't you fear he might still be ahead of us in the mind-game? Valentine ventured, to a chorus of nods. 'I have this debilitating sensation that he's inside our heads and already knows what we'll do next.'

'Don't fall for that, none of you,' Lorenzo implored forcefully 'Yes, he's banking on spooking us, making us disconsolate morale jettisoned, so that we start questioning our own judgment. If he can create disarray in our ranks, he'll divide and conquer. It's imperative that we don't start thinking of him as superhuman, because he's not. Despite his cerebral method-ology, he's nothing but a low-life criminal; no different from the rest of the roaches.

'Contrary to impressions, he's making mistakes all the time. Like a shark, a Great White, that has a whole ocean in which to swim, hunt and kill, eventually he'll make a wrong turn, a wrong move, and be snared, if our nets are correctly placed. I'm not exaggerating when I say I expect a wrap within 48 hours. Now let's go to it.'

Lorenzo scanned the faces. He estimated that there were only two believers in that room and he was one of them. Valentine was the other, though no doubt Judas, the original double agent, had appeared just as loyally supportive.

Tricia sounded less wrung-out.

'You'll get him now,' she said confidently. There was an affinity between them that enabled them to communicate in shorthand; no need for her to introduce the subject matter. 'I was awake all night thinking about it.'

How therapeutic, thought Lorenzo. 'Better than dwelling on your own problems. It's not even your case; not even one of your cold ones.'

'True, but like an avid reader of Agatha Christie whodunits, it had me hooked. There's also an advantage in being detached.'

That was something with which Lorenzo certainly identified.

'What fascinates me most of all in a macabre way is how it began. What was the trigger?'

'I'm getting the feeling that you don't believe it was a long-term life-plan. He didn't tell his careers teacher that he wanted to become a highly acclaimed Jack the Ripper and wondered if there was an appropriate apprenticeship or course at Oxford or Cambridge.'

Tricia tittered politely; just once.

'He's definitely a Jack the Ripper obsessive. But when and why did he cross the line from student to practitioner?'

'Has burning the midnight oil fired your imagination?'

'As a matter of fact, yes. I remembered my last visit to my doctor's surgery to collect a prescription. There was a queue of about four patients waiting to speak with the receptionist. When it was my turn, I explained why I was there and gave my name, of course. As she was fishing out my prescription from a box, she requested my address, a routine procedure as a security measure. The two people behind me would easily have heard me give my name and where I lived. Now, just suppose I'd been Mary Walker and your aspiring Jack the Ripper had been directly behind me in the queue. Name combined with address could have been the detonator, tipping him over the edge, making him believe it was an omen, God calling; something like that. What do you think?'

'It's nuts. But that's exactly what's needed: something that fits the mindset of a nutter.'

'So what you do, Mike, is find out if Mary Walker was a patient at the same surgery as one of the men on your list. And if the answer is affirmative and he was at the surgery on the same day that Mary last collected a prescription, it's time to think about organizing a close-of-case knees-up at your team's favourite hostelry.'

'And watch everyone else get legless while I'm on orange juice all night.'

'I'm sure you're capable of getting inebriated on the euphoria, which has two very attractive components: it comes free of charge and also without a hangover.'

'It's just possible, Tricia, that you're a genius.'

'Bet on it, Mike!'

By mid-morning next day, they had a name: Ronald Fleming. He'd flown Virgin Atlantic to New York on September 28th on a return ticket, returning on October 1st. He'd been a low priority on the list of Land Rover owners; a remote 'possible' rather than a 'probable' and hadn't yet been knocked up. Age and profile seemed all adrift: 68, widower with adult children and grand-children. Desirable address on Bournemouth's East Cliff. One factor, irrelevant before, now upgraded his status as a suspect, irrespective of his quick round-trip to New York, wrapped around the murder date: he lived in the catchment area of a doctor's surgery that could easily have served Mary Walker. He was also only a five-minute drive from Boscombe.

'Make discreet inquiries,' Lorenzo instructed Valentine. 'Talk with his neighbours. Look for the Land Rover. I'm familiar with the block of flats where he lives. There's an underground carpark for residents' vehicles. Snoop around. Find out if he's been seen recently. By *recently,* I mean during the past 24 hours.'

'He must be aware we're closing in,' said Valentine. 'He'll have read the morning newspaper, same as we have. I can't believe Kingdom hasn't been blasting your eardrums with vitriolic abuse.'

'One good reason why not, she's jumped ship; taken a week's leave. Like a fire chief pushing off to the opposite side of the world in the middle of an inferno.'

'You're kidding?'

'Straight up. So enjoy. She'll be recharging her batteries, which means we'll be in for an electric storm on her return.'

'If we close down this case while she's off, she won't be able to steal the stardust,' said Valentine.

'Don't you believe it.'

After a moment's rumination, Valentine said, 'You haven't forgotten that this guy has unfinished business? There's still a Mary Kelly to come – or should I say to *go?*'

'Of course I haven't forgotten.'

'The date – November 8th – will be just as important as the name,' said Valentine. 'The two will go together like grave and burial.'

'Just where's this leading, Matt?'

'He has five weeks to evade arrest. Surely he's not simply going to sit at home, ticking off the days on his calendar? He must know we'll be propelling his front door from its hinges long before then.'

'So you suspect he'll be preparing to do a moonlight flit?'

'No, I believe he's *already* taken off. He won't have come home. He'll have gone nomadic. Shacking up in motels or B&Bs. Biding his time.'

'Impossible to get away with that for five weeks, if not five minutes,' said Lorenzo. 'The moment he uses plastic, we'll bag him; even if it's just to milk money from an ATM.'

'He could have more than one vehicle,' Valentine continued in negative vein. 'Even if his Land Rover is parked under the flats, he could be miles away, moving every day in another car.'

'Do another check with Swansea,' Lorenzo said crisply. 'See if he owns a second vehicle.'

'Which shall I do first, chat up residents or Swansea?'

'Swansea. You'll have an answer in ten minutes max. Let me know the score before you set off for the East Cliff.'

Valentine threw a mock military salute as he exited Lorenzo's office.

The answer to the question Valentine put to Swansea was no. Fleming was a one-vehicle owner. And there was no record of the Land Rover having been sold or exchanged, though that could have occurred in the last few days and the paperwork was still in the post.

Bert Morrison was the resident caretaker of the apartments where Ronald Fleming resided. Morrison and his wife, Mavis, occupied a suite of rooms on the ground floor, next to the unostentatious entrance, which was permanently locked. Visitors had to announce themselves via the intercom and be let in, by remote control, by a resident. No hawkers. No canvassers. No junk mail. Providing security and peace was a strong selling point that added considerable value to the properties.

Mr Morrison went to the tradesmen's entrance to speak with Valentine, first closely inspecting his ID and comparing the photo with the flesh in front of him. Not until he'd released the electronic catch on the door, was Valentine able to enter.

'You say you want to ask me about one of the residents: am I allowed to know what it's all about?'

'Not at this stage; maybe later.'

'Oh, well,' Morrison shrugged. 'Who are you here to talk about?'

'Ronald Fleming. Know him?'

Morrison frowned, as if to say, *You've wrong-footed me there. That's the last name I expected you to bowl at me.*

'What can you tell me about him?'

Morrison was in his sixties, a retired plumber, who also knew something about electrical wiring systems. Dabbling in DIY had been his hobby for forty years, just the man to be janitor of a block of apartments that only the affluent could afford.

'Fleming and his wife, Constance, moved in around ten years ago. She passed away five years ago; some kind of cancer. You don't like to pry too much about those sorts of things, do you? Until then, he was a very outgoing, active sort of bloke. He was also chairman of our residents' management committee.'

'But his wife's death changed him?'

'Dramatically. It hit him hard. He became withdrawn and secretive.'

'*Secretive?*' Valentine pounced.

'Didn't want to chat about anything. He used always to be talking about his rugby-playing days and when he served in the Army – the Parachute Regiment, I believe. Mind you, he keeps very fit, very strong for his age, but he resigned from the management committee and cut himself off from his old friends. Until Constance passed away, other residents were routinely in and out of his apartment.'

'What for?'

'Oh, just to gossip or play cards. He and Constance were keen bridge and golf players, but that all stopped.'

'I assume he's retired?'

'He packed in his job within a month of Constance dying. He'd been a professor of history at Southampton University, after his short military career. A very intelligent and well-spoken bloke. Sort of posh, I suppose, but not snobbish. Always going on about the legacy of the Victorians, how we owe them so much. Mind you, I was never a part of his high-brow clique.'

'So he doesn't work at all now?'

'Oh, yes, he does. On and off at one of the libraries. Part-time I think it's the large Central one in the Triangle.'

'And he drives a Land Rover?'

'Yeah, a black one. A strange vehicle for the kind of people who live here, I remarked to my wife, only the other day. Out of character, especially with him. He used to drive a Jag.'

'When his wife was alive?'

'Yes, but as I said, everything about him has changed of late.'

'When did you last see him?'

'Only this morning. I was looking out of our kitchen window and saw him returning with newspapers under his arm.'

'I believe he's been abroad recently for a few days,' Valentine remarked casually.

'Really? That's news to me.'

While Valentine was quizzing Morrison, Lorenzo was talking on the phone to the chief executive of the local Primary Care Trust.

'You appreciate our practices are bound by strict medical ethics and doctors are forbidden from discussing the conditions of their patients,' Hilda Manning said, preacher-style. 'This is non-negotiable, regardless of the seriousness of any crime committed.'

'I'm as *au fait* as you with that part of the legal bible,' Lorenzo retorted; tone barbed, balking against being lectured. 'I've just spoken with the partner of the late Mary Walker. He tells me that Mary was a patient of the Clarendon Green surgery. I've two questions. One: is a Mr Ronald Fleming also a patient of that surgery? Two: did he have reason to be in that surgery on the same day that Mary Walker was last there? That's all. I don't give a fig about their medical records.'

Hilda Manning had envisaged a testy stand-off, followed by a mental arm-wrestling contest, so her relief was palpable.

'I don't see an obstacle to question one. However, to help with question two, I require clarification. Do you want to know if they were both there for a doctor's appointment or for any reason at all?'

'The latter.'

'Fine. I'll see what I can do. Give me half an hour.'

'I'm obliged.'

Hilda Manning was as true to her word as you'd expect from someone in her position.

'The answer to your first question, Inspector, is yes; Mr Fleming is a patient of the surgery you named,' she said, without embellishment. 'As for question two, records indicate that both he and Ms Walker did have repeat prescriptions to collect on the same day. However, there's no way of confirming if they were on the premises around the same time.'

'Many thanks for all the trouble you've gone to.'

'No trouble at all. I hope the information is of use to you.'

'Oh, it is, believe me, Ms Manning. So much so, that in future I shall always refer to you as the tin-opener.'

22

As in most investigations of this nature, the denouement was as sudden as the hatching of a chick from an egg. One minute the darkness of the shell, swiftly followed by light, with everything seen and taking shape.

The weight of evidence against Ronald Fleming was crushing. As a librarian temp, he had ready access to all literature on Jack the Ripper and the Victorians, including their vices, hypocrisy, crime and the underbelly of society, without leaving a single footprint. Motive was missing, of course. Often in serial killer cases, the motive never surfaced until the trial; and not even then in many instances.

Many people, probably the majority, wrongly assumed that serial killings were motiveless. Not so. There was always a reason; a very rational one to the moonstruck perpetrator, however barmy and barbaric to the sane mind.

'What now?' Valentine enquired.

'No more finessing,' Lorenzo decreed tersely. 'We arrest him. We move fast. We get inside his place. Get inside his head.'

Accordingly, Valentine rounded up a posse, while Lorenzo tipped-off the Scene-of-Crime unit.

Ronald Fleming was on the sea-facing balcony of his apartment, when he observed a fleet of six black Ford Mondeos turn left from the coastal road towards the rear of the building, where the entrance was situated. He'd been looking across the water to the sharp, white Needles at the western tip of the Isle of Wight.

Seven floors beneath him, the gardener attended the manicured communal lawn, on which there were benches and wooden picnic tables.

'Six cars, of the same make and colour, all in a row!' he said to himself, as if reciting a nursery rhyme. 'What odds of that being a coincidence? Must run into millions. So they're on their way. Sooner than expected. No matter. Everything has been taken care of.'

Slowly but purposefully, he walked from the balcony to the door of his apartment – and waited. But the intercom didn't buzz. *Of course, not!* he chided himself. *They won't be taking any chances. They'll have got Bert to smuggle them in. Some will use the lift. Others will bomb up the stairs. So much excitement and adrenalin. All for nothing! They'll re-group in the corridor. Hearts pummelling ribcages. The leader will give a signal and one of them will knock.*

Shouldn't be long now. They'll be so eager, itching for a showdown that they're not going to get. What a spoilsport I am! All police officers of the masculine gender are little boy-racers at heart. They join the force to become legal law-breakers, but there's not going to be any fun for them here today.

Knock, knock, knock. Three firm raps.

No rush. Ronald Fleming coolly took off the chain, levered the bolt sideways, and swung open the door. Nothing tentative about his action. No inching open the door, as in the normal case of an elderly person living alone and conscious of the threat posed by armed burglars or violent tricksters

'Mr Ronald Fleming?' It was Lorenzo who spoke, with the rest of the invasion party swarming around and behind him, rottweilers straining to be released from the leash.

'Inspector!' said Fleming, as if greeting an old friend, who, although calling uninvited, was nevertheless very welcome.

'You are Mr Fleming?' Lorenzo pressed, slightly bemused by the unexpected and confusing convivial reception.

'But, of course, dear chap! Come in. All of you! Make your-selves at home. Looks like you've brought your whole extended family, Inspector. May I get you something to drink?'

The gang piled in, as if a dam had been breached. Raids such as this were crack to cops.

'We have a search-warrant,' said Lorenzo, anticipating a challenge at some point about the validity of the mob intrusion.

'Of course you do. You're not a novice at this game. Now, how about that drink?'

Fleming was ignoring the script, which was disconcerting for Lorenzo.

'Don't you want to know why we're here in such numbers, Mr Fleming?'

'I know already, silly boy! I've already acknowledged that you're no novice, please have the courtesy to reciprocate. Just go about your business, but understand that I shall not, under any circumstances, be answering questions.'

Fleming didn't look in his sixties. Most people above a certain age, male or female, quickly lost their upright posture, but Fleming was astonishingly well-preserved. No stoop, no awkward gait, no shakes. He had also kept most of his hair and there were only a couple of small grey patches. His facial features twinned well with his manner. Widowers were known for losing their self-esteem once their partner of decades had departed, but everything about Fleming was redolent of a proud, contented man. A thinly-disguised mocking expression was engraved on his aristocratic features; his opalescent eyes were as bright as those of a child; not a speck of rheum and certainly no milky way. He wore neatly-pressed grey trousers, fake crocodile-skin loafers, and a white cotton shirt, with the sleeves folded up meticulously, so that both sides were level, revealing biceps that hadn't been allowed to go saggy or wrinkled.

'Let me get this straight,' said Lorenzo, 'you're flatly refusing to co-operate?'

'About *what*, exactly, Inspector?' He was playing games and enjoying himself.

'You've already stated you're aware of our purpose.'

'But you haven't confirmed.'

'OK, we're here to ask you about three recent murders, one overseas. How's that?'

'Not very interesting for me, Inspector. You may talk and I'll listen. You may ask as many questions as you like, but I shall not be responding.'

Both Lorenzo and Valentine were astonished by Fleming's sangfroid in such circumstances; his speech and manner were incredibly measured.

'We shall be taking away your vehicle as well as searching your property,' said Lorenzo, hoping that this might lever open a window of communication.

'Be my guest, you good people. Look around all you like. As for my vehicle, I have a feeling I shall not be needing it again in my lifetime. And certainly not in the next life. It has a small dent. Maybe you'd care to have it repaired for the next owner?'

'How do you expect to manage to complete your journey on November 8th without a vehicle, Mr Fleming?' Lorenzo said provocatively, attempting to goad him into participating.

Not a single brick was dislodged in the wall of peaceful non-co-operation.

'OK, go to work,' Lorenzo instructed the rank-and-file of the advanced party, who immediately fanned out, feathers ruffled, like a flock of scavenging magpies.

'You keep our *friend* company while I take a look around his comfortable *shack*,' Lorenzo said acidly to Valentine.

The split-level living-room was spacious and airy. The sliding glass doors to the balcony faced south, designed to snare the best of the sunshine. The walls were white and black stucco, and white prints accentuated the pastel décor. A cream-coloured mini-grand piano on the elevated level was more than a tad OTT and pretentious, Lorenzo thought, perhaps a shade churlishly. The lower-level doubled up as a dining-room and lounge. The dated furnishing, showing wear but not tear, had clearly been expensive when bought. Nothing in the apartment was cheap, apart from the cops.

The main bedroom was preserved as a shrine to Constance;

the four walls were plastered with framed photos with Constance in every one of them.

Kitchen-knives were bagged. The computer hard-drive and software were confiscated. Examples of Fleming's handwriting were carefully placed into evidence-bags and sealed. A long-handled hammer was found in the rear of the slightly damaged Land Rover. There was no sign to the naked eye of blood or human hair on the implement. While all this was going on around him, Fleming carefully filled in the *Daily Telegraph* crossword puzzle.

'There! All done in 36 minutes. Not bad for a man of my age,' declared Fleming, without a flicker of trepidation. 'What do you say, Inspector?'

'I say we're finding more clues than the crossword and we'll soon have all the answers to our own puzzle, though it'll take longer than 36 minutes, I grant you.'

'*Touchez!*' Fleming said good-naturedly, embellishing the enigmatic aura around him.

As soon as the search was complete, Fleming was formally arrested. By that time, it was early evening.

'I'm usually thinking of preparing my dinner around now,' said Fleming, as Lorenzo snapped on the handcuffs.

'Don't fret, I'm sure we'll be able to rake up a mug of stewed tea and a chip butty,' said Lorenzo.

Valentine drove, while Lorenzo sat in the back with the prisoner

'I'm not one for late nights these days,' said Fleming. 'I do hope you're not going to keep me up beyond my bedtime with boring questions which will amount to your simply talking to yourself. Monologues are tedious at the best of times.'

'You weren't concerned about an early bedtime when you were in Kettering, dragging Anne Chapman to that hole in the ground,' said Lorenzo, seizing the opening.

'There you go again, Inspector, spoiling everything by stepping into no-go territory.' He'd resisted an urge to say, '*For historical accuracy, it should be Annie – not Anne – Chapman*'.

Nothing else was said until Lorenzo and Valentine had Fleming in an interview-room, with audio and video recording equipment ready for action.

When asked if he wished a solicitor to be present, Fleming replied, 'Good heavens, no! What a dreadful waste of public money that would be. There isn't going to be a conversation for a lawyer to hear. I fully appreciate that this is going to be awfully frustrating for you, but all that frustration will be of your own making.'

After the routine formalities, the recording equipment was started and Lorenzo began with questions about Fleming's recent trip to the USA.

'What was the purpose of your visit to New York City?'

Fleming folded his arms across his chest and began humming a military march.

'I suggest you were there on business, murderous business?'

The humming continued, volume raised a little.

'Through Internet searching, you had identified and located a Liz Stride.'

Lorenzo waited in vain.

'You were enjoying the sick game, still are, right?'

All Lorenzo's cajoling and needling failed to budge Fleming from his stubborn resolve.

'You had no chance of getting to a Liz Stride in this country. The risk would have been too great. We'd closed all doors. We were getting to grips with you, closing in, trimming your options, and we've finally won. You've lost. You may have killed three innocent women, but your goal was to finish the historical cycle, to rub out a Mary Kelly in her own home on 9th November, to complete the circle. But it's not going to happen. Failing to finish a mission, like a crossword puzzle, rankles with you, doesn't it? Jack the Ripper would be disappointed with a third-rate groupie like you. You're a failure, by anyone's standards, especially those of the *real* Jack. Far too old for the job you undertook. A right, rip-roaring failure! How does that feel?'

Now Fleming stopped humming and grinned, but didn't speak. Just blew Lorenzo a kiss.

And this is how it went on until 3 a.m., when Fleming closed his eyes and feigned a snore, all provocation having failed ever to dent the bubble he'd ballooned around himself.

Valentine summoned the station gaoler.

'Take him to a cell,' said Lorenzo, yawning, far more tired than Fleming.

Just as Fleming was being led out of the interview-room, he turned to Lorenzo and said, still grinning, 'I shall be forever your 8-1-1-2-8. Remember that because you'll be haunted by it to the grave.'

And they were Fleming's last words.

23

The veteran gaoler, PC Joe Garside, began his morning rounds at seven o'clock. Fleming's cell was the third for Garside to peer into through the hatch.

Fleming was sprawled on the floor, his head in a pool of vomit.

Garside grabbed his bunch of keys, which were attached to his leather-belt, and opened the cell-door. Fleming was alive but motionless. Garside, a first-aider, turned the prisoner onto his side and checked vital signs; pulse was weak, spume frothed round his purple lips. The gaoler raised one of Fleming's eyelids, but was met by a fixed, sightless gaze.

Dr Owen Montague, a police physician, arrived tieless and panting within ten minutes. He took one look at Fleming and summoned an ambulance.

Lorenzo was still at home when informed that his prized prisoner was in a coma and on his way to hospital. Lorenzo, in turn, apprised Valentine and the two of them met at the Royal Bournemouth Hospital.

'He's in intensive care,' said Valentine, who had arrived first, by a few minutes.

'What's up with him? Food poisoning? An allergic reaction to our nick's bacterial breakfast?'

'Dunno. The quacks wouldn't tell me anything. Not important enough – me, not them.'

'Well, they got that right. Show me the way.'

Two uniformed officers had been posted outside the double

doors of intensive care. A notice above a red bell-button read *Ring for admission. Do not enter without permission.*

Lorenzo, on his best behaviour, rang.

The sister in charge of the unit admitted the detectives, saying quietly, 'Doctors are with Mr Fleming now.' She pointed to a cubicle enclosed by green curtains.

'Has he regained consciousness yet?' Lorenzo asked eagerly.

'No, but you'll have to speak with the senior doctor for more information. Wait here.'

Their wait stretched into almost half an hour before Dr Rosemary Sutton emerged from the curtains around Fleming's bed and approached them briskly.

Routine handshakes over, Lorenzo said, 'Is he faking it?'

'Inspector, I haven't yet encountered any patients in hospitals who have accomplished the feat of faking their own death.'

Computing what they had just heard took some time for both detectives. Expressions flatlined.

Stupidly, Lorenzo said, 'Are you telling me that he's dead?'

'Death tends to be the consequence of dying,' Dr Sutton said, no modulation, face as straight as a Roman road.

'Heart-attack?'

'Unlikely.'

'Poisoning?'

'It's a mystery, Inspector. I'm afraid you'll have to await the outcome of a post mortem examination.'

Another friggin' mystery! Lorenzo groaned to himself. *It's not just God who acts in mysterious ways, the Devil has caught on, too.*

Chief Constable Kingdom's first question was, inevitably, 'Is there any indication of physical injury?'

Lorenzo knew exactly what she was alluding to: had Fleming been worked over while in custody?

'Not that the medical staff mentioned,' said Lorenzo.

'But you didn't ask, *specifically?*'

'No, not *specifically*, but if there had been, I think the doctor would have raised the matter when I asked about probable cause.'

'Let's hope you're right ... for a change. A blow to the stomach could result in vomiting and convulsions, without physical evidence.'

'Except for a dirty great torso bruise,' Lorenzo pointed out dryly.

'Yes, well. Have you arranged the PM?'

'Yes, 2 p.m.'

'Update me the moment you have the result.'

Not once that day, did Kingdom ask the one question that should have topped her agenda: *Are you absolutely sure that Fleming was our man?* If there was a sliver of doubt, then it was premature to declare the all-clear for November 8th.

Although Kingdom hadn't posed the all-important question, Lorenzo forged ahead as if the investigation still had traction.

Forensic analysis couldn't be hurried. Thoroughness was paramount. Cutting corners cost lives, whether on roads or in laboratories. But two items taken from Fleming's apartment were of special significance; diaries dating back five and six years. They were two large, A4-sized, leather-bound jobs, with a whole page devoted to each day. One entry read:

Constance found a leaflet on VD among my papers. I didn't think she was one for snooping, but there you are! I couldn't keep the truth from her any longer. I had to admit that I'd been given penicillin treatment at a clinic for sexually transmitted diseases. What an embarrassment! She went into a rage; quite unlike her. She kept on at me until I had to confess I'd been associating with the demi-monde. She couldn't seem to appreciate that it was mere research on my behalf, not lust or prurience. She couldn't understand my curiosity and I couldn't understand her prudishness. Quite extraordinary! She talked – no, screamed! – of betrayal and infidelity, yet we hadn't indulged in sex together for years. She couldn't seem to accept that there was no emotional intimacy when I was experimenting with female creatures of the night. I was simply studying, sampling firsthand something that was not the least pleasurable but perfunctory and academic; the physical bonding of two people without any spiritual binding.

Another entry read:

Constance no longer speaks to me, unless we are in public, when she pretends that everything is hunky-dory between us. It is farcical but appearances are everything to Constance, something I hadn' realized until I was forced to come clean! I have to wash and iron my clothes and cook all my meals, and Constance even refuses to eat with me at the dining-table. This is becoming mentally exhausting, espe cially when having to put on an act in front of other residents Constance shows no sign of relenting and at times I feel as if I could strangle her. What a terrible emotion to harbour about the woman I've always loved and still do – so very dearly! But it's the frustration and injustice of being ostracized, a pariah in my own home, that is so depressing. I have ceased my experimental night-time excursions, bu Constance continues to refuse to be reasonable. She is so judgmental So Victorian! Such a closed, straight-laced mind! If I don't go mad it'll be a miracle.

In the second diary, an insertion on December 17th read:

My beloved Constance died today. Whatever the medics say, know that the real cause of her death was a broken heart. I killed her as if by my own hand. Another silent Christmas approaches: no different, in that respect, from the last five. Being alone in the festive season is my Christmas story. Am I feeling sorry for myself? No What am I feeling then? Anger, yes. Hatred, yes. A desire for revenge, oh yes, yes. But against whom? I think I have the answer though it is only just beginning to crystallize. What is important is that my adventures of the night and exploration of social history, at street level, are not squandered.

The autopsy was undertaken by Prof. Henry Goodman and was finished by early evening. Lorenzo was alone in his office awaiting Goodman's call from the hospital, which came at a few minutes after 6 p.m.

'Interesting,' Goodman began. 'I enjoyed that. Quite a fit and healthy chap for his age. Couldn't find anything seriously wrong with him organically, except for his liver, which was a mess. A mess as in meltdown!'

When once asked by Kingdom to describe Goodman, Lorenzo

had said, 'My stereotype of a nuclear physicist; a weasel with wiry glasses and maniacal eyes.'

Kingdom had retorted, 'Jealous are you, because he has a brain?'

'Alcohol abuse?' Lorenzo speculated to Goodman.

'No evidence of that. No, his liver was destroyed by the over-the-counter painkiller paracetamol. Massive overdose. Enough to knock out an elephant. Stomach still clogged with the residue.'

Lorenzo's brain was a windmill in a cyclone. 'But he'd been in custody almost 24 hours,' he said lamely. 'How many tablets did he swallow?'

'Probably between thirty and forty, maybe even more. Irrelevant, really. Eight can be enough in some circumstances.'

'Jesus! But how and when?' The question was as much for himself as for the professor. 'The police station staff would have searched Fleming before locking him away. Anything on him that might have been deployed for self-harm – shoelaces, belt, necktie and certainly tablets – would have been confiscated.'

'All too late, old chap; after the horse had bolted. Surely, Inspector, you're familiar with the time-lag problem associated with paracetamol?'

'Sort of,' Lorenzo said vaguely, not wishing to advertise his ignorance.

'Well, here are the facts: however large the OD of the drug, it can take up to 36 hours – or indeed longer – before the walking-dead become ill, by which time it's too late to reverse the damage to the liver. A paracetamol OD is an insidious assassin. There's no steady build-up of external symptoms: no stomach pain, sleepiness or slurred speech, no overt evidence of being drugged; just sudden convulsions and vomiting, leading rapidly to visceral shutdown. A sneaky death. People who have OD'd accidentally on paracetamol are lulled into believing they've got away with it. Fool's paradise, as you know, can be a vipers' nest.'

'If your time-frame is correct....'

'It is, rest assured,' Goodman interposed irritably. Although the professor was normally affable, with a droll sense of humour, he could turn prickly when his professional conclu-sions were challenged.

'Ronald Fleming could have taken the tablets the night before we arrested him?'

'Very likely. No, I'll amend that: almost certainly.'

'Anything else?'

'Isn't that enough?'

'No external injuries?'

'A couple of old bruises, very faint. Some fading scratches to his hands. An ancient appendix scar. That's it. Nothing to get excited about.'

'Good job, Prof. Just email me your written report, will you?'

'Don't I always?' That was Goodman's inimitable way of signing off.

Despite instinctively having the urge to rubbish anything relayed to her by Lorenzo, Kingdom could hardly disguise her delight with the findings of the post-mortem.

'So he killed himself, but not on our time,' she virtually chirruped. 'How convenient and thoughtful of him! He must have seen the end coming and decided to implement his own ending to replace ours. His prerogative, I suppose. And he has saved taxpayers a lot of money, so he wasn't all bad. Just goes to show there's a streak of goodness in the wicked.'

'Perhaps a statue should be erected as a memorial to his public-spiritedness,' Lorenzo suggested caustically.

'Not funny, Inspector!'

'I agree,' said Lorenzo, just to irk her. Kingdom was always nettled whenever Lorenzo was agreeable towards her.

'Fleming's action can justifiably be interpreted as a full admis-sion of guilt,' the Chief Constable declared, almost ebulliently. 'I've a feeling I shall soon be in a position to make a highly satis-factory closure statement to the media.'

'Don't jump the gun,' warned Lorenzo, smiling wickedly.

'I'll jump when *I'm* ready, without any prompting from subordinates,' Kingdom said, her waspish streak quickly relit.

The following morning, Lorenzo visited the Central library and spoke with some of Fleming's ex-colleagues.

'Ronald was what I'd call a real, old-fashioned gentleman,' said one of them, Dorothy Avery, who looked every bit the middle-aged, bookish woman that she was. 'He was a dying breed. They don't make them like him any more. He was always *Ronald* to us, never *Ron*. You couldn't wish to meet a kinder or gentler human being. He'd do anything for anyone.'

Even kill them! Lorenzo mused.

'He loved his work here and was very popular with customers, too. They'd make a beeline for him whenever they wanted to know where to find a certain book. He was very knowledgeable, especially about the Victorians and also obscure cultures. We're all absolutely gutted by his death. So tragic! He'll be sorely missed. I don't suppose you're yet able to shed light on how it happened and where?'

'All will materialize in the fullness of time,' Lorenzo said evasively.

Mrs Avery also revealed that she was aware that Fleming was ambidextrous.

'He didn't boast about it, nothing like that,' she said. 'He wasn't a show-off, but I once saw him writing with his left hand. I remember saying, "Ronald, you're right-handed, aren't you? Yet here you are writing beautifully and clearly with your left hand." That's when he let me into his little secret. A man of many hidden talents was our Ronald! He actually sent me a Christmas card, using his left hand to write a message and my name and address on the envelope.'

'How do you know that?' Lorenzo asked.

'Because he wrote in it, "A left-handed seasonal greeting just for you!" '

Yet she didn't respond when we appealed in the press for anyone who recognized the example of handwriting that was published. Obviously she didn't give it a thought: how could such a perfect, old-

fashioned gentleman be a contemporary Jack the Ripper? Unthinkable
I bet Fleming had forgotten about that card. Not so clever, after all, as
he reckoned he was!

'I don't suppose you've kept that card?' said Lorenzo, more
hopeful than optimistic.

'I'm certain I have it at home somewhere, stored away with
old Christmas tinselly leftovers. Would you like me to dig it out
for you?'

'Oh, yes, please,' said Lorenzo, drooling.

Within 48 hours, Fleming's left-handed writing had been
scientifically matched to the killer's cryptic notes – from his
diaries as well as the Christmas card. Human hair and fabric
fibres, extracted from Fleming's Land Rover, a Limited Edition
model, established conclusively that Anne Chapman had been
in his vehicle. However, not a drop of blood was detected in
laboratory tests on all knives lifted from Fleming's kitchen.
Lorenzo assumed that Fleming would have had sufficient
forensic knowledge to have used bleach to eliminate blood-cont-
amination of any blade.

'How smart are you at solving conundrums?' Lorenzo said to
Tricia during another of their late-evening phone chats.

'Try me.'

'What does 8-1-1-2-8 mean to you?'

'Pardon?' she queried, perplexed, wondering if she had heard
correctly.

Lorenzo explained that Fleming's last words to him had been:
'I shall be forever your 8-1-1-2-8.'

'Beats me,' said Tricia. 'Could be a phone number or a math-
ematical formula. Wait a minute....' An elongated pause, then,
'Something about it does begin to ring a little, distant bell. Leave
it with me.'

'Glad to. It's all yours.'

Lorenzo had just been sucked into the dark tunnel of soothing
sleep, when he was jerked out of it by his noisy, attention-
seeking bedside phone.

'Solved it!' Tricia trilled, obviously very pleased with herself.

'Let's hear it,' Lorenzo beseeched groggily.

'I called an ex-FBI colleague on the US west coast. I had a hunch and he's one of the agency's magpies; collects and stores in his head an amazing anthology of useless data. But not so useless on this occasion: 8-1-1-2-8 was the coroner's case number in Los Angeles in the early 1960s for Marilyn Monroe. Did the iconic movie star OD voluntarily or was she murdered by the Kennedys or the Mafia? One of Hollywood's eternal, classic conspiracy quandaries. Now you can sleep in peace.'

She was wrong, of course. Lorenzo remained awake, brain cells chattering, for the rest of the night.

November 8th came and passed.

A collective sigh of relief resonated through every county police HQ in the south-west. Even Kingdom was on a relative high, and Lorenzo got a buzz from overdosing on sleep.

Still, for a week afterwards, Lorenzo logged on to the crime record databases of all the world's major law enforcement agencies, but there was no murder victim with the name Mary Kelly.

Astonishingly quickly, Jack the Ripper, Mark 2 had become as consigned to the historical graveyard as his more infamous progenitor.

Yet Lorenzo couldn't rid himself, however hard he tried, of the grinning image of Fleming as he spoke his last words; the riddle of the number, solved by Tricia and her US contact. There had been something so evil and diabolical about that smug expression; the grin of a Mephistopheles who knew when the time came, he would claim his Faust and have the last laugh.

The calls between Lorenzo and Tricia became less frequent. Tricia put her property on the market. Lorenzo said he'd vacate 'The Barn'. Tricia said there was no need until a sale was completed. Lorenzo said it made sense to find alternative accommodation before it became a matter of urgency. The chasm between them had become far greater than the distance from Bournemouth to London. Lorenzo deliberately avoided asking questions about Luke, to avoid the risk of opening another front in the theatre of matrimonial warfare.

Friday, November 21st was a day Lorenzo would never forget. Like most momentous dates, it began blandly and inauspiciously. Daybreak overslept. The clouds of Thursday's night-sky were bloated and waddled overhead like gluttons who had over-indulged, so that it was mid-morning before Friday had fully woken up, bringing with it a steady drizzle and anti-social winter-air from Russia.

Lorenzo and Valentine were looking into a spate of racially-motivated assaults on foreign students at some of the local private English language tuition colleges. Bread-and-butter work. Nasty crimes but not sexy.

Then it happened, just as Lorenzo was slipping into his over-coat to go for lunch. On the other end of the phone was Sam Ravello, the lieutenant with the New York City Police Department who earlier had delivered the news to Lorenzo of a Liz Stride's demise in the Big Apple.

'Got something else for you,' said Ravello, as dispassionately as if merely about to offer candy.

'Not another murder, I hope?' said Lorenzo, tensing.

'I'll leave you to be the judge of that.'

What an odd, destabilizing comment, thought Lorenzo.

'I was catching up yesterday on news from the foreign press,' Ravello continued. By *foreign,* he meant out-of-state. 'A small item in the *Miami Herald* grabbed me. A woman in New Orleans had killed herself in her home with a knife: cut her throat; bled to death. An unusual way to take your own life and the only reason it was newsworthy. And you know what?'

'Just finish the story,' said Lorenzo, not in the mood for amateur dramatics.

'Her name was Mary Kelly.'

Poleaxed, Lorenzo went into auto-pilot. 'When?'

'The self-inflicted deed was done on November 8th. Interesting, eh?'

'Was it *definitely* suicide?'

'Debatable. I called the New Orleans PD, spoke with a detective from Homicide. Apparently, on November 6th Mary Kelly received in the mail a letter wrapped around a voodoo doll. At this point, it's worth noting that Mary Kelly was second generation Haitian/American. In the letter it was claimed that the sender had a lock of Kelly's hair, some of which had been burned and the rest thrown away.'

'What's the significance of that?' said Lorenzo, his voice stumbling along.

'We're talking Louisiana voodoo here; quite different from Haitian voodoo. The hair-burning ritual is a prelude to harming someone. The letter stated that the only way Kelly could cleanse herself and save her soul from the claws of Satan was to take pre-emptive action, using a domestic knife to slit her throat on November 8th, when the arms of God would be waiting to embrace her, and so deprive the Devil of his intended catch. The letter was signed: *Mari D, Disciple Queen of Marie Laveau.*'

'And that carried weight?'

'For someone rooted in voodoo superstition, believe it. Louisiana voodoo was introduced into the US by African slaves. Marie Laveau, a devout Roman Catholic, became the original Queen of Louisiana voodoo in the 1830s. Her name is routinely shouted by gamblers in the US looking for "Lady Luck" when throwing dice in casinos. Even today, more people visit Laveau's tomb on pilgrimages every year than those who pay homage to Elvis Presley.'

Lorenzo's brain was struggling. 'You say the package was received on November 6th.'

'Correct.'

'But when was it posted?'

'November 3rd.'

Days *after* Fleming's death, Lorenzo computed.

'Do you know where it was posted?'

'Locally. As in New Orleans.'

'How about the ID of the sender, apart from Mari D, etc.?'

'Ah! That's another dead end! But the state of Louisiana is awash with charlatan voodoo practitioners who claim to be able to put evil – even deadly – spells on someone's enemies, at a price.'

'Do any of them work?'

'Only if the receiver is a true believer, which all uneducated Haitians are. Sticks and stones can hurt them, but voodoo words will kill!'

'Did this Mary Kelly have enemies?'

'Not according to my contact. She was a simple woman of simple faith. Mother of four, all grown up. Husband died from a snake-bite in the swamps a few years ago. Brought up to fear voodoo by her Haiti-born parents. A very impressionable sort, open to suggestion, it would seem.'

Lorenzo wanted to believe it was just a coincidence and yet...

'What are the police doing about it in New Orleans?'

'Not breaking sweat, that I guarantee.'

'Tip me off if anything else turns up, won't you?' said Lorenzo.

'You can rely on me.'

Instead of going to lunch, Lorenzo summoned Valentine and told him to bring all records of emails sent by Fleming in the month before his death and his bank transactions during the same period.

By late afternoon, all was transparent. Two days after his return from New York, Fleming had emailed a Mari Devereaux. A week later, he had transferred electronically the equivalent of $1,000 to the Chase Manhattan bank account, in New Orleans, of a Mari Devereaux.

Now the malevolent grin of Fleming's was suddenly explained. He had put his extensive knowledge of arcane cultures to evil use, knowing that, from the grave, he was virtually assured of completing his heinous mission.

Jack had come a long way since his crude introduction into Victorian folklore and the psyche of successive generations the world over. Jack of all trades was the master of one.